FRENEMIES LIKE THESE

HEIRS OF ANDIS BOOK ONE

LILY SKYY

December 2024

ISBN 978-1-962071-85-7 (ebook)
ISBN 978-1-962071-86-4 (paperback)

Published by Books to Hook Publishing, LLC.
www.BooksToHook.com

CONTENTS

PROLOGUE

Ashlyn

The celebration in the Grand Ballroom of the Bevair mansion was inspired by the legendary Festival of Wonders, a rare event known for its magical displays and exotic marvels. Billowing clouds of red-and-gold silk were draped across the ceiling, mimicking the skies of the festival's desert origins. Hovering lanterns enchanted to glow like warm embers floated overhead, and tiny starlit crystals strung around the hall added to the magic, each cluster reflecting light like a shower of shimmering stars across the room.

Above, aeromancers in iridescent costumes glided gracefully, their wings of translucent fabric catching the light from the crystals as they spun and twirled, leaving trails of glimmering reflections. Below, illusionists conjured creatures made of mist—glowing ethereal phoenixes, twisting serpentine dragons, and phantom unicorns that pranced and danced through the crowd before dissolving into wisps. Musicians filled the air with haunting, otherworldly melodies played on instruments of glass and silver, each note echoing the enchantment that surrounded us.

I watched, wide-eyed, as the aeromancers swooped low like phantom swans, spreading their arms to create sweeping arcs of light. The entire scene felt alive with magic, and I gasped, caught up in the wonder of it all.

Magic always had that effect on me. When I reached my eighteenth birthday in two years' time, I would discover my own gift, and I'd always wanted to be an aeromancer—the ability to fly away and soar with the birds whenever the ground got a little bit crowded was my idea of bliss. Not that I was unsociable. At least, I didn't consider myself to be unsociable, although I often felt like a caged animal at these events, trapped behind invisible bars where the adults could view me at leisure and award me marks out of ten for grace, charm, and fashion sense.

My eyes widened as one of the acrobats curled into a ball and dove through a flaming hoop above the banquet table, straightening midair and skimming past enormous crystal bowls filled with iridescent starfruit pearls and slices of moon citrus on beds of frost crystals. In one corner, pyromancers juggled blazing orbs that flickered with colors beyond ordinary fire, while across the room, cryomancers conjured sparkling ice blossoms that hovered above our heads, glinting like suspended stars. The Bevairs had outdone themselves again, which wasn't easy when they hosted more celebrations and feasts than any of the other industry Lords.

Andis, where we lived, was divided into five realms of influence known as industries: Mercantyl, governed by Lord Bevair, managed all matters of trade and commerce; Elementum, my father's domain, controlled power and natural resources; Technomancy, regulated technology and advanced magical innovations; Vitalis focused on healing and restoration; and Illumina presided over arts and revelry. The five ruling families weren't considered monarchs, but they helped oversee the nation's affairs alongside the Council of Arcane Governance. While laws were set by the Council, the realms—and therefore the families—held considerable sway in decision-making.

Which meant that all eyes were generally on the governing families at these events. And the industry heirs. In other words—me.

It sounded worse than it was, and I wasn't complaining. I mean, who wouldn't enjoy attending an endless round of parties with their best friends?

Parties at our mansion were generally more dignified, more... understated. Lady Bevair loved to put on a show; she thrived on the adoration, on the oohs and aahs, and the *congratulations on providing spectacular entertainment once again, my dear.* My mom, however, never ever forgot that she was the wife of Lord Grove, ruler of the Elementum industry. It was like duty ran through her veins instead of blood, and she couldn't bring herself to lighten up and throw a few starlight flares into the fire. Our home was powered by solar, water, and wind energy. The most extravagant display my mom had ever organized featured a shimmering stream winding around the grand gazebo in our enchanted gardens, complete with shadow-winged swans and water nymphs draped in iridescent scales, splashing on the rocks and singing their haunting songs.

I loved the water nymph scene. I loved that my mom had been creative enough to envisage it *and* pull it off, but I think my dad gave her the pursed lips seal of disapproval, and every event we've hosted since has been the usual boring stuff: food, drink, stuffy business chat, and even stuffier music.

As if reading my thoughts, an aeromancer hovered above my head, her shimmering arms encircling me, and then she drifted away again, blowing me a kiss from somewhere near the tented ceiling.

"Quite the spectacle, isn't it?" a smooth voice cut through my reverie.

I turned to find myself face-to-face with a boy I'd never seen before. He looked to be around my age or maybe a few years older and was undeniably handsome, with piercing green eyes and a sharp jawline. His expression was neutral, yet there was a flicker of something—amusement? Curiosity?—in his gaze. He wore a tailored waistcoat of midnight blue with silver threading that caught the light like stardust, layered over a crisp, dark shirt that emphasized his lean build. In his hand, he held a slender crystal flute filled with starling nectar, the effervescent drink sparkling like tiny galaxies as he brought it to his lips.

"It's beautiful," I replied, unable to keep the wonder from my voice. "I've never seen anything quite like it."

He raised an eyebrow slightly. "Beauty and danger, intertwined. One has to admire the Bevairs' flair for the dramatic."

There was a touch of dry humor in his tone that made me smile despite myself. "You don't sound particularly impressed," I said as I turned to resume observing the performance.

"Let's just say I've seen my fair share of... elaborate entertainments," he said, his lips quirking into a half-smile. "Though I must admit, the aeromancers are a nice touch."

Just then, one of the aerial performers swooped particularly low, causing me to step back instinctively. My elbow connected with something solid—the boy's hard abs—and I heard the distinct sound of liquid splashing.

I whirled around, horrified to see starling nectar dripping from his chin onto his elaborately embroidered waistcoat. "Oh, Spirits, I'm so sorry!"

His eyes flashed with momentary annoyance, quickly masked by a tight smile. "Well, I suppose that's one way to liven up a conversation."

"I didn't mean to—I'll get something to clean that up," I stammered, frantically looking around for napkins.

He held up a hand, stopping me. "No need for a fuss. It's just clothes."

"Still, I insist on covering the cleaning costs," I said, feeling my cheeks flush. "My name is Ashlyn Grove, and I—"

"Ah," he interrupted, something shifting in his expression. "Ashlyn Grove. I should have guessed."

I blinked, surprised. "You've heard of me?"

"In these circles, it would be remiss not to," he replied, his tone carefully neutral. "Though I must say, your... enthusiasm for aerial displays wasn't quite what I expected from the Elementum heir."

There was a subtle edge to his words that I couldn't quite decipher. Was he mocking me? Or just making conversation?

"And you are...?" I prompted, trying to regain some footing in the conversation.

He smiled, but it didn't quite reach his eyes. "Just another face in the crowd, Ashlyn Grove. Nothing for you to concern yourself with."

Before I could press further, he glanced down at his stained waistcoat. "If you'll excuse me, I should probably see to this before it sets. Do try to keep your feet on the ground for the rest of the evening. I'd hate to see what would happen if you actually tried to fly."

With that, he melted into the crowd, leaving me staring after him, a mixture of confusion and indignation swirling in my chest. I smoothed down my dress, only to realize it had slipped dangerously low during the starling nectar fiasco. Wonderful.

As I adjusted my neckline, I couldn't shake the feeling that I'd just been subtly insulted, though I couldn't quite put my finger on how. The man's parting words echoed in my mind: *I'd hate to see what would happen if you actually tried to fly.* What was that supposed to mean?

Where were the boys when I needed them? I knew they would back me up, and I really needed the support. Come to think of it, I hadn't seen them since I arrived. I glanced around the crowded ballroom, but there was still no sign of them, which made me wonder if they were planning some kind of childish prank to catch me unaware. It wouldn't be a new occurrence.

All of us were heirs to our respective industries, and coincidentally, we were all born around the same time. It was almost as if our parents had all taken a fertility potion at once, ensuring that none of us became an heir before the others. Naturally, we gravitated toward each other at parties and became best friends over the years. When things were dull, we would sneak outside, lay on our backs on the grass, and stare at the stars, making up ridiculous stories about fantastically strange creatures and the battle between good and evil. Sometimes, we even climbed into the treehouses that our parents built for us when we were younger and ate food stolen from the banquet table. During winter, we bundled up and had playful snowball fights wherever we gathered. Silly, childish games. Because when we were together, it felt like the only time that we could really be ourselves.

Although things had shifted lately. I couldn't quite put my finger on what had changed, and it was probably nothing more than the five of us growing up, but sometimes I noticed how they looked at me differently. Like the last time we were all together at Kris's house, and I pounced on him right in the middle of a crystal-racer duel with Shane. The game was intense, with enchanted crystals controlling holographic racers darting through twisting, illusion-filled tracks. Kris lost his focus—and the match—but instead of the usual pile-on to wrestle me off him, the guys all kind of froze like they were afraid I might unleash a magical curse on them or something.

I wouldn't have. Also, we don't get our gifts until we're eighteen, and curses are not really a thing in Andis.

My dad had already started making comments about marriage to one of the heirs. At sixteen? Ugh! We haven't even gone to university yet, and there's a whole world outside of Andis waiting to be discovered, not to mention learning how to run the industry when I take over from him. I'll be the first female Lord in our nation, so no pressure. It terrified my father, a fear that he'd never tried to conceal.

"Maestra Ashlyn Grove?" Someone tapped my shoulder, and I turned around to find a waiter watching me with a bland expression. "Master Cole Bevair would like to speak with you privately..." He cleared his throat. "In the downstairs parlor." He clicked his heels together and walked away before I could ask what Cole wanted.

Cole, more than the rest of us, seemed to revel in his position as heir to the Mercantyl industry. He'd take over now, given half a chance, and learn on the job because he has that much confidence; it's almost like he was born to carry out the role. Which he was, I guess. So, if this is a prank, he's providing the distraction.

I made my way around the edge of the ballroom, avoiding my parents, whose gazes kept skipping my way intermittently like they were a tag team tasked with keeping an eye on me. But I didn't get far because Kris stepped out in front of me, making me jump.

"There you are," he said.

"Here I am." I smiled, relieved to finally have someone to talk to.

Perhaps I was wrong to choose a favorite out of my friends, especially as we spent so much time together, which would continue even when we inherited our respective industries, but if anyone ever asked, I would tell them that Kristopher Reeve was the one I had the most affinity with. He was kind of nerdy—as heir to the Technomancy industry, I guess that was a given—and quieter than the other heirs, more thoughtful. When they took things too far and got a bit boisterous, Kris was the one who protected me, even if it earned him a whole bunch of ribbing from them.

I noticed now that he wore vision crystals—small, enchanted lenses placed directly on his eyes—that made them appear even larger, giving him an intense, almost otherworldly gaze. He was dressed in a sharp suit, though he looked anything but comfortable in it, twisting his neck and tugging at his bowtie as if it were conspiring to strangle him.

"Do you want to dance?" he asked.

I narrowed my eyes at him suspiciously. Kris knew that I had no sense of rhythm and that his shiny shoes would be scuffed by the time the song ended. "I'm going to find Cole. Do you know what he wants?"

"Cole?"

"Uh-huh. You know, Cole Bevair, your friend?"

"Oh, Cole," he said, his eyes widening.

"O-kay," I said, grinning at him. "Whatever game this is, I'm onto you."

Kris chewed his bottom lip the way he did when he was concentrating. "No game, Ash. I just wanted to talk to you." He pulled me away from the dance floor, forgetting that he'd just asked me to dance, and out onto one of the balconies overlooking the park that was the Bevairs' garden.

I waited.

Kris didn't seem to know where to look, so I surreptitiously glanced down at my chest to make sure that nothing had slipped out. It hadn't.

"Ash..."

"Yes?" I peered back into the ballroom, expecting the others to jump out at us, but we were alone on the balcony, and no one else seemed to have noticed that we were missing.

"Do you...? I mean, I've been thinking... I wanted to..."

"Spit it out, Kris."

"Hey, Kristopher," someone called from inside the ballroom.

Kris's shoulders seemed to deflate like an undercooked cake, and he stared out at the garden, blinking furiously.

"You should go," I said. "I'll see you later."

He sucked in a deep breath, kissed me on the lips, and scurried away without another word while I was left standing there, the imprint of his lips on mine and a furious burning in my cheeks, still wondering what was going on.

The cool air on my bare arms and neck wasn't enough. I needed to go outside and walk. It wasn't like the five of us were not touchy-feely—we were—but in the way children are when they pull each other about and punch each other playfully on the arm. This... This was different, and I wasn't sure how I was supposed to feel about it.

I peered over the balcony. People were chatting on the patio, glasses of bubbly in their hands, so I couldn't exactly climb over the railings and jump down without getting noticed. Head down, I wandered back into the noise and lights of the party, circling the ballroom until I reached the lobby, which was equally as grand with a high ceiling and crystal chandeliers taller than me, and out onto the wide curving steps at the front of the property.

I sat on the top step and hugged my knees to my chest. I could feel my heart thumping inside my ribcage. *No, no, no.* If that kiss was what I thought it was, then it would change everything, and I wasn't ready for that. I wasn't ready to grow up. I closed my eyes and replayed it in my head. Perhaps I was wrong. It was over so quickly that I might've imagined the whole thing, and all Kris was trying to do was give me a distracted hug. That was it. That had to be it.

"Ash? What are you doing out here?"

Shane sat beside me, his brow furrowed with concern. He wore a red velvet jacket over a frilled white shirt paired with black-and-ivory boots with sharply pointed toes. As heir to the Illumina industry, Shane Aster could pick up a lutecrystal and play any tune you requested, his fingers weaving enchanting melodies as effortlessly as breathing. He was unmatched in our year's storycraft, always cast as the lead in every hall of tales performance. Now, he rested his chin on my shoulder, our noses almost touching. And somehow, he'd inherited all the artistic gifts among us, with a spark of creativity that made everything he touched feel alive.

"I was hot," I said.

He nodded. "It's cooler out here."

"Do you know what's going on?"

"Going on?" He sat back and wrinkled his nose, flicking his ginger hair out of his eyes. "What do you mean?"

"Cole wants to see me in the downstairs parlor."

"Cole?"

Okay, so that was the same reaction I got from Kris. The game was already wearing thin.

"The prank," I pressed him. "You guys are up to something,

and I wish you'd just get it over and done with so that we can all laugh about it and get some food."

"No. If they're messing around, they haven't included me." His tone was genuine, which didn't exactly fill me with confidence that Kris's kiss wasn't real.

"I'd best go find him then." I went to stand up, but Shane placed a hand on my arm.

"Stay," he said. "We don't get much time alone, just the two of us."

I couldn't stop myself from smiling. "We see each other through the Echo Panels at least twice a week, just the two of us. Aren't you bored with my company already?"

Shane shook his head. "How could anyone get bored with your company? I mean... The thing is... I like you, Ash."

Heat flooded my cheeks, and I wished one of the cryomancers would come out here and sprinkle me with ice.

"I'm not very good at this," Shane said, his own face turning rosy. When he faced me again, our lips were almost touching, and I could feel the heat from him like a furnace.

I rose abruptly and almost lost my balance. Shane was on his feet in a heartbeat. He grabbed my shoulders to keep me steady, his gaze so intense that I had to look away. "I should go find Cole."

I left before he could stop me, even though I heard him calling out behind me.

This couldn't be happening. Was there something in the air tonight? I didn't always pay attention at these events, but I'd heard whispers of "things" being adrift among the adults, like "things" had been trundled onto a rowboat without oars and pushed out to sea. I didn't understand what else it could be, unless—

I wasn't watching where I was going and collided headfirst into Jase Branson in the ground-floor hallway, which stretched from the lobby to the library, the family dining room, and the kitchens. The Bevairs, of course, had multiple kitchens—one simply wasn't enough to cater to events like these.

"Whoa, Ash. In a hurry?" He blocked my path and grinned at me, arms folded across his chest.

Jase's family ran the Vitalis industry. He was the athletic one in our group, the one most likely to complete an endurance run through the Ember Fields—not that I'd ever considered doing something so grueling—the one who ate healthily and rose early to practice his dawn sprints. The one who could launch a moonstone orb into the far ring with his eyes closed and never miss.

"Sorry," I said. It was turning out to be a night for apologies. "Cole is waiting for me."

"Cole?"

There it was again.

"Let me guess," I said, "you want to talk to me about something."

Jase smiled. "Yeah, actually."

I peered into his eyes. They didn't look glazed. In fact, Jase had huge eyes, the kind that drew people in, but he wasn't conceited about his looks the way some guys in school were. It was part of his charm how oblivious he was to the way girls looked at him.

"Ash..." Jase stepped closer. "Can I kiss you?"

He didn't wait for my approval but grabbed my hands and moved closer, his lips inching toward mine.

What the hell? I ducked, wrenched my hands free, and darted along the hallway, bounding into the library and leaning against the door, my heart hammering and pulse racing. This could not be happening. What had gotten into my friends?

"Ashlyn? What are you doing in here?" Cole was sitting on the leather Chesterfield sofa, one arm draped casually across the back, an empty starling nectar glass on the coffee table in front of him. He patted the seat next to him. "Come and sit down."

I crossed the room mechanically. If this was a prank, now

would be a good time for them to all jump out and say, "Surprise!" Part of me still hoped that was all this was; the childish part of me remembered cozy winter evenings spent in front of the fire in the library, reading books, eating hot, buttered toast, and drinking hot chocolate. The other part of me, however, the part that chose this dress to wear tonight because it revealed more flesh than the dress my mom had chosen for me, knew that this wasn't a game.

"You look beautiful tonight," Cole said.

"You mean I don't look beautiful every other night?" I was still trying to keep this lighthearted before they all succeeded in embarrassing themselves and me.

"Of course you do. I know I've never told you this, but you are the reason I attend these parties. I could make some excuse— my mom would always buy it—but I don't because it would mean that I don't get to see you all dressed up."

"Cole... I don't know—"

"You don't have to say anything. You know it's only a matter of time before you and I get together, right? We would make the best match for our industries. The other heirs might try to sway you, but our families want this, too."

"Our families?" The words struck a nerve, sending shivers down my spine. What about what I wanted? What about what Cole wanted, too? How was I supposed to know what any of the heirs wanted with the pressure of our parents pushing us together to form the best alliance for the industries?

I went to stand up, but Cole was fast. He grabbed my wrist, pulled me close, and kissed me before I could tug my hand free.

The door opened then to reveal the other heirs gathered outside the library. Cole sat back with a sly, lopsided smile spreading across his face. As I gazed at my friends, at the hurt expressions on their faces, someone passed along the hallway behind them in a silver suit and scarlet cravat.

Cole's father, Regalis Bevair.

CHAPTER ONE

Ashlyn

Two years later...

I covered my mouth with my hand and stifled a yawn, although I couldn't stop the ensuing tears from welling in my eyes. Blinking, I nodded at a woman standing nearby in the auction room, studying the ugliest vase I'd ever seen, and flashed her a smile that I hoped said *Go on, buy it; I dare you.* Ignoring the way she jutted her chin and raised her nose toward the ceiling as though I'd stepped in something nasty going through the doors, I kept on walking, doing what I always did at formal events these days, pretending that I was having fun.

"Ashlyn, smile like you mean it." My mom flashed me her own well-practiced smile as an example of the effect I should be trying to achieve.

Although we looked alike, with thick chestnut-colored hair, wide brown eyes, and flawless creamy skin, my mom always resembled a moonstone statue while I just looked like—me. Today, she wore a classic white pantsuit with a turquoise silk shirt underneath and coordinating turquoise shoes. My pantsuit was emerald-green, with large gold buttons. But my hair was long and unruly, cascading over my shoulders, which my dad said made me look feral, while my mom's hair was styled into a sleek bob, which made her look elegant.

I'd tried to get out of coming today, but my father insisted that I show my face as it was the last event before I left for Aurora University. What he meant was that he wanted me to follow him around and act like nothing had happened two years ago, to prove to everyone else who socialized in the same circles that there was no rift between the five heirs.

I was here. That was as far as I was prepared to go.

The heirs and I hadn't spoken since that night at the Bevair mansion, and if I ever saw them again—which I was bound to as we were all headed to the same university—it would be too soon. They'd blamed me for what transpired at the ball. Admittedly, Cole had been the most vocal of the four of them, accusing me of playing them all off against one another, but none of them had given me a chance to explain things from my perspective. They'd all looked hurt, standing there in the doorway of the library, Kris accusing me with large, damp eyes, while Jase kept repeating, "What the hell. Like, seriously, what the hell, Ash? Is this some kind of a sick joke?" while Shane didn't say a word.

They'd stood together, Cole in front of them, the leader as always, while I tried to defend myself alone, my self-esteem shrinking with every word they muttered. Cole said that he'd seen a future with me, but he could never trust a girl who used him to drive a wedge between him and his best friends. Jase said he'd never trusted me, anyway. Shane simply shook his head like he was trying to erase the image of Cole and me kissing from his mind, while Kris was numb, silent, and broken.

It didn't matter what I said; they refused to listen. They acted like they were the victims in the situation, as if they hadn't cornered me. As if I had sought them all out. I became furious just thinking about it. In the end, I'd pushed past them and stumbled blindly along the hallway and back into the ballroom, where I found my mom and told her I needed to go home. She didn't question it; it didn't do to discuss intimate female stuff at a formal event such as that. So, she bundled me into the chauffeur-driven luxury Terra Cruiser and took me home, where I stood in my ensuite shower until I was shivering and cold, trying to rinse my ex-best friends out of my life.

The more I thought about it that night, while I tossed and turned in bed, the more I realized that what hurt the most was that not even one of them cared about how I was feeling. Not even Kris. Shane tried calling me on the Echo Panel a few days later, but by then, I'd made up my mind never to speak to them again, so I'd rejected his calls and switched off my device. I didn't need friends like them. Each time I thought about one of them, their actions that evening replayed inside my head, but it wasn't until months later when my dad was talking about Cole Bevair over dinner, that it occurred to me that Cole had been waiting for me in the library when the waiter had told me to meet him in the downstairs parlor.

I didn't know if it was significant. By this point, all I wanted to do was block the whole situation out of my mind—difficult enough when I'd been ostracized by my four best friends—so whenever their names popped up in conversation or I saw one of them around Andis, I repeated a mantra under my breath until they went away.

The heirs mean nothing to me.
The heirs mean nothing to me.
The heirs mean nothing to me.

In the auction room, my parents were chatting with Geoffrey Aster, Shane's dad and Lord of the Illumina industry. Shane inherited his ginger hair from him, and each time the man flicked it out of his eyes, I felt a pang in my chest of missing his son and instinctively surveyed the auction room, seeking him out. He wasn't there. The boys hadn't attended any of the same events that I'd been to in the past couple of years. Whatever had passed between them that night, they'd cut me out of their lives completely and clearly had no intention of sealing the cracks before we went to Aurora.

So be it. If that was the way they wanted it, I would never let them see how much they'd hurt me.

My father chuckled at something Lord Aster said then, jolting me back down to Earth. "We haven't played shadow cards in a while. We should arrange a game soon."

"Indeed," Lord Aster replied. "You know how I enjoy losing to you."

My father smiled at him, a smile that I rarely saw at home. I wondered if he smiled when he and my mom were alone or whether it was something he reserved for friends and acquaintances, a front that ensured he was well-liked among his peers.

"And look at you, Ashlyn," Lord Aster turned to me. "You're positively blossoming. I'm sure that we won't recognize you when you return from Aurora."

Heat rose in my cheeks. The Lords all knew about my disconnect with the heirs, but Lord Aster had always been kind to me, and I wondered again how much they knew of what had transpired that evening. I remembered seeing Cole's father outside of the library door when everything went down, but I wasn't sure if he knew what actually happened since he didn't stick around.

We parted ways, my parents and I heading into the large auction room where the most expensive artifacts would be sold, all money to be donated to the buyer's charity of choice. When he was certain that no one was within earshot, my father hissed, "I suggest you fix things between you and the heirs at Aurora. Sooner rather than later. Our industry's future depends on it."

"What about *my* future?" I blurted out before I could stop myself. My father had never asked what happened between me and the other heirs, and I now realized with absolute clarity that either he didn't care or blamed me, too.

His face turned an unhealthy shade of red, as if someone had switched on a radiator somewhere deep inside him. "I need to know that the Elementum industry is in good hands when the time comes," he said, clenching and unclenching his fists.

"And my hands are not good enough?" It was the first time I'd ever squarely stood up to him, and I knew that I was crossing a line, but the injustice of all that had happened weighed heavily on my shoulders, and it was either this or cry, something that I'd been brought up not to do, especially in public.

"You know nothing of the business, Ashlyn." He smiled at a couple of the upper class walking by. Impressions were important. He couldn't let the facade drop, not even for his daughter.

"Whose fault is that?" I snapped.

"Enough!" he hissed.

My mother's hand rested on my shoulder. "We'll discuss this later, honey," she said sweetly, the smile fixed in place.

We followed my dad into the auction room, where gravitons levitated the artifacts waiting to be auctioned above the guests' heads so that they were visible from all angles, and cryomancers walked around with chilled trays of starling nectar. It was the staple drink at industry events. I wanted to take a glass and down it in one, but I'd pushed my father far enough already, and he would be even angrier if word got around that we'd been arguing in public. His daughter causing a scene and being the center of a scandal? Spirits forbid!

I avoided making eye contact with anyone.

As usual, I scoped out the room from beneath lowered eyelashes, ignoring the stares of the other patrons as I looked for the guys.

"Ashlyn," my mother interrupted me, "do you remember Councillor Edna Mirelli, and have you met Ethan Weiss?"

I'd met Edna several times before. She was a tiny woman with curly, gray hair and gold-framed spectacles that seemed to perch on the end of her nose. I'd always found her to be adorable in a cute grandma way; she was one of the few people I met at these events and galas who wasn't ostentatiously judgmental but always asked how I was getting on at with my studies and if I was looking forward to Aurora.

I aimed a smile her way as Ethan Weiss stepped forward. Familiarity tingled my spine as he came closer. Oh my goodness! It was the boy from the Bevair ball the night my life changed forever, the boy I'd spilled starling nectar on before everything went wrong. He certainly wasn't a boy anymore. I burned with embarrassment, as it seemed he recognized me as well, a smug smile appearing as he raised his eyes toward the ceiling, a reminder of the one and only conversation we'd ever had. A conversation I would never forget since he'd seemed so rude for no reason.

Ethan Weiss.

So he had a name, one I'd heard before. Everyone had. He had the rarest magic: Celestial. Only two other people in the history of Andis had been awarded the gift of Celestial magic, which was why everyone had been so shocked to hear about Ethan Weiss. He was from a middle-class family with no heritage to hint at the future gift, so it was no wonder that there were rumors about new magical powers being unlocked. Most magic was elemental. But Celestial was primordial, the most coveted magic of all, and it wasn't long before people were fawning over the young man, which must have made his ego even bigger than it already was.

No wonder he had been so rude the last time I'd seen him. I kept a carefully blank look on my face, what with my mother beside me. A complacent smile lingered on his lips, curling the edges in a way that hinted at mischief, his green eyes gleaming like emeralds.

He looked even more handsome tonight, his hair in unruly waves around his head, a curl hanging down over his forehead.

"Ashlyn, you have grown into a beautiful young woman." Edna Mirelli reached across and touched one of my own curls. "You must be off to Aurora soon."

I nodded, fighting the urge to stare at his square jaw. The last thing Ethan needed to know was just how attractive I thought he was. "In just a couple of days."

Ethan gazed all around, disinterested in the conversation. Why was I interested in him? Maybe it was his gift. I was so close to getting mine that my curiosity about the gifts had risen. Maybe that's all it was. Yes, it had to be. Because nothing else could explain the way every mention of his name had my pulse revving this fast.

"How exciting! And before we know it, we'll have our first female Lord."

My heart swelled with the unexpected comment. It was the first time I'd ever heard anyone mention me taking over the Elementum industry, and her smile made me realize that she was eager to see it happen.

On cue, my father said, "That's a long way off. Besides, Ashlyn has no inclination for the industry yet. I'm hoping Aurora will help her to understand where her priorities should lie."

The heat in my chest evaporated as quickly as it had arrived, but I kept the smile in place and kept my eyes somewhere above Edna's left shoulder.

Edna pushed her spectacles further up her nose, and they slid straight back down again. "Ethan, maybe you could give Ashlyn a few tips before she goes to Aurora."

Ethan sipped the amber liquid in his crystal tumbler. His hands were rough and tanned, and I hated myself for noticing these things. I hated how I felt about noticing those things even more. He caught me staring and shot me a fast wink, making my cheeks flare with color. "I went to Polaris," he said, his tone dismissive. "I'm sure Ashlyn can handle figuring out Aurora on her own without any input from me."

Edna gasped.

My parents shared a loaded glance.

Seriously, what did they expect? He hadn't had the same upbringing as the Lords and their families. His social standing had come purely from being a Celestial, so what need did he have for etiquette and manners?

And wasn't he perfectly right, too?

The dinner gong sounded, and I quickly said goodbye, rushing to the restroom before my parents could stop me. I stared at my reflection in the mirror. It wasn't even what he'd said that had floored me; it was simply the man's arrogance coupled with my father's refusal to believe that I was a worthy heir to the industry he was so proud of. I didn't understand why. I graduated from the preparatory academy at the top of my class. I spent all my leisure time, now that I didn't have the guys around, learning about the industry, but it would never be good enough for my father.

I dabbed my eyes with tissue, touched up my lip gloss, and tidied my hair before heading back outside. One day, I would make him notice me, and then it would be my choice to take over as the first female Lord. Or not.

I hadn't expected to see Ethan there, but as I stepped out of the bathroom, I found him leaning against the wall, his arms crossed and his gaze distant, as if he'd been lost in thought. The moment he noticed me, he straightened, unfolding his arms and looking me over with a sharp intensity. His brows knit together slightly, and his usual air of casual confidence seemed to fade, replaced by a flicker of concern. His eyes softened, but his tone remained steady, almost cautious. "Were you crying?" he asked, his voice low, as if he didn't want anyone else to hear.

I refused to give him the satisfaction of a glare. He was insufferably arrogant, lounging there as if he expected me to stop and talk to him after what he'd just said inside.

"No." I lifted my chin, determined to make my point. His gaze remained steady, and I felt my heart trip faster in response.

Ethan pulled his hands from his pockets and fidgeted for a second, as though uncertain how to bridge the gap he had created. I watched him, refusing to step back or give way.

He gave a one-shoulder shrug and met my eyes squarely. "Despite what you think, I was simply pointing out back there that you're more than capable of navigating Aurora and your industry and that you don't need my help."

Was that really all there was to it? His expression was unfathomable, but his tone seemed genuine. "Well, you could've worded it better."

He nodded, and an apology flitted through his eyes. "You

seem like a strong woman, Ashlyn. I thought you might've handled them differently." Then he turned around and walked away, leaving me alone in the hallway. I watched him go like the first time, my thoughts swirling in a murky mess.

What did he mean? Was he trying to be mysterious? He'd been the one who hadn't thought to make his meaning clear. I rolled my eyes hard to the ceiling. I wouldn't be giving Ethan Weiss another thought. It didn't matter that my heart was still thudding dully.

Back inside, my dad was talking to Regalis Bevair about the crystal sector. "I think it will turn out more profitable than solar or wind if we give it enough time. I have a few crystal farm beds already set up back in Rhiannon, and they're running at full capacity, outstripping solar by 10 percent and wind by 30. A rollout has the potential to begin within the next ten to twenty years."

I soaked up the information like a sponge. If my dad refused to teach me, I would learn as much as I could from everyone else.

"I bet Cole is eager to get to Aurora," my dad said now. "Hopefully, the heirs will move forward after this ridiculous spat and reconcile their differences. We should all be working together before they receive their magic."

I couldn't hear the response, and then Regalis Bevair was moving away, mingling with other people before the bidding commenced, no doubt checking out his rivals, although everyone knew that if an item took his fancy, they didn't stand a chance.

I followed him, hoping to hear more about the crystals. He nodded at several people, stopped to chat with Lord Aster briefly, and then joined his wife, who was studying an old painting of a young woman holding a daisy to her nose.

"You must speak to Cole before he leaves for Aurora about the *problem*." Lord Bevair's tone altered, his voice little more than a whisper. "Kenneth is keen for the girl to befriend the heirs again —he's still hoping that marriage is on the cards—and Cole needs to stay focused. I know what they're up to, and I will not let it happen."

I slipped into the shadows and back out to the hallway, grateful that Ethan was no longer around, the Lord's words spinning around inside my brain. What did he even mean? Enough. I was done having my future dictated by men who had no idea what I was capable of. I would show them who Ashlyn Grove really was—just as soon as I worked it out for myself.

Ashlyn

"You don't have to take your entire wardrobe, you know, Ashlyn."

I was due to leave for Aurora the following morning, and I'd spent the entire afternoon pulling clothes out of my walk-in closet and tossing them onto the bed. Now, glancing around my bedroom, I realized that at least 50 percent of my clothes were on the floor in a tangle, and my travel trunk was empty apart from a pair of gold moonshadow cat-ears that I used to hold my hair back while I was doing my makeup.

My thoughts were buzzing like wasps around a sweet treat. All my efforts to hide the events of two years ago at the Bevair mansion in a locked cabinet at the back of my mind had been in vain because, since the charity auction, I'd replayed them a hundred times. I recalled every word—how I remembered them anyway—every mannerism, every touch of hands and cheeks and lips, and I still couldn't figure out why they'd all chosen to make the same move on the same night.

Was Regalis behind it? He'd made it clear at the auction room that he had no intention of Cole and me forming any kind of alliance with or without wedding rings. The thought made my cheeks hot. So many people were trying to control my life when no one, not even my own father, ever stopped to consider what I wanted. I found Regalis' stance odd since Cole had said that it was inevitable that he and I would end up together and that our parents wanted it. Something wasn't adding up.

Or were the guys' childish attempts to kiss me at the Bevair mansion all a setup by Cole? He'd always been the one who considered himself above the rest of us, untouchable, ambitious, the one above whom there was no question mark over his future success, and part of me wondered if he'd manipulated the others to deliberately drive a wedge between us so that he could blame it on me. It made sense, even if it broke my heart to think that we used to be so close. But that night had forced us apart, and now all Regalis had to do was make sure that it stayed that way.

But what was his issue with my dad?

My dad trusted the other Lords; he'd worked closely with them his entire adult life and probably spent more time with them than he did with his family. Or *did* he trust them? Was he pushing me to mend the rift because he didn't trust them, and he knew they could make life difficult for our industry if I didn't eventually marry one of them?

So many thoughts were battling to be heard in my mind, and my emotions were rising and dipping like a ride at the festival that visited Andis in the fall.

"What's wrong, Ashlyn?" My mother held up my silver, sparkling one-piece romper between her thumb and forefinger as if it might burn her. The outfit was elegant—a sleeveless garment crafted from shimmering fabric that draped gracefully over my frame without clinging. It featured a fitted bodice that cinched at the waist with a delicate, jeweled belt and flowed into wide-legged trousers that swayed with every movement. Her eyebrows lowered in concern.

"Nothing," I said a little too brightly.

I didn't know that I'd made the decision *not* to tell her about Regalis Bevair until the word came out of my mouth. She would go straight to my dad, and he would immediately accuse me of causing more drama to deflect the attention from me. I would sort this out myself at Aurora, one way or another. It would be difficult as I still didn't want anything to do with the guys, but there were other ways to get to the bottom of what was going on, and I intended to find them.

Besides, I would soon have my gift.

"Sorry." I shook my head, hoping my thoughts would settle. "It's a lot to process." I flopped onto my bed, taking the outfit from her and dropping it into my case. That was two things packed. I wasn't originally going to take the outfit, but my mom's obvious distaste was too tempting to ignore. "What do you think my gift will be?"

"It's difficult to say. It's generally connected to whichever element resides within you and isn't always dictated by bloodline."

Well, we only had to look at Ethan Weiss to know that was true. Something else I was struggling to process was the man's obvious dislike for me, which was completely at odds with what he said when we were alone at the charity auction, if he was telling the truth, anyway.

My dad was a cryomancer, which was predictable as he was such a cold person and never showed his emotions. My mom, whose personality was much warmer and far more sociable, was a pyromancer. If I were using them as criteria upon which to guess my own gift, I should be an aquamancer, as I like to go with the flow in whatever situation I happen to find myself in. I would be happy with that. Who knows, I might even dye my hair green, the color of the ocean surrounding Andis on a summer's day.

"Your father and I met at Aurora. We spent many warm evenings in the forest, strolling along by the stream and enjoying the tranquility away from the busy hallways." Her eyes adopted a dreamy gaze, and I couldn't help wondering if my dad was different when he was younger and, if so, what had changed him. "You never know; you might meet '*the one*' there, too."

"What if I don't want to, Mom?"

Her smile wavered as she tried to work out if I was being serious. "Well, maybe not straight away, but Aurora has that effect on a lot of students. It's such a beautiful, magical place, Ashlyn. Just keep an open mind, is all I'm saying."

I nodded. If the guys had taught me anything two years earlier, it was to stop defining myself by their standards. The point everyone seemed to overlook was that I had the opportunity to make history—I would one day be the first female Lord of an industry, and I intended to make that title my own.

I was going to make history! The enormity of this thought changed everything, and I smiled at my mom, buoyed by that knowledge tucked tightly away inside my chest.

———

I WAS STILL BUZZING about my epiphany when I went down to dinner. We always ate at the formal dining table, using the finest silverware and drinking from crystal tumblers, and tonight was no exception. The cooks had prepared my favorite meal for my last night at home: herb-crusted pheasant in a rich, spiced cream sauce, golden root gratin with melted sharp cheese, and a crisp greens salad drizzled with a light honey-almond dressing.

My dad came in and took his seat shortly after the food arrived, as usual; time was precious. Time also meant money.

"Busy day, dear?" my mom asked as she sliced her pheasant. She ate straight-backed, poised as if she were dining with a room full of nobles.

"Regalis called again," my dad said. He ate quickly, barely chewing his food before he swallowed. "That man is relentless."

Silence followed the statement.

"Ashlyn has been packing for Aurora," my mom said.

My dad glanced at me as he raised a forkful of food to his mouth. "Maybe you'll have some classes with the other heirs."

And there it was. The constant reminder that he expected *me* to repair the shattered remnants of our friendships. If he'd only said to me: *Work hard, Ashlyn. One day, you'll be the first female Lord Andis has ever seen. One day, you'll make us all proud*, and then perhaps the conversation might've taken a different turn. But he didn't. He was so stuck in his outdated mentality that a woman could never lead an industry that he was basing his legacy's entire future on me marrying a man who could move it forward for me.

"Or"—I set my fork down on my plate, my appetite fading—"I could make new friends and new connections for the Elementum industry."

I ignored my mom's sharp intake of breath.

My father swallowed, washed his food down with a mouthful of Silverdew wine—a pale, shimmering drink made from fermented moonberries—and studied the liquid in his glass as it caught the light. Finally, he looked up, eyes narrowed, and jabbed his fork in my direction. "I've had about as much of your attitude as I can take, Ashlyn. You should be repairing friendships, not discarding them like dolls you've outgrown. Without the other heirs—"

"Without the other heirs, I'll still be the first female Lord."

I couldn't keep the tremor from my voice, but I doubt he even recognized it for what it was. This was my second time speaking back to my father, and to be honest, it scared the life out of me, but I was so desperate for him to see how important it was to me that I'd have even told him I'd consider marrying one of the guys —one day—when I'd had the chance to prove I was worthy of my title.

His mouth opened and closed, and then he wiped his lips on a napkin, scrunched it up, and set it down beside his plate, his fingers drumming the table. "Nothing is set in stone, Ashlyn," he said quietly.

"Wh-what does that mean?"

"It means that you are my heir, but the decision to hand over the industry to you is solely mine."

Several moments passed before I realized what he was trying

to say. I swallowed, and my throat clicked. "You mean, you might not allow me to take over."

"One day, when I'm no longer around, people will be looking to you for answers. I've yet to see those answers in you, Ashlyn."

"Because you never look at me." I realized that I sounded like a spoiled child whining for sweets before dinner, but his words were seeping in through my pores and making me feel nauseous. He couldn't do this to me. He couldn't snatch my entire future away from me without even giving me a chance to prove myself—the injustice of it made tears sting my eyes. I blinked. I would not let him see me cry. "You have never taken me to work with you. You've never taught me anything about our industry, or what it means to Andis, or even to the people who work for us. I had to learn about the crystal sector from Lord Bevair."

His eyes flashed my way. "And I had to learn from him about your little tantrum that saw you cast aside by the other heirs."

"That's all you care about, isn't it? You don't even care about what really happened," I said, my pulse racing.

"Ashlyn," my mom said, reaching out a hand to placate me from across the table.

"No, Mom. You don't get to silence me now. I'm not five years old; I'm almost eighteen. I'm going to Aurora tomorrow, and soon I'll receive my gift. I'm going to learn everything I can about our industry—everything I should've learned from you, Dad—and I am going to do it without the other heirs because, guess what, I don't need them. Who wrote the rule that said a female heir would never be as good as a male heir? Expecting me to hand over what should be mine to my *husband*," I cringed as I uttered the word, "is such an archaic way of looking at the world. You say you're worried about the future when you're so stuck in the past that you can't even comprehend that I might carve a new future for our industry."

My voice caught in my throat. Don't cry, I told myself. *Don't cry.*

My father kept his eyes on his plate. His fingers had stopped drumming, but a tic had appeared in his jaw. He was angry. No, he was furious that I'd dared to answer back to him. Finally, he said, "I only want what's best for the industry."

I shook my head. I'd tried to get him to see things from my perspective, but all he cared about was the industry, tradition, and stupid laws that were centuries out of date. "Please may I be excused from the table?" I whispered.

I didn't wait around for their response. Once outside the dining room, I ran to my bedroom and threw myself onto my bed, waiting for the tears to come.

CHAPTER THREE

Jase

"Are you packing any clothes, or do you intend to walk around Aurora naked?"

"Is naked the operative word in that sentence?" Kris glanced up from the cords he was untangling, his eyebrows dancing comically.

"Hmm... Is it not?"

Kris was the nerdy one whose love of gadgets completely surpassed any obligation he might have felt as a kid who would one day inherit the Technomancy industry. So far, he'd filled a case with more handheld devices than I'd ever possessed in my life, all of them yet to be made available to the paying public. A perk of being a Reeve, I guessed.

"Well, you seem to assume that I'll be walking around Aurora for starters," Kris said. "I'm going to find myself a tech lab, make myself comfortable, and you all can come and feed me whenever I'm looking a bit gaunt."

I grinned at him. The thing was, he wasn't joking. That would be like a dream come true for him, the same as making the Stormball and Pathrun teams would be for me. I could practically feel the weight of the stormball in my hands, the rough grooves etched by lightning itself, and hear the roars of the crowd as I dodged an opponent on the unpredictable Stormground. Or, in Pathrun, feeling the Living Trail shift beneath my feet as if testing me with each twist and incline, daring me to keep pace and outmaneuver whatever came next. Yeah, that would be my dream come true.

"I heard you and Beatrice broke up." Kris stretched his arms wide to release a knot in a cord before spooling it back up and tucking it inside a pocket in the lid of his travel trunk. "Never saw that coming," he snarked.

"What? I thought you liked her."

"I think the real issue here is the fact that I'm not the one who's supposed to like her."

He could be such a jerk at times, even if I knew he was right. Beatrice was the bubbly Skylance captain at school. The way she maneuvered that skystone through rings with her lance, leaping and spinning with the kind of agility that won her almost every match, it was hard not to be impressed. One of the popular girls, for sure, with a thing for athletes. None of us had dated anyone before that fateful night at the Bevair mansion; I guess we'd all kind of thought back then that no one would ever live up to Ashlyn because she was one of us. But it was only a matter of time before we started gravitating toward other people. So, when Beatrice asked me to go to the Starspire—a place where the constellations light up the dome with tales of ancient battles—I accepted.

It was fun while it lasted, I guess.

"Makes sense," Kris said absentmindedly. "Guess she's following in Bellis's footsteps." His cousin Bellis Reeve had recently graduated from the TruthForger program and landed a position at one of the news facilities. Bellis was a few years older than us and had always been known for her curiosity. If there was any drama at an event, she'd be the first to find out.

Cole used to joke that all girls had that instinct and that we would have eventually grown apart from Ashlyn anyway. But with Bellis, it was something deeper—like a relentless need to uncover every detail. Now, as a TruthForger, her job was to do exactly that:

find and shape the truth with a precision that sometimes felt almost too intense for those around her.

I spotted an old stick then sitting on the bookshelf across the room and grabbed it, wielding it above my head like a sword. "You kept this?" I asked. It was about as long as my arm, the top of it stripped of bark so that it formed a point, with two handle-like prongs at the bottom.

Kris glanced up, blinked when he saw what I was holding, and then went back to the device in his hands, his cheeks growing hot. "Yeah. I keep forgetting to throw it out."

"Do you remember when I accidentally whacked Cole over the head with this?"

"Accidentally?" Kris grinned.

Shane had found the stick on the grounds of the Bevair mansion and declared that it was his sword, and that made him king. This resulted in four eight-year-olds chasing each other around the gardens, trying to grab it until Ashlyn arrived and told us off in her prim, maternal tone, at which point she claimed it for herself and proceeded to chase us around. I was the fastest. I snatched the sword from Ashlyn and whacked Cole over the head as he tried to take it from me.

I replaced the stick on the shelf.

After *that* night, Cole had convinced us that Ashlyn had been leading us all on, toying with our emotions, manipulating the whole scenario to make us feel stupid. He'd made us vow to cut her off and stick together. A woman in power was a dangerous commodity. He'd sounded exactly like his father when he'd said it, and we'd all agreed because we'd all gotten stung, and our egos needed soothing somehow.

But, on reflection, I couldn't help wondering if we were wrong. That wasn't the Ashlyn I remembered.

Silence filled the room. This was what happened whenever an old memory of the five of us snuck back in, especially when Cole wasn't around.

"Do you ever think about just skipping university and just going to work?" I asked.

"Nah," Kris said. "I like working with Dad, but I'm not so sure about the office politics."

"What do you mean?" Kris had never mentioned anything like this before. He loved working with his dad, and he was a natural-born techno-geek. Most of the time, the subtle nuances of relationships and differences seemed to wash over his head.

"I don't know. Lord Bevair is putting pressure on Dad to form some kind of merger. I don't know the details."

"Sounds like Regalis." We all knew that was where Cole got his bossiness from.

"Yeah." Kris shrugged. "Maybe he went too far this time."

"I'm sure it'll all be sorted by the weekend."

I didn't add that it wasn't our concern right now. When I finished my time at Aurora, I still had three years at the Healer's Academy to navigate, and sometimes, I felt like it set me apart from the other heirs. My industry was always just out of reach, whereas they could already see the finish line.

"We'll probably see her there. We might even be in the same classes."

Kris finally powered off the device and looked at me. "What do you think she'll say?"

My stomach twisted. All this time, with university looming closer and closer, I'd imagined how I would react when I saw Ash again, what I might say to her when we came face-to-face, but I'd never considered how she would react in the same situation. Did that make me the biggest jerk of all?

All I did know was that I was dreading the moment but longing for it at the same time because—and I'd never admit this to the guys—I missed her.

———

Shane

I stared out the darkened window of the Bevair Terra Cruiser —a sturdy vehicle designed to navigate the varied terrains of Andis—seeing only my hazy reflection on the glass, which made me appear like a shadow: gaunt eyes, hollow cheeks, and stringy, gray hair. Was this how I would look when I grew old? We were on our way to Aurora, and the closer we got, the more my stomach twisted; it would be practically performing somersaults by the time we arrived.

For two years, I'd listened to Cole carrying on about how we were going to rule Aurora, how they'd probably never seen four heirs attending at the same time in the university's entire history, and each time, I'd wanted to remind him that there were five heirs. I'd gotten so close to it, but then I looked at Jase and Kris and bottled it, realizing that they wouldn't back me up.

Two years beating myself up for being a wimp of the highest order. I hadn't even told my mom what happened that night; I knew exactly what she would've said: *You get right on over there and apologize to Ashlyn... now!*

I tried contacting Ash after, but she never answered, and I gave up trying, and then the more time that passed, the more awkward it became, and an apology two years down the line would just be... lame. So, now, we don't even speak about it anymore. I wouldn't blame her for hating us all. If I'm honest, we deserve it.

Cole sat next to me in the back of the Terra Cruiser, talking about magic. He was wearing a gray pinstripe suit, black shirt, and formal, silver tie, perfectly knotted, like he was on his way to a meeting rather than university. But that was Cole: a suit for every day of the year. He was more like his dad than any of us realized.

"Rumor has it that we can invoke the Divine and awaken our elements before initiation," Cole said. "It would put us ahead of the game."

"Or we can be patient. I'm not going to screw things up by doing that."

"Lack of confidence, brother, every time." Cole fixed his already perfect collar and tie. "I've been waiting all my life for this. I'm going to get the most powerful element of all."

"Fire?" I asked.

"Ha!" Cole shook his head. "Celestial."

I chuckled. "Yeah, good luck with that."

I caught his frown before he replaced it with a devious grin. "Laugh all you want. When it happens, you'll be the first I practice on."

"Whatever, Bevair."

"Imagine the power. My industry already leads the others through money alone, but with Celestial magic running through my veins..."

He left the sentence hanging, probably picturing himself as some kind of demi-god sitting on a gold throne and wielding an invincible sword. It wasn't an image I wanted to dwell on—he'd cut Ashlyn off without a second thought; what would stop him from doing the same to us?

"Think about it," he continued. "There are only three humans known to have acquired Celestial magic."

"Yeah, and one of them is in jail, and the other is dead."

"You're a coward, Aster," he said, his eyes narrowed. "I'll get Celestial, and then maybe you'll listen."

I tried to see beyond my ghostlike reflection in the passenger window and watched the landscape change. It was a ten-hour drive from Cole's family mansion to the university, and we'd left early in the morning to arrive before dinner. We'd already left behind the sprawling cities with their glass towers and air of busyness, and now we were entering the Eldergreen Forest, where the colors became more vibrant, and the trees seemed to reach for the sky. I wondered if that was why Aurora had been built here—not only for the peace and its connection to nature but because it was setting an example of aiming high.

Cole said I read too much into things and that not everything in life has a deep, philosophical theme, but I couldn't help smiling at the breathtaking scenery of our land. I'd studied the images displayed on my Echo Panel—an enchanted, palm-sized device that revealed distant places with a touch and so much more. Crafted from smooth crystals embedded with swirling threads of light, it responded to my thoughts and fingers. Through it, I could access information, send messages, and even communicate face-to-face with others, seeing and hearing them as if they stood beside me. Using the Echo Panel, I explored the thick woodlands, misty waterfalls, and massive canyons contained within the Elder-green Forest.

I already knew that Cole had no interest in any of this. He was here to study. I'd switched off hours ago to his steady stream of chatter about how he believed that one day, Andis would be ruled by one leader—meaning him—and how everyone knew it was time for change. There was something brewing. There'd been an unexpected Celestial four years ago, and Aurora was hoping for magic to set a precedent now with the heirs all attending the university at the same time.

When he said all the heirs, he didn't include Ashlyn, of course. It was as if he'd erased her from his memories that night and never looked back. Was he simply going to pretend that she didn't exist at Aurora? Look the other way whenever he saw her in class or in the hallways? Because no matter how often he told himself that she was no longer a part of our lives, we'd grown up together, and whether we cared to admit it or not, she'd helped shape us into the people we were.

He was right about one thing, though—something was going to change, but not in the way he expected. Ashlyn was still an heir, and rather than planning our futures without her, we should've been hoping that one day, she would find it in her to forgive us.

"Once we graduate," Cole was still speaking, still in full-on we're-the-kings-of-the-world mode, "we'll all be ready to take over our industries, and Jase can head off to Vitalis school..."

"This is true." I agreed just to confirm that I was still listening.

But then the forest opened up, and I spotted the large, white arches in the distance, the towers in the four corners of the school, and the wide moat complete with white shadow swans and tall, green rushes, the heavy bridge lowered, ready to greet the new students.

"We're here!" I said.

CHAPTER FOUR

Ashlyn

I spent the whole journey to Aurora with my stomach twisted into knots like a coiled storm serpent ready to strike. The argument I'd had with my father the evening prior had played on my mind all night, causing me to toss and turn, watching the sky darken and lighten again through the open drapes while my thoughts continued to replay every harsh word we'd exchanged. My parents didn't travel with me; my father had a Council meeting, and my mother was attending an event for which she was a patroness. Perhaps that was a blessing, although it didn't make me feel any less anxious.

Until I saw the university looming ahead.

I'd visited once before, but arriving now, knowing this would be my home for the next four years, felt entirely different. Aurora consisted of several buildings, all constructed from red brick that gleamed in the sunshine like polished rubies. There were two dorms, both five stories high, with towers at each corner resembling the ancient castles from Andis's own legends. I could almost imagine a maiden standing at the highest window, her luminous hair cascading down the tower walls, while a daring hero or mystical creature awaited below, seeking a way to ascend to her.

Excitement swirled inside me, gradually replacing the

mounting anxiety I'd been feeling over the prospect of bumping into the guys—this place was huge. The chances of seeing them in the hallways or even sharing the same classes with them were minimal.

Inside, the university was even more magnificent—if that were at all possible. The lobby walls were decorated with sumptuous crimson and gold brocades, and as someone who'd grown up with luxury, even I had to stop and blink, turning in a full circle to take in the cavernous space. A grand moonwood reception desk dominated the center, its surface shimmering with veins of silver light. Luminescent crystals mounted on ornate sconces cast a soft glow, their light refracted through shades of deep sapphire. It elevated grandeur to a whole new level, and I entered with a feeling of pride and determination to prove that I was a worthy heir. Perhaps it was designed specifically for this reason. Aurora was a prestigious academy with an impressive Pathrun record, which was why the heirs had all been given unconditional offers to attend—in return, we were expected to excel in our chosen fields.

Wheeling my travel trunk behind me along the corridor of Tower C, I wandered open-mouthed, eyeing up every piece of ancient artwork, every bronze statuette, every crest, and candle on the walls, and believe me, there were plenty of them. By the time I located my room, 412, on the fourth floor, my mouth was dry, and the glowflies in my chest had grown wings the size of golden sparrows. My dorm room was nestled at the end of a hallway adjacent to the tower. On tiptoes, I peeped out of the tower window, watching the steady stream of arriving Terra Cruisers crawling across the university grounds like glimmer ants carrying crumbs.

Dumping my travel trunk outside my door, I investigated the tower first. The first room I came across was huge but cozy. Comfy couches with plump cushions and tasseled throws scattered across the arms were arranged in a semicircle in the center—for socializing, I guessed—while desks were set closer to the walls, which were lined with bookcases. A huge arched window allowed the sunlight to stream through, casting golden shadows across the entire room, making it feel even warmer and more inviting. I decided instantly that I would be spending all my leisure time here curled up with a book, which was basically how I'd spent the past two years between excruciatingly dull social events.

Feeling calmer and more positive about my first year at Aurora than I felt when I arrived, I wandered back to my room and unlocked the door using the key card I'd been given at the reception desk.

My heart fluttered as I stepped into my new home. It felt surreal, like I was outside my body watching someone who looked like me wandering through a scene set for a grand performance. *So, this is what happens when the first female heir arrives at the academy.* I even glanced around, half-expecting to find hidden observers behind the tapestries.

The room was larger than some of the grand inns I'd stayed in with my parents. T-shaped, it was more like a luxurious suite, and I felt a rush of fear as it dawned on me that, overnight, we were expected to behave like adults. I hoped the other heirs had received the same message. It would make everyone's life easier if we could stop behaving like spoiled children and at least try to get along.

There was a small kitchen area to the left of the hallway with a polished stone counter and cream-colored cabinets—very elegant and totally in contrast with the rest of the building, but I wasn't complaining. Especially when I pushed open the door to the right and discovered the bathing chamber with the moonstone tub standing on gold-clawed feet, a spacious shower enclosed by etched glass panels, and a huge mirror framed with softly glowing crystals. Aurora had gone out of its way to make this feel like a slice of home.

By now, I was buzzing. Back out into the hall, I tugged my travel trunk along the cream-colored rug, praying that the wheels wouldn't leave scuffs that I'd be expected to scrub clean, and entered the bedroom.

I'd definitely saved the best for last.

The room was divided into two identical halves, split down the middle by another pale rug—didn't they consider footprints? In front of the large arched window were two identical desks. But the showpieces—the things that made my cheeks ache because I was grinning so widely—were the oversized, four-poster beds draped with gold-fringed curtains and crimson comforters, the school crest picked out on them with gold embroidery.

I knew which bed was mine—the boxes I'd had shipped to Aurora ahead of my arrival were stacked neatly by the moonwood headboard. I left my travel trunk upright next to the boxes and set my bookbag down on top of them, tracing the crest with my fingertip: the lit torch with a golden ring encircling it. I wondered if it represented the flame that they expected every student to carry high above their heads as a mark of respect and loyalty to the university.

Ignoring the moonwood wardrobe and nightstand, I quickly glanced around the room, double-checking that I wasn't being watched, before slipping off my comfortable shoes and leaping backward onto the plush bed, limbs spread wide. I stared up at the crimson canopy above my head, grinning like a child who'd just discovered a hidden treasure, and wriggled my body, grabbing handfuls of the smooth fabric and scrunching it up. I let out an excited squeal. Okay, so maybe I was overreacting, but after the argument with my father and my anxiety over seeing the heirs again, this was my chance to let it all out unnoticed so that I could relax and greet my roommate later like a normal person. Well, semi-normal, anyway.

"Ashlyn Grove?"

The voice startled me, and I sat up, dragging the comforter with me. I flexed my fingers, trying to smooth it back across the bed, and blew hair out of my eyes. Typical. I didn't even have a chance to brush my hair and straighten my tunic, which had ridden up in all the excitement.

"Sorry, I didn't mean to frighten you. I'm Jenny Webber. Your roommate."

I hadn't heard her come in, and I wasn't sure how much of my childish behavior she'd witnessed, but at least she was smiling at me.

Jenny Webber was petite, with a tiny frame and slim, tanned legs beneath her short, deep-blue dress. As she stepped closer, I noticed the sparkling stars scattered across the fabric like a galaxy. She certainly knew how to make a girl feel underdressed. I tugged my tunic down to cover my waist, wishing I'd chosen anything but dark leggings to wear on my first day. What was I thinking? Comfort—that's what I was thinking, but apparently, my roommate had no such qualms. She was barefoot, with shimmering anklets around each ankle, making it look as if she wore intricate sandals. She had short, almost-black curls, freckled cheeks, and pale lips that glistened softly and wore delicate crystal spectacles. The overall effect was that she looked like a fragile moonstone figurine. An extremely cute moonstone figurine.

"Shall I go back out and come in again?" She gestured to the front door with a smile.

"No, please don't."

I jumped off the bed and stood facing my new roommate. I was at least a head taller than she was, and for the first time in my life, I felt kind of clumsy and awkward, like a flower that had spent too long in the bright sunlight and outgrown all the other delicate blossoms in the garden.

"Hello, Jenny." I didn't know whether to shake hands or hug or just offer a wave from across the room and ended up clutching my hands in front of my chest. Seriously, who knew what kind of first impression I was making on her? "How did you know my name?"

"My mom's a guidance counselor here—she told me that we were going to be roommates. I was so excited when I found out. I mean, I've seen you around at parties in the Bevair mansion, so I knew that you were just normal like the rest of us, but still... I'm sharing a room with Ashlyn Grove! That'll be something to add to my credentials when we leave Aurora: *shared a room with the first female heir.*" She giggled, and the sound was light and playful, and I decided instantly that I was going to like sharing a room with her.

"We've been to the same parties?" I asked. How did I not notice her before?

"Not exactly. My uncle works for Lord Bevair, so I've seen you around. Well, I used to see you around, not so much lately."

I'd already noticed that Jenny talked a lot, her tongue trying to keep pace with her thoughts as they scrambled in different directions. Which suited me just fine. I inhaled deeply, wondering what I should say. Everyone knew about the rift, but I'd bet that few people knew what really happened that night. "You know about that, huh?" I said.

Jenny shrugged. "Cole Bevair didn't exactly keep it quiet, and then I didn't see you with your parents at the next party, so I guessed something had happened to split up the group."

I let out a groan. "Great. Do you think everyone here will be expecting drama when we all meet up again?"

"Absolutely!" she said brightly. "It's just the way people are. As they say, curiosity snared the mooncat and all that. Doesn't mean you have to give them what they want, though."

"I don't want to."

"That's the spirit." Jenny grinned at me. "If the guys want to cause drama, then let them. They'll only make themselves look ridiculous. And, you know, it is kind of a momentous occasion—all five heirs starting at Aurora at the same time. Even if there weren't any tensions between you all, people would be watching your every move."

"Even better," I said. "I was kind of hoping I could just blend in."

Jenny shook her head, hands on her hips. "Have you looked in the mirror recently? You're never going to blend in looking like this, so if you want my advice, embrace it. Get yourself noticed. Work hard and show them what you're made of."

I laughed out loud. "Are you always so positive?"

"Oh, I have a whole journal packed full of inspirational sayings." Jenny glanced behind me at the rumpled bed. "You're new to all this, aren't you?"

"Does it show?"

I followed her gaze.

"A little."

She lifted her travel trunk onto her bed, unzipped it, and started unpacking, hanging her clothes in her wardrobe. I could tell at a glance that Jenny didn't care much for stretch fabric. Everything that she pulled out of her case was stunning, carefully chosen to suit her petite frame and dark hair. She was every girl's idea of a best friend: fashion advice, clothes to share (if only they would fit), motivational quotes.

"You're positively radiating curiosity and excitement," she said. "I'm quite jealous. I'm a first-year student like you, but I visited my brother often when he was here a few years back, so I don't feel new." She paused and watched me open my own trunk, a violet-colored dress with an elegant, off-the-shoulder neckline in her hands. "There are plenty of intriguing spots around Aurora, especially beyond the other side of the wall."

I knew which wall she meant—it was the one that separated the immaculate grounds from the woods. My mom had told me that it contained a magical spell to protect the students, but most students ignored it and ventured into the woods anyway.

"I'd love to show you around," Jenny said.

CHAPTER FIVE

Ashlyn

Jenny gave me the guided tour en route to the bookstore; my Arcane Mathematics book hadn't been delivered to my house, and I had enough on my plate without worrying about missing textbooks.

She explained the rules of the women's dormitory: no mischief after curfew, no unauthorized gatherings, and be considerate of your neighbors. Pretty standard stuff. Her friend from the preparatory academy was also at Aurora, which made my stomach twist a little; I hoped that Jenny wouldn't abandon me for her old friend at the first opportunity. Not that I wanted to become dependent on one person, but she already seemed like a cool person to have around, and since we were sharing a room, I didn't want things to get awkward whenever it was just the two of us.

"She already doesn't like her roommate, though," Jenny said. "I'm sure she'll explain later. You'll love Emma. She's one of those people you can't help liking, kind and generous and selfless. Unlike me."

She laughed the statement off as we stepped into the lift. I suffered from motion sickness and winced as the doors closed, and I felt the unpleasant dip of weightlessness. I would tell Jenny once I knew her better, but for now, I was determined not to give anyone a reason to talk about me. Even my roommate.

"Couldn't she ask to switch rooms or something?" I suggested.

"Maybe," Jenny said. "The same thing happened to my brother Harvey when he was here. That situation was easily sorted, though, because other people had complained about the same kid."

Harvey Webber. For some reason, the name rang a faint bell at the back of my mind, but I didn't have a chance to pursue it because the lift doors opened onto the first-floor hallways, where a group of girls watched us emerge like we were roaming the corridors without clothing or something. One even leaned closer to her friend and whispered behind her hand, her eyes following me so that there was no ambiguity over what she was doing… Like I wouldn't notice!

"Yeah, yeah, we have an heir in our midst," Jenny said loudly enough for all to hear. "Get over it, girls. Her blood's still red, and she uses the bathroom just like everyone else."

She kept walking, her arm linked with mine as if nothing had even happened. I glanced over my shoulder at the girl who'd done the whispering; she didn't look so sure of herself now, and I found myself smiling as I matched my stride to Jenny's. I felt like I was floating. It was good to know that I'd already found someone who didn't treat me differently just because I was an heir and who was also prepared to fight in my corner to help keep my life as normal as possible.

This was my lucky day. After two years of planning my entire existence around avoiding the other heirs, I finally felt like I was back on track.

Jenny was a knowledgeable tour guide—another bonus. The center of campus was like a marketplace, a courtyard surrounded by buildings of various shapes and sizes; it was the Student Commons, where we could find all sorts of stuff: books, stationery, guidance, medication, and even directions around the grounds. The red-bricked buildings housed the administrative offices, the guidance counselors' salons, campus security, conference halls, and last, the bookstore.

Before we entered, Jenny pointed out that the Dining Pavilion was the halfway point between the Student Commons and the boys' dormitories. She didn't mention the other heirs. She didn't need to; I was already picturing them standing in line behind me while I dithered over a frosted moonbrew or a spiced embertea, Cole breathing down my neck and making snide remarks about girls never being trusted to make important decisions.

There was a strict no-magic rule for unsupervised students, but I spotted a couple of students displaying their gifts between the buildings, sparks of electricity popping above one guy's hands, while a random gust of wind lifted a passing student's skirt. The girl caught it before it revealed anything above her knees and glanced around for the culprit, who had turned his back and was acting like he was completely oblivious. I couldn't help smiling. That would be us soon. While I'd never been the kind of student who chose to break the rules, I guessed it must be difficult not being able to practice a new gift. It would be like giving a child a precious toy and telling them they could only look at it but not touch it.

The bookstore was two stories high. Inside, the central atrium soared all the way up to the vaulted ceiling, where an enchanting display had been crafted to make it appear that the ceiling contained all the constellations in the night sky. I stood beneath it, staring open-mouthed, as the sky slowly faded from midnight black to mauve, to pink, and then finally blue—the kind of blue one might see in the crystalline waters of the Sapphire Lakes or in the deepest hues of a twilight horizon.

"Wow," I breathed.

"I know." Jenny followed my gaze. "You could never get bored with that view."

She dragged me through the store to the math section where I would find my Arcane Mathematics—apparently, she'd had to pop in earlier to buy one, too, so she knew her way around. While I pulled out my Echo Panel and double-checked that I was looking for the right book, Jenny sat on an old-fashioned wooden stool, her knees hugged closely to her chest, making her appear even more doll-like.

"How do you think you'll feel when you see the other heirs?" she asked.

I froze, my fingertips hovering in front of the book that I needed. It was a good question. I'd spent many restless nights playing out different scenarios in my head about what would happen when we finally came face-to-face with each other again, but ultimately, it was impossible to predict because I had no idea how they were going to react either.

"I don't know," I said truthfully, turning to face her, the book in my hand. "They made it quite clear that they wanted nothing to do with me, which is why I've spent the past two years avoiding them." It felt wrong to be speaking about my former best friends this way, especially when I'd only known Jenny for a little over an hour, but at the same time, it felt good to talk to an outsider, someone who didn't know me or the guys, someone who could perhaps offer impartial advice.

"You can't avoid them forever, though," Jenny said. "Seems unfair to me that you've been the one who skipped parties, so you didn't bump into them. I didn't see them rearranging their social calendar."

Even though I'd probably never seen Jenny at the Bevair mansion, it was obvious now that she'd paid a lot of attention to me. It was only natural—everyone knew about the five heirs, and although we'd attended regular schools and tried to fit in, our family names alone set us apart from others our age. Aurora was going to be no different. I'd already seen proof of that.

The coils in my stomach that had started to unwind when I

met Jenny twitched a little more tightly, hugging my anxieties close. "If that's the way they want it to be, I won't try to stop them," I said. There. I'd said it out loud. It was the first step to proving to myself that I'd managed perfectly well without them and that I'd continue to thrive without them, too. I ignored the pang of missing my old friends. That was all in the past.

Jenny smiled. "You don't need them, Ashlyn. They'll soon learn that they can't order you around just because you're a girl."

"I don't think—" I began. Why was I still defending them? Jenny was right. That was exactly what they'd done; they manipulated the situation to make me look foolish because it was easier than owning up to their own silly games.

"Hey, I know it's disheartening to think that they deliberately cast you aside to make themselves look good, but seriously, they're not worth it." She jumped off the stool and took my hand in hers. It was a maternal gesture, one that made me smile, given how tiny and delicate she appeared beside me.

I nodded. "I always thought they were worth it, you know. We were so close when we were younger."

"Yeah, and boys grow up and let their baser instincts take over —like they can't think past that sudden rush of energy in their blood."

Was that what this was all about? It made sense, given what the guys had all said to me that night.

"I'm sure they'll grow out of it eventually," I said, the queasiness in my stomach starting to settle again.

"I wouldn't count on it." Her voice rose a notch. "Cole Bevair is an arrogant twit who thinks he's better than everyone else, and the others will cling to him like starfire moths to a flame, afraid of getting the cold shoulder too. They haven't got a backbone between them."

That was when Kris stepped out from behind the bookcase, his face pale as he swiped his floppy fringe away from his eyes.

I almost dropped the book on my foot but caught it before it landed, grateful for the distraction as my face flooded with heat. How long had he been standing there? Had he heard the whole conversation?

"Oops," Jenny said, straightening herself to her full height, the top of her head still barely reaching my shoulder.

"Kris..." I managed.

He swallowed, his gaze flitting between me and my roommate. "Is that what you really think of us?" he asked.

"I-I..." I hated myself for stammering.

This had never happened in the reunion scenes inside my head. I'd secretly hoped that I'd be able to stand tall and defend myself because I was innocent. The fear that they were still ganging up on me, blaming me for what happened that night, crept inside my stomach, and the serpent finally uncoiled.

"Yes," I said. "That's exactly what I think of you. Not even one of you asked for my version of events two years ago, and in all that time, none of you cared how it felt to be me, ostracized by the other heirs." My heart was racing, and I hoped he wouldn't notice the way my hands trembled.

"Ashlyn..." He studied the toes of his shoes as if afraid to look me in the eye. "I didn't think—"

"No, you didn't, Kris," I interrupted him. I couldn't bear to stand here watching him any longer. It was obvious now that two years had done nothing to alter their feelings toward me. They had no intention of reconciling our differences and trying to get along, even if it was what was best for the industries. "So, if you don't mind, I'm going to pay for my book and go back to my dorm." I went to step around him and hesitated. "Perhaps you could warn your friends to keep out of my way, too. That way, we'll all be happy."

I approached the counter, afraid to look behind me, but sensing Kris's eyes boring into the back of my skull. I handed over the money for my book and left the bookstore with Jenny.

Outside, she gave me a big hug. "You were brilliant in there," she said. "Now they know they can't walk all over you, and it's only day one."

As we headed back to the girls' dorm, Jenny peered over her shoulder at the entrance to the bookstore, a broad smile on her face, and it was only then that I wondered if she'd known Kris had been there all along.

CHAPTER SIX

Kristopher

I stared at my reflection in the mirror. I'd hardly slept the night before, and it wasn't because I was sharing a strange room with a guy I'd barely spoken to. My roommate was called Fredrick, and although he seemed like the kind of guy I could get along with—he'd pulled a couple of handheld devices from his travel trunk and set them up before he even looked at his clothes—he'd yet to make eye contact with me. I knew it was buzzing around the hallways that the five heirs had finally entered the building, but he could at least try speaking to me before he labeled me as unapproachable.

I mean, I considered myself to be a regular kind of guy. I wasn't a scowler like Cole, or competitive like Jase, or a bit weird like Shane. I was just normal.

So, why didn't I feel it this morning?

When I'd heard Ashlyn talking to her friend about us, my heart had skipped a beat the way it always used to when we were still friends. The familiar smile spread across my face, and I was about to surprise her when I remembered all over again that we were no longer part of the same group and that what she was saying about us wasn't exactly favorable. How could I have erased the past two years just like that? Was it wishful thinking to hope that when we finally saw each other, everything would be okay again? And why was I so disappointed to find that it wasn't?

I mean, we'd cut her off without a second thought. Ashlyn was right when she said that we hadn't given her a chance, and if I was honest with myself—which perhaps I should've tried being sooner—it was all because of Cole. He said she'd played us, and we all knew how much Cole hated being played.

But what had kept me awake the most last night was her friend's comment: *They've not got a backbone between them.* Was that what people really thought of us, that we were Cole's lackeys?

I hadn't mentioned it to the guys last night—I knew how Cole would react, and I didn't want it to make things even worse between us and Ashlyn—but I had to warn them. If Ash had come to Aurora with the intention of causing trouble, we needed to get our heads together and come up with a plan.

I'd already missed breakfast, so I messaged the guys and asked them to meet me in the Dining Pavilion for lunch. Then I let myself out of the room quietly so as not to wake Fredrick, who was still sound asleep, hoping that I didn't keep him awake all night with my tossing and turning. Thank the Spirits the beds didn't creak.

There were six eateries in the Dining Pavilion, each offering a different specialty: a bistro serving handmade kinds of pasta and stone-baked flatbreads, two stalls featuring steaming bowls of spiced noodles and ocean-fresh sashimi, a classic tavern with hearty fare, a fiery grill known for its spicy ember wraps, and a self-serve counter where students could grab anything from a savory herb-stuffed roll to a sweet honeycake and a frothy cream brew.

I instantly spotted Shane with a tray of ocean-fresh sashimi and Jase, his tray piled high with a stacked meatroll and seasoned root wedges, scanning the area for a quiet corner to sit in. I flinched. Was this what it was going to be like now—the four of us trying to keep out of Ashlyn's way? My cheeks grew hot. If that was how she wanted it...

I grabbed a herb-stuffed cheese roll and a bottle of fizzy berry tonic, knowing I wouldn't be able to eat it even though my stomach was rumbling. I joined the guys as Cole strolled into the Dining Pavilion, eyeing a table full of girls who were all watching him with wide smiles and sidelong glances. I didn't know how he managed it, but girls were like that wherever he went. Maybe it was his presence—he did have a certain kind of bold, well-groomed charm about him. Or maybe it was the fact that he was heir to the Mercantyl industry. That tended to sway things in his favor.

Cole slid into his seat with a glass of sparkling crystalstream water and a bowl of seasoned rice noodles. Even then, he was still scanning the rest of the Dining Pavilion to see who'd noticed him. It wasn't easy being Cole Bevair. "Hit me with it, Reeve," he said.

From my position, I could see every entry point into the Dining Pavilion, and I skimmed the area again, reassuring myself that Ashlyn and her friend were not there. "I saw Ashlyn yesterday," I said, pulling a crust off my roll and tossing it back into the wrapper. I never did like crusts.

"How is she?" Shane asked.

I avoided full-on eye contact with my friend. I knew that he'd tried calling Ashlyn after that night, and I guess I'd always felt guilty that I didn't make more of an effort with her, too. "Hard to tell," I said. "She was with a friend."

"And?" Cole rolled his eyes. Like I said, it wasn't easy being perfect.

"She shut me down before I had a chance to ask, told me to warn you all to keep away from her."

"Ash or her friend?" Shane asked.

"Does it matter?" Cole snapped. "What did she look like?"

"Ash or her friend?" I realized my mistake when Cole squeezed his eyes shut, waiting for the rest of us to keep up. "Short girl, glasses, black curly hair, cute. Cute with attitude."

Cole's eyes narrowed. "Interesting."

"What's that supposed to mean?"

"Nothing." Cole shrugged. "Only that I have a feeling Ashlyn Grove is going to cause trouble for us this year."

"Not if we bring her down first." Jase had already polished off his stacked meatroll before I'd even swallowed a mouthful.

Shane flinched. "Come on, guys, this is Ash we're talking about."

"And I seem to recall you taking her side one time too many." Cole jabbed a fork in Shane's direction. "It's clear that Ashlyn Grove has already started spreading rumors about us. Why else would she have gotten all argumentative with Kris in front of her friend?"

Shane shook his head. "That isn't like Ash. There's no way she would do that."

"You don't even know her," Cole said.

"Whose fault is that?" Shane glared at Cole.

"I seem to recall that we all agreed to exile her." Cole sat back in his seat. "If you all want to go sucking up to her now, be my guest. Don't come crawling back to me when you realize she's been leading you on all along."

Cole had always been the forceful one, and he had a point that we'd all agreed to cut Ashlyn off, but that didn't give him the right to go making up ridiculous stories about her.

"She's just angry at us," I said. "Maybe we should give her time and—"

"And what?" Cole interjected. "Her father has been trying to get his hands on my industry for years. He wanted her to marry me so that it would give him a foot in the door, not the other way around. The man is power-crazy, and he's using his daughter to drive a wedge between us to cause a distraction."

"For what purpose?" I asked. It sounded to me like Cole had just described his own father, but I kept that to myself.

"Wait and see, Kristopher. All will be revealed soon enough." He swallowed a mouthful of his drink. "Look, we should steer clear of Ashlyn and keep our eyes and ears open. Our friendship is more important, and we need to keep it strong. Agreed?"

"Agreed." Jase nodded. "I don't trust her."

"Me either," I added, avoiding Shane's gaze.

Shane inhaled deeply. "Agreed," he said with no conviction. Because how could we refuse?

Jase

Yeah, so perhaps Cole was being a little bit dramatic over the whole industry takeover thing, but Ashlyn had given us no reason to trust her. She'd given us plenty of reasons not to. *I think.* I mean, she played us all that night at the gala ball, and Cole wasn't fabricating the scenario in which her dad was desperate for her to marry one of us. Looking back on our childhood, she'd always kind of been the bossy one, choosing the games and then manipulating them so that she always won. The Elementum industry was never going to work if that was how she proposed to run it, through manipulation and tyranny.

The only problem was that fond memories of Ashlyn still crept in occasionally. Like the time I'd tumbled off my riding cart and scraped the skin off both my knees and elbows and she sat me down in her mother's washroom, carefully picking out every tiny stone and piece of grit with a pair of enchanted silver tweezers that glowed faintly as they soothed the raw skin. She'd kept talking the whole time, pretending she didn't notice the pain etched on my face.

I shook my head, flinging the mental images as far away from me as possible. Cole was right about one thing. People change, and that night had proved that we didn't know Ashlyn at all.

Kris was still checking out the corridors over his shoulder on our way to our first lesson at Aurora. "Calm down, will you?" I said. "What are the chances she'll end up in our class? You've got to keep a little faith." He nodded in agreement, but I knew Kris better than anyone, and what he was really doing was trying to quiet me so he could focus on the other students approaching the alchemy lab, watching for a glimpse of long, chestnut hair.

A couple of pretty girls entered the room, and one paused to glance our way before turning back to her friend and squeezing her arm. It was always an ego boost getting noticed by charming girls. So what if our reputation as heirs preceded us? We were young, and I intended to make the most of my good fortune while I had the chance. I still had seven years of study ahead before I had to knuckle down to the serious work, so no one was going to deprive me of a little fun along the way, especially not Ashlyn Grove.

The lab, when we stepped inside, was a scholar's haven. It was larger than any classroom at Terrace, the preparatory academy the guys and I had attended, bigger, even, than all those prep labs put together. Aurora didn't do anything by halves, that was for sure. Shelves lined the walls, filled with vials and a labyrinth of glass tubes containing liquids in every color imaginable, fueled by bubbling cauldrons on the counters below. I wasn't sure if the cauldrons were powered by magic or something else, but the overall impression was a mesmerizing maze of liquid in motion. From the ceiling hung woven holders filled with lush, green plants; a myriad of apothecary jars containing preserved specimens floated in some sort of solution, displayed in glass cabinets. A small creature with tufted fur and iridescent wings darted around in its glass enclosure, tapping against the sides as it took its morning exercise. Above our heads, a skeletal model of a winged creature pieced together from ancient bones hung as if it might spring to life at any moment.

It was like stepping into a contained enchanted garden, one

where an eccentric scholar had decided to install an alchemy laboratory. I was impressed.

"Whoa," Kris said, trying to take it all in. He was clearly impressed, too.

"Let's sit in the back." I smacked his shoulder to bring him back down to reality and led him toward the rear of the room, grabbing a long bench with two stools.

Alchemy wasn't my best subject, which was a bit unfortunate considering I was heir to the Vitalis industry. I had to work hard for my grades, which were average at best. Kris, on the other hand, was a natural. He seemed to view alchemy as just another branch of Technomancy, seeing the body as some kind of living mechanism, so he just got it.

He must've sensed my confidence wavering because he said, "Hey, don't stress. We'll buddy up for assignments. It'll be fine."

The two girls who'd entered before us were sitting diagonally across the room. One gave me a tentative smile, and I flashed my most charming smile back—the one that had worked wonders back at the preparatory academy, even on Madam Kendall, our math tutor, when I'd hand in assignments late and should've been getting reprimanded. Her friend was eyeing Kris. I elbowed him in the ribs. Someone had to get him to pay attention; all through the academy, he'd been too hung up on Ashlyn to date anyone, but that was about to change—at least if I had anything to say about it.

I'd thought that the class was full, but then the door opened, and Ashlyn walked in with a short girl who must've been the roommate Kris had seen her with in the bookstore. I ducked, my chin almost resting on the bench, hoping that they wouldn't spot us behind the other students. "Don't look," I hissed at Kris.

Too late.

"I said, 'Don't look.'"

Kris lowered his head, too. "Here's the thing, when you tell someone not to look, it's the first thing they do. It's in our nature."

"Have they noticed us?"

Kris raised his eyes and lowered them again. "Yes." He chanced another look before I could stop him. "Might as well have a flashing target above our heads that says: HERE WE ARE."

"Don't keep staring at them," I whispered.

A pair of vibrant green, wide-legged pants approached our desk and halted right in front of us. I followed them with my eyes, up to a bright yellow, embroidered overcoat layered over a pale-green linen tunic and finally to the graying hair and silver-rimmed spectacles of the alchemy instructor, Professor Anita Harpe. "When you're quite ready, Master Branson," she said, "perhaps you wouldn't mind joining the rest of the class." She rapped the desktop with her knuckles twice as if to reinforce the statement and then drifted back to the front of the room, her long coat swirling lightly behind her.

All eyes were on us. Of course, they were. She'd already mentioned my name, and the lesson hadn't even begun; if Ashlyn didn't know that we were hiding from her before, she did now.

Sometimes, things seem like a good idea, and it's only after they play out differently than you'd imagined that you realize just how misguided and unoriginal they were. Straightening, I glanced at the back of Ashlyn's head. Her spine was rigid. I knew her well enough to see she was forcing herself not to look our way.

Her friend had no such qualms, though. A slow grin spread across her face as she shook her head and turned her attention to the professor.

Heat flooded my cheeks as Professor Harpe introduced herself as a practitioner of geomancy, which was hardly surprising since she taught alchemy. I needed to get a grip. If Ashlyn wanted to make fools of us, she was doing a great job without even trying.

Professor Harpe reached under her desk and retrieved a clay pot, which she placed on top. "So, who can tell me what alchemy, particularly biological alchemy, is?"

Ashlyn's friend's hand shot into the air, and since they were sitting in the front row, the professor aimed a wide smile her way. "Jenny Webber?"

"Yes, ma'am," Jenny said. "Biology is the study of organic life."

Ugh. I could already tell she was the type to suck up to every teacher. No wonder Ashlyn seemed to like her.

"Precisely. Biology is the study of living organisms and the energy that flows through them." Professor Harpe reached below her desk again, pulled out a small bucket, and began filling the pot with soil. "Without the natural laws that govern our world, there would be no life."

Her hands hovered over the pot as she closed her eyes, inhaling deeply, then raising her hands in a cupping motion toward the ceiling. A collective gasp went up as a purple starlily sprouted from the soil, its petals tilting toward the students as if waiting for applause.

"We may have a few geomancers among you, but we will find out soon enough." The professor moved to the front of her desk and leaned back against it. "It takes energy to move this planet, to grow forests and mountains and streams. Think of the energy a predator needs to hunt and how that predator absorbs the energy from its prey, which, in turn, absorbs energy from its own food source. This is the circle of life. It is also the circle of magic."

This was it. This was what every student here was excited about—tapping into the magical spectrum, as per our contracts with the Spirits. I didn't know much about these contracts—Ashlyn's family handled them—and I often wondered just how much control they had over them. Our contracts were written at birth and stored securely until our eighteenth birthday. Come to think of it, did Ashlyn already know what powers each of us would receive? Did they discuss magical contracts over dinner, the way my family talked about new medicinal discoveries? I stared at the back of her head, wondering if she'd deliberately caused this rift between us because she feared her powers weren't going to measure up and needed to secure one of us in marriage to protect her status. That would explain why her father had never taught her anything about the Elementum industry.

Professor Harpe placed the potted plant in front of Jenny Webber with a smile. "I'm the one who keeps the flowers blooming around campus all year round, in case you were wondering." She moved to the lesson panel and asked the class to open our books to chapter one.

The lesson continued smoothly. Professor Harpe had a casual teaching style that suited me, and by the end of the double period, I was feeling more confident about the course. Aurora was going to be good to me; I could sense it. All I needed now was to get picked for the Pathrun club, and I'd be cruising all the way.

"Okay, class, I know this is day one, but we're here to work hard, right?" Professor Harpe stood at the front of the room, acknowledging each student with a steady gaze. "We're going to begin a semester-long project that requires working in pairs. And before you start nudging your friends to buddy up, I must inform you that I will be choosing your partners."

A collective murmur swept through the room. I didn't dare look at Kris—I wasn't about to give the rest of the class another chance to dissect our reactions and chew over them during lunch in the Dining Pavilion.

"I get the same reaction from my students every year, and it never gets old. So"—Professor Harpe clapped her hands—"listen for your names, please."

She proceeded to recite names from the register in pairs, a glint of amusement visible in the faint lines fanning from the corners of her eyes. I was beginning to think that the bright clothes and soothing voice were all a facade—she was getting way too much joy from mixing up the class.

My pulse raced as she worked her way through the list, and I still hadn't heard my name or Ashlyn's. The Spirits wouldn't do that to me, would they? I even found myself wishing she'd get paired with Kris if only I could work with someone else—anyone else—and it scared me how uneasy I felt about the whole situation. We used to be friends, for Spirit's sake. Ashlyn wasn't a monster with two heads and acid breath.

"Nolan Milligan," Professor Harpe announced, "you will be working with Jenny Webber."

I saw the girl peer around the room and averted my eyes.

"Kristopher Reeve... You'll be working with Danielle Taylor."

The cute girl who'd been watching him all lesson beamed at Kris from across the room. Lucky man.

Before I had a chance to remind myself that Ashlyn's name was yet to be called, Professor Harpe said, "Jase Branson, you'll be working with Ashlyn Grove."

No, no, no, no, no.

I covered my face with my hands. I didn't even know if I'd groaned out loud, but I sensed Kris's entire body tense up beside me as the snickers around the room penetrated my thoughts. Don't give them anything to gossip about, I told myself. But I couldn't help but glance at Ashlyn, who kept her head down while the professor walked back around the desk, apparently satisfied with the announcements.

"If anyone has any issues with their partnerships," Professor Harpe said, "please address them with me in private." Her eyes zeroed in on me, her mouth turned down at the corners. She clearly disliked having her choice questioned so vocally and expected better from her new students, especially the industry heirs. "I want you all to meet up with your partners and exchange contact details, and I'll share the project details next time. Class dismissed."

I barely had time to reach for my satchel before Danielle was standing in front of Kris, twirling her hair around her fingers. "Um, would you like to sync our Echo Panels? For, you know, assignments and... stuff?"

Kris whipped out his Echo Panel and dropped it onto Danielle's foot. She yelped and jumped backward. Then their foreheads collided as they both stooped to pick it up at the same time.

I watched it happen without really seeing any of it. Ashlyn hadn't moved. Jenny Webber was on her feet, her gaze hopping between us and Ash as if uncertain if she should intervene. A tiny part of me was glad that Ash had a friend to look out for her, but a much bigger part of me, the wave of emotions that were growing and squeezing and making it difficult to breathe, wished that I'd been paired with anyone else in the room apart from Ash. I needed to get out of there, but I wasn't so far gone that I'd forgotten everyone was staring.

Shouldering my bag, I strode toward their table, Kris practically running to keep up with me. Perhaps I could still salvage this. I could be the bigger person—I was Jase Branson, heir to the Vitalis industry.

Only, it wasn't until I was standing in front of Ash, her large eyes peering up at me, that it all came flooding back, and I recalled how upset she'd been that night at the Bevair mansion. We'd been cruel to her that night. Maybe she deserved it, maybe she didn't, but I didn't want the reputation of a troublemaker hanging over me.

"Look, do you still have my Echo Panel details?" I asked, swallowing the lump in my throat.

She stared at me for what felt like ages. She'd warned us to stay away, and here we were, the first class of the semester, forced to work together on an assignment. Finally, she said, "No, Jase. I got rid of it a long while ago."

Jenny's eyes widened.

Ash had done it again. Any misgivings I might've had about the way we'd treated her blew away with those few words. "Well, I still have yours. I'll reach out to you later."

"Fine." Ash grabbed her satchel and left the room with Jenny by her side.

Was this the way it was going to be, the two of them joined at the hip? I had no foundation on which to base my opinion, but I had a sneaking suspicion that Jenny was going to get a lot of enjoyment out of watching the battle of the heirs this year.

"Master Branson?" Professor Harpe called me over to her desk. Kris came, too. "Is there an issue that I need to be aware of?"

The class had emptied; it was now or never.

"Yes, Professor," I said, surprised at the confidence in my voice. "Do I have to work with Ashlyn Grove? We don't exactly get along."

"Based on your unnecessary reaction when I called out your names, I think I get the point. I'll try to find you a new partner, but I'm not promising anything." She eyed me coolly. This wasn't the best start to a school year I'd ever had, and I was guessing she felt the same way. "As heir to one of the five industries, I expected better of you, Master Branson. I don't appreciate distractions in my classroom. Do I make myself clear?"

"Yes, Professor."

"Great class, Professor Harpe," Kris said, attempting to lighten the mood that had settled around us like a thundercloud.

"I don't appreciate flattery either, Master Reeve."

The professor turned her back on us. We were dismissed.

CHAPTER EIGHT

Ashlyn

A few days later, I was in the dorm, working on an Arcane Mathematics assignment. I'd gone up to the tower study hall first, but it was packed with other students, so I'd chosen to work in the privacy of my room instead. Not that I didn't get along with the others—most of the girls were friendly —but I still hadn't heard from Jase about our alchemy project, and it was making it hard to concentrate on anything else. How would he handle it? Would he be the confident, sometimes brash Jase I remembered from childhood, or would he be blunt, even cold, making it clear that any feelings he might have once harbored had long since faded? Not knowing was the worst part.

"Hey, Ash." Jenny came in and flopped onto her bed before curling her legs up and sorting through the pile of stuff she'd been carrying. She had a habit of sneaking up on me without me hearing her, like she'd somehow magicked her footsteps away, even though that was impossible as none of us had our gifts yet. "What are you doing?"

"Arcane Math assignment." I peered at her over my shoulder.

"Hurry up and get it finished. I have something to tell you, and everyone knows Professor Tate can be a real twit if assignments aren't turned in on time."

Rooming with Jenny was already proving useful—between her and her mom, their knowledge of the professors was invaluable, like having my own personal guidebook to Aurora.

"He's a non-user, which explains it all," Jenny said without glancing up.

"It does?" I'd assumed that all the professors were magical, given that Aurora was dedicated to nurturing elite magic users.

"Professor Tate married a user. They both taught here until she left him and transferred to another school. How are magic users even allowed to marry non-users anyway?" She shuddered dramatically.

I thought about it. Magic was tightly regulated by our families and the Council. If magic users married non-users, they'd be treading on thin ice since family lines were so sacred. And I had no idea how it would affect any children they had. I kept quiet.

"I think the Council should ban the option," Jenny continued, launching into a rant about the Council's incompetence. I only half-listened, my gaze drifting back to the nearly completed assignment on my desk. It wasn't that I wasn't interested in Jenny's opinion, but I knew that one day I'd be working closely with the Council myself, and I wanted to keep an open mind until I could form my own opinions, grounded in knowledge and experience.

"Anyway, what have you got there?" I asked when her rant finally wound down.

She grinned at me and waved a packet of pastries in the air. "The prefects are giving them out for free if you sign up for study teams," she said. "You should've come along."

"Yeah, maybe next time." Jenny opened her mouth to more than likely say something about me hiding away from the guys, and I quickly added, "I want to join some clubs, too. The sooner, the better."

"Well, I might just be able to help you with that. What are you doing tomorrow evening?" Her eyebrows danced above her glasses, and I couldn't help giggling.

"Probably more homework. Why?"

"Wrong!" She sat cross-legged on her bed and gestured for me to join her. "There's a first-year party in the Student Commons. Eek!" Her curls bounced as she shook with excitement, making her hair appear almost fluid around her face.

My shoulders slumped as I sat down and faced her, ripping open the pastry packet to distract from the look of disappointment on her face. "I don't know…"

"A lot of students are going. It'll be a cool way to meet everyone."

"Yeah, I already know some of them."

"Hey," she said, reaching for my hand. "You can't let those guys control your first year at Aurora. You have as much right to enjoy yourself as anyone else, and their presence should not stop you from having the time of your life."

I knew she was right, but it didn't make it any easier. I'd spent the last two years avoiding them, and it had become second nature.

"Besides," she said, "I want you to meet some friends of mine."

"Really?" She had my attention now. "Who?"

"Remember I told you about the club I joined before term started? The League of Magical Theory? A few of the members will be at the party, and I really want to introduce you. I know you're going to love them."

Her enthusiasm was infectious, and the club sounded intriguing, especially since they'd invited Jenny to join before she even started at Aurora. "Okay, okay," I said, rolling my eyes. "But only to meet your friends. Then I'm leaving."

Jenny threw her arms around me and squeezed. Not only did she talk a lot, but she and her mom were both tactile—something that would take some getting used to. "Deal," she said, pulling away. "But I guarantee you'll end up staying once you've met them."

Jenny leaped off the bed. "We should decide what to wear

now. I've seen those pretty dresses you stuffed in your wardrobe. We could have a fashion show. I could go find Emma."

"I don't know." I hated being such a downer, but Professor Tate's assignment was still looming over my head. My first week had already tossed enough challenges my way... so much for blending in. "Why don't you look through my wardrobe while I finish up?"

Jenny was getting ready to unleash her most persuasive arguments on me—and I'd already seen how convincing she could be —when there was a knock at the door. "Stay right there," she said. "Don't you dare move, Ash. I'll be right back."

Obedient as ever, I sat on her bed and didn't move. I heard Jenny squeal, and then she returned, arms linked with Emma, her friend from her preparatory academy.

"Look who's here," Jenny said. "Now you have to let us choose an outfit for the party. No arguments. Tell her, Em."

Emma grinned at me—she knew from experience that it was pointless to argue once Jenny made up her mind. I'd already been introduced to Emma, and I liked her from the start. She was every bit as sweet and kind as Jenny had described, and to top it off, she had a body that could turn heads, with curves to rival anyone's. Despite her perfect figure, long blonde hair, and wide gray eyes, she seemed oblivious to the stares of the boys in the hallways, and I had a lot of respect for her.

"Humor her," Emma said. "It's the easiest way."

Jenny released her arm and flung open my wardrobe doors. "How about this one?" She pulled out a shell-pink wrap dress.

"Nuh-uh." I shook my head. "My mom made me pack that one."

Emma winked at me and joined Jenny. I hoped that meant she was on my side and would choose something a bit more conservative, something that wouldn't get me noticed—at least not by the heirs. "Oh, by the way, I have news," Emma said. "My roommate, Samantha, has moved out, and I heard her father got his magical contract revoked."

Jenny gasped. For once, she was quiet... and still. It was rare to have a magical contract taken away; it generally meant that the person had broken it somehow. I'd only ever heard of it happening a couple of times.

"How did you find out?" I asked.

"I heard it from Ranya Mirelli. She's a prefect this year; she helped sort out the roommate situation."

"Ranya Mirelli?" She must've been Edna Mirelli's grand-daughter. I vaguely recalled meeting her at a family event.

"Whatever Samantha's father did, it involved a non-user," Emma said.

"What a fool," Jenny said, rolling her eyes. That was another thing I'd learned about Jenny. She lived for gossip, lived and breathed it, and devoured it for breakfast. "Why throw away a magical contract for a non-user? It's blasphemous."

I couldn't help smiling at her dramatics. "He must've had good reason. It isn't a decision you'd take lightly."

"I wouldn't take it any which way," Jenny said. "Once I get my gift, that's it. I'm hanging on to it until the end."

"How does it even work, Ashlyn?" Emma's expression was serious. "Doesn't your dad handle the contracts?"

"Uh-huh." I didn't want to confess that I didn't know exactly how it worked, thanks to my father keeping me in the dark. Everything I knew about it I'd learned from Jase.

"So, not only are the Lords in charge of the industries, but they control contract distribution too?" Emma pressed.

Jenny was still quiet.

I swiped my hair behind my ears. "Well, from what I understand, when a child is born with magic potential, my family gets notified and starts the process. The contract gets vaulted until the child is eighteen and unlocks their element, and then my parents release it from the vault, sign the contract, and that person becomes a documented user. It was assigned to my family by the Council years ago."

Emma was wide-eyed. "That's a lot of people to keep track of.

Just look how many of us will unlock our elements this year at Aurora alone."

"Well, there are more non-users than users," I clarified. "And my parents have a court of individuals to help keep up with the records." I realized that it made it sound like my parents knew everything there was to know about every magic user in Andis, but it wasn't like that at all.

Jenny waggled her eyebrows. "That's so cool. You get to see it all in action, huh?"

I shook my head. "Not really. My father doesn't want me learning about our industry because he doesn't think that I'm... He doesn't think that I'm ready."

A groan of outrage escaped Jenny's lips. "Men and their stupid egos and their refusal to believe that women can do anything they can do."

"And do it better," Emma added.

"Still, one day, you'll get to show him," Jenny said.

"Years from now." I didn't add that I would have to battle my father all the way if he was ever going to hand over the reins to me.

"Are all contracts the same?" Emma asked.

"I don't think so. I've never seen one. In fact, I don't think users ever get to see their own contracts."

"So, how does someone get caught breaking one then?" Jenny's curiosity was getting the better of her, and even the fashion show had been put on hold.

This was something I did know. "The contracts are magically bound and break of their own accord if a violation occurs. The contract turns to gold dust, and my parents get notified after the event. There's nothing they could do to prevent it from happening."

"That must be so sad," Emma said. "Imagine losing your magic just like that."

"Serves them right," Jenny said. "Anyone careless enough to break their contract and lose their magic is an idiot in my book."

"But what if it wasn't their fault?" Emma asked. "What if

circumstances outside their control meant that it was taken away from them?"

I recognized the fear in Emma's eyes. I'd never considered the possibility that a magic user might have their contract broken through no fault of their own, and I hoped to the Spirits that this was impossible. If it were true, and contracts could be broken by another individual, then would any magic user be safe? I squeezed my eyes shut to block out the image of Regalis Bevair at the charity auction, urging his wife to keep the other heirs away from me.

CHAPTER NINE

Ashlyn

The following day was warm and sunny, the buildings sparkling like they were putting on a show for the students. My stomach was still twisting at the thought of going to the Student Commons welcome party despite telling myself that I was being ridiculous—I'd been attending parties since I was old enough to walk. I guessed the past two years had affected me way more than I'd realized. Which made me angry with myself for allowing it to happen. Which made my stomach churn even more when I pictured the outfit the three of us had chosen for me to wear.

Jenny and Emma had squealed when I'd pulled out the sparkly silver romper from my closet. It was one of the few outfits I'd chosen entirely on my own—no input from my mom, who had eyed it with clear disapproval as I packed. The romper—a sleeveless, shimmering one-piece that draped gracefully without clinging, was elegant yet bold. When I'd tried it on in our dorm room the night before and paraded across the room, hips jutting playfully and ostentatiously flicking my hair over my shoulder, I'd barely even recognized my reflection in Jenny's floor-standing mirror.

I was overthinking everything. Should I dress to impress and show the other heirs what I could do when given the freedom to be myself, or should I hide inside the kind of clothes my mom insisted I bring to keep up appearances? I could imagine her narrowed eyes and pursed lips as she judged the romper. *Everyone will be watching you, Ashlyn, judging your every move. Do you think this outfit is wise?*

Did I? It had been a tough first week, my brain skipping between new lessons and the very real fear that I would bump into the guys in every corridor, and I'd been left feeling a little frazzled.

It's week one, I told myself. *Get a grip, Ash!*

"Wow, are you feeling all right?" Jenny's eyebrows created funny shapes behind her glasses. "You look a bit green. Come on, I'm taking you outside." She grabbed my hand and practically dragged me out to the field surrounding the Pathrun and athletics complex.

I followed willingly. Sure, I'd resolved to be more assertive in Aurora, to stop being bossed about by everyone around me, but when Jenny took control, she did it with kindness and good intentions, and it was impossible to refuse.

We found a secluded spot under the dappled shade of a Silverleaf Apple Tree, its shimmering leaves casting silvery-green light over us as we sat on the grass and stretched out our legs. I lifted my face toward the sun and closed my eyes, soaking up the warmth. Moments like these were exactly what I needed to help me see beyond the trivial problem of what to wear to a party. I was Ashlyn Grove, heir to the Elementum industry. My mom was a fashion icon who was probably born looking elegant.

I heard a soft groan from Jenny and opened my eyes.

Jase was near the Living Trail, talking to a small group of older students dressed in light training gear, their vests marked with the Aurora Pathrun insignia. He had his back to me, but I could tell by the way he kept glancing at the trail that he was itching to show them what he could do. I knew Jase well enough to know that making the Pathrun team would have been at the top of his list of goals before he arrived at Aurora.

"Do you want to go back inside?" Jenny asked.

Deep breath. I couldn't keep running away from them forever. "No, it's fine."

I watched Jase walk to the starting line on the Living Trail—he was up against another guy of similar height and build, even though he looked a few years older, so it seemed like a fair race. One of the other students blew a whistle, and they shot off around the Pathrun circuit. Unlike a typical track, the Living Trail was unpredictable. It could change its length, width, and incline without warning, throwing low-hanging vines or shallow water crossings into a runner's path. It tested more than just speed; agility and cleverness mattered just as much.

Jase immediately took the lead, moving with practiced ease. He'd always had a knack for reading the trail's subtle hints to anticipate its changes—maybe it was fate that the heir to the Vitalis industry would be a fitness fanatic who excelled at every sport he touched.

I sipped my carton of citrus nectar and watched the race unfold. They were halfway around the Pathrun, on the far side of the field from where Jenny and I were sitting, when the other guy sped up. He overtook Jase, who glanced sideways at him in surprise and pushed himself harder, trying to keep up. By the time they approached our side of the field, Jase's face was flushed, and he looked winded—something I'd never seen before. The other guy crossed the finish line well ahead of him.

Beside me, Jenny giggled. "Man, it's just horrible when that happens."

"When what happens?" I asked.

"When you're completely confident you're going to win, and someone else comes along and shows you up."

She was smiling, but I didn't find it amusing. Jase went to the same preparatory academy as Jenny, so maybe he'd been a little too sure of himself back then, but something about this competition didn't sit right with me. The other guy had deliberately held back until... he didn't.

"Do you think he cheated?" I asked her. "Did he use his gift to win?"

"Probably." Jenny shrugged. "Not everyone here thinks the heirs are that special." She glanced at me, and when she saw I wasn't smiling, she nudged me with her elbow. "Apart from you. I just wish you'd realize how special you are, Ash, instead of keeping up this ridiculous belief everyone drilled into you—that the other heirs are somehow better than you just because they're boys."

I couldn't help smiling now. She was right. Of course, she was right, and I couldn't keep letting that old belief hold me back.

———

LATER THAT MORNING, as Jenny and I headed to the Dining Pavilion to meet up with Emma for lunch, we passed the tech labs. The doors were open now that morning lessons were over, and I spotted a group of students gathered around one of the large, enchanted screens. I didn't need to look closely to know they were watching Kris.

A cheer erupted from the group, and Kris leaped from his seat, arms raised above his head like he was celebrating some kind of victory. "Beat that!" he said to the other students clustered around him.

I couldn't help smiling. Kris was completely in his element with technology, almost like he'd already found his gift and didn't need the Spirits to bestow another one on him. He was lucky. The Technomancy industry suited him so perfectly, and I wondered briefly how he'd feel if he were in my place, destined for Elementum instead. Would he be this enthusiastic about harnessing natural resources? Or had his family's legacy simply shaped his interests as he grew up?

Jenny muttered something under her breath that sounded like *They're all a bunch of showoffs.*

"Kris isn't like that," I quickly jumped to his defense. It was true. Kris would probably be mortified if he knew that's how others perceived him.

Jenny's eyebrows slid upward, making her look exactly like her mom. "Why are you still defending him?"

"Just because ... I know he isn't like that. I mean, Kris knows his way around an enchanted screen the way you know your way around a closet."

Jenny laughed out loud. "That's okay, then. For a moment there, I thought you were going all gooey-eyed over a guy who chose his friends over you."

"No, never!" I widened my eyes in mock horror. "Note to self: remember my worth."

"Exactly." Her smile quickly faded. "Also, say it like you believe it."

"I do believe it. It's just..." I hesitated, realizing that until a few moments ago, I'd been Ashlyn, heir to the Elementum industry, but watching Kris had stirred up doubts about my place in the family legacy. Jase had Pathrun and every sport the university offered. Kris had technology. What did I have? "I'm heir to the Elementum industry," I said flatly.

"Uh-huh. So you keep telling me. Only kidding." Jenny quickly turned her attention back to Kris, her eyes narrowing with realization. "Seems to me you have the whole world at your fingertips."

I grinned and shook my head. "How do you mean?"

"Well, look at them. What are they doing?"

"Playing a game?"

"Maybe." She shrugged. "The point is, they're playing with technology, and what does technology need in order to work?"

"Energy?"

"My, you catch on quick. Watch this."

Without warning, and before I could stop her, Jenny snuck into the lab, ducking behind the desks closest to us, and pointed at the master socket near the door. On her hands and knees, she crawled across the floor, switched off the plug, and then ran back to join me just as the boys realized the power had gone out.

"What happened?" one of them said.

"Did the power go off?"

"What did I do wrong?" This must've been the one who'd replaced Kris in the hot seat.

We both giggled and linked arms as we carried on our way to the Dining Pavilion.

It might have been a little childish, but I understood Jenny's motive. She didn't do it just to make Kris look foolish—though she'd probably enjoy that, too. She did it to remind me that one day, I'd wield power of my own.

And it worked for a while.

Until I saw Shane that afternoon, who added his name to the audition list posted on the main notice board in the Student Commons. Jenny and I were on our way to the bookstore—Jenny wanted to pick up a book for a class I wasn't in—and I sensed her roll her eyes when she spotted him with his back to us. I knew how she felt. It seemed like we couldn't go anywhere without running into one of the guys.

I'd have recognized Shane by the clothes alone. He wore a patchwork waistcoat over loose, ivory-colored pants and an ivory cap tilted jauntily to one side—an outfit most guys wouldn't be caught dead in for fear of annihilating their social credibility. With his curly ginger hair, he somehow pulled it off.

"You should audition, too," Jenny whispered.

"Me? No. Acting really isn't my thing." I shook my head so she'd know I was serious.

"How do you know? Have you ever tried?"

"Yes. In preparatory academy, I was chosen to play a modern-day princess in the end-of-year production."

"And?" Jenny adopted her mock-maternal tone again.

"And... I tripped over the hem of my ballgown, knocked over the cardboard carriage I was supposed to be traveling in, and would've landed on my butt in front of the entire audience if the prince hadn't caught me."

Jenny chuckled and then bit her lip to stop herself. "You have to admit, that's funny."

"It wasn't at the time."

"Only because they chose the wrong role for you."

That was exactly it. I still had no idea which role I was supposed to fill. The boys had all found their niches, seemingly without effort, but I was still searching for mine. Maybe meeting Jenny's friends from the League of Magical Theory would give me a nudge in the right direction. I didn't know much about the club —if I was honest, I knew zero about it—but I'd promised myself I'd join as many extracurricular groups as possible, and this was at least a start.

There was still the small problem of what to wear, though.

For the rest of the afternoon, I pictured myself walking into the welcome party between Emma and Jenny in various outfits. Some were too prim—the kind my mom would want me to wear. Others were too casual—Jenny and Emma were both wearing stunning dresses, and according to Jenny's mom, most girls took this opportunity to dress up and shine. But it was clear that no matter what I wore, I'd get noticed, so maybe I should embrace it, as my new friends suggested.

An outfit I'd previously overlooked—a bold choice I'd packed without my mom's approval—came to mind. It was a bit daring, but if I was going to do this, I might as well do it with style.

Back in the dorm room, I filled the tub with steaming bubbles and climbed in, laying back and closing my eyes. I'd run into all the guys today except for Cole, which was almost more unsettling than seeing him everywhere. What was he up to?

CHAPTER TEN

Ashlyn

"Wow!" Jenny eyed me up and down, hands on her hips, making me wonder if I'd gotten my outfit completely wrong. "I'm not surprised you kept that hidden. I'd totally have stolen it for myself."

Emma squealed and clapped her hands like a child spotting the cake at a birthday party. "I love it. It's bold but still classy. Very you."

"Is it? You don't think I look silly?" I asked, turning to examine myself in the mirror. The crimson off-shoulder top draped elegantly over my left shoulder, leaving the other bare, while its fitted design hugged my waist snugly. The fabric shimmered faintly in the light, giving it a rich, almost liquid quality that made every movement feel fluid and deliberate.

Below, the high-waisted black ebonhide pants added the boldest touch to the outfit. Ebonhide was a rare, enchanted material woven from threads spun in darkness by skilled magicians, who infused it with shadow magic to create its unique properties. The process involved binding strands of twilight essence, collected at dusk when shadows are longest, with fine mineral threads to give it durability. When completed, ebonhide held a shadowy sheen that absorbed and reflected light in a way that gave it an almost living quality.

The fabric's magic allowed it to mold to the wearer's form, creating a tailored fit without feeling restrictive, and its resilience was unmatched, as if the material itself resisted wear with a quiet, mystical strength. The sleek cut emphasized the length of my legs, while the subtle gleam along the fabric added just enough edge to make the entire outfit feel daring.

The finishing touch was a pair of strappy crimson ankle boots that tied the entire look together. Their slightly glossy finish complemented the top perfectly, while the slight lift in the heels gave me an added sense of confidence. For the first time in a while, I felt like I was stepping into a version of myself I wanted the world to see—bold, confident, and unafraid to stand out.

"You look amazing." Jenny stepped beside me and rested her head on my shoulder.

Jenny herself wore a navy halter-neck dress with tiny white polka dots, strappy sandals, and a string of white beads around her neck, making her look even more like a moonstone doll. Emma, on the other hand, wore an emerald-green silk wrap dress with a decorative bow on one hip. The fabric accentuated her green eyes and her curves, ensuring every eye in the room would be on her. They'd be crazy not to notice.

Standing between the two of them, I felt a shiver of anxiety. I would get noticed, too, but for the first time, that didn't feel terrifying. Tonight, I wasn't hiding. I was stepping out.

"Let's go, girls," Jenny said, her voice bubbling with excitement.

I pulled on a sleek black jacket with subtle gold embroidery along the cuffs, adding a final edge to my look before linking arms with my new friends. I forgot all about the promise I'd made to Jenny earlier—to meet her friends from the League and then slip away quietly.

The party was being held in one of the conference halls in the

Student Commons. We joined the line of students waiting to get in, and I took the opportunity to study what everyone else was wearing. Madam Webber hadn't been wrong—most of the girls wore gowns fit for a high-society ball, the kind that wouldn't have looked out of place at an event in the Bevair mansion. As we moved closer to the entrance, I saw the other girls catching their reflections in the windows, adjusting their hair, and smoothing their dresses. Watching them, I caught a glimpse of the old me—the girl who used to care so much about looking polished and perfect.

Everyone turned to stare as we passed, their gazes lingering on my outfit. At my exposed shoulders, my long legs, and those crimson boots. I smiled back at them. This was me. Love it or hate it, I wasn't going to change for anyone.

"Ashlyn, did you hear me?" I glanced at Jenny, who was watching me with a curious expression. "I said Shane Aster just walked past, and his eyes almost popped out of his head when he saw you."

"They did?" I scanned the room, hoping to catch Shane still in the act of staring, but I couldn't see him anywhere. A thrill traveled down my spine. My entire life, I'd felt like I was walking in the shadow of the other heirs, like a sapling that never got to see the sun. Now, I was finally stepping into the light.

Emma squeezed my arm. "Feels good, huh?" she whispered in my ear.

I laughed. It did feel good, and we hadn't even stepped inside yet.

Music spilled out into the hallway as we entered. The conference hall was hung with silver streamers and strung with enchanted fairy lights, while a large crystal orb suspended from the ceiling cast shimmering patterns across the room. The DJ in the corner played the latest tunes from the Illumina industry, nodding along to the beat beneath oversized earecho panels. Round tables draped in black cloth with silver centerpieces were scattered throughout, and a minibar had been set up in one corner, staffed by professors disguised as waiters serving snacks and sparkling sodas.

Nearby, a large crystal punch bowl sat on a table alongside glass tumblers, paper umbrellas, and sparklers.

We headed to the punch, and the server filled a glass for each of us. His eyes lingered on me a moment too long, and I felt heat rise to my cheeks. I turned away, pretending to survey the party while willing him to look somewhere else.

Students had already started dividing into groups. Some claimed tables near the dance floor, clearly there to let loose, while others hovered near the minibar. I scanned the room for the guys but couldn't see them anywhere. A flicker of disappointment surprised me. I didn't want to talk to them or even have them gawking at me all night, but somehow, their absence felt... unnatural.

"I haven't seen my friends yet," Jenny said.

I'd nearly forgotten about meeting the League of Magical Theory members. Part of me inexplicably hoped they wouldn't show, even though they were her friends. It was only my first week —I wasn't sure if I was ready to meet them yet. But when I glanced at Jenny's eager face, guilt pricked at me. The least I could do was make an effort. Meeting them didn't mean I had to join the club. Not yet.

Danielle, the girl who partnered with Kris for our alchemy project, approached me then, her sparkly floor-length gown catching the light with every step. She smiled warmly and complimented my outfit.

"It's stunning," she said.

Her sincerity caught me off guard. Danielle wasn't just beautiful; she carried herself with a grace that I'd once envied. In the past, I might've resented Kris spending so much time with her, but those thoughts felt distant now, like they belonged to someone else.

Emma's elbow gently jabbed my ribs, reminding me to return

the compliment. "Your dress is gorgeous," I said with genuine sincerity.

We mingled for a while. Emma and Jenny stopped to chat with everyone they knew from Terrace while I trailed behind, feeling awkward, like I was intruding into a world I didn't quite belong to. There was still no sign of the guys, and I was surprised when a couple of girls from my old preparatory academy called me over, asking how my first week had gone. We hadn't run in the same circles back then, but things felt different now that we were all at Aurora. Here, we were equals, and the warmth of their welcome boosted my confidence even more than Jenny and Emma's enthusiastic comments about my outfit.

I caught up with my friends again by the punch bowl. The student filling drinks brushed his fingers against mine as he handed me a glass, leaning close as if to whisper something just for me. Before he could, Jenny grabbed my arm and said, "They're here." She took the punch from my hand, gave it back to the student with a look that said, *she's got better things to do than talk to you* and pulled me away. I glanced back over my shoulder, but he was already chatting with Danielle and her friend.

In a quiet corner of the room, three people—two men and a woman—sat around a table with an air of serene authority. It was as if they were wrapped in a faint aura of shimmering light, visible only if you looked closely enough. I couldn't pinpoint exactly what gave me that impression, but perhaps it was their poised posture, the woman's ankles crossed neatly to one side, or the way they'd settled at the table, clearly expecting others to bring them food and drinks. It might have been the black velvet cloaks resting over their shoulders, held in place with intricate silver brooches shaped like ancient sigils, or the red shirts peeking from beneath their collars, almost as if they were branded with some quiet, personal magic.

Even from across the room, I could tell they were older than the other students. I wondered how they'd come to be at a first-year gathering, but I didn't ask Jenny; she was already steering me toward them as if afraid they might vanish like mirages.

They looked up as we approached, their expressions cool and knowing, smiles widening when they saw me on Jenny's arm. They'd clearly been expecting me. I swallowed hard, wishing Jenny had let me bring the glass of punch. My mouth had gone dry, and my heart was beating faster. Why was I so nervous?

"Well, Jenny, who do we have here?" The man closest to us rose and extended his hand, an oddly warm light dancing in his amber-flecked eyes. He was tall, his head nearly brushing the delicate hanging silver strands woven into the ceiling above, with high cheekbones, slick, jet-black hair, and a faint shimmer about him, as if he was standing just a fraction outside the present moment.

Jenny beamed with pride, like she was introducing a treasured jewel she'd discovered deep underground. "This is Ashlyn Grove, heir to the Elementum industry."

I tried to look away and tease her for the formal introduction, but the man's gaze held mine with an intensity that felt like the whisper of magic.

"One of the five elite," he said. "I'm Howard Patel, President of the League of Magical Theory." He gestured to the man beside him, whose platinum-blond hair seemed to reflect a soft, ethereal light, and the woman beside him, whose green eyes sparkled like enchanted jewels. "This is Benji Kuhns and Carla Reign."

They shook my hand in turn, each with a strange, subtle warmth that lingered longer than expected. Their aura was undeniable; it felt as if they'd brought a small slice of the ancient world with them. I almost wanted to bow, the way I'd seen done in the old tales. Carla's eyes sparkled as though she could read my mind.

"Please, sit down." Howard gestured for us to take the remaining seats at the table.

As I sat, I realized they had an unobstructed view of the entire room. From here, I'd be able to see the guys as soon as they arrived —and they'd probably see me. I wasn't sure how I felt about that, but perhaps it wouldn't hurt for them to notice I was already making connections.

"So, how have you enjoyed your first week?" Howard asked, sipping from his punch, his movements fluid, almost like the flow of water.

"It was okay," I said as Jenny nodded vigorously.

Howard gave a knowing smile, one that hinted at secrets hidden within the halls of Aurora. "Soon, you'll both unlock your gifts. That's when things will really... come into focus." His words seemed to resonate like a bell softly ringing in my chest.

"Howard," Jenny blurted out, unfazed by his almost lyrical tone. "Ashlyn is interested in joining our club."

I flashed her a look, but she didn't notice. I hadn't actually said I wanted to join; I'd only agreed to meet her friends because she was so convinced I'd like them. Still, I didn't want to make things awkward, so I stayed quiet.

"Can you tell me what the club is about?" I asked instead. Though I was intrigued by the League's name, the surreal calm surrounding them made me feel like I'd stepped into an enchanted circle, the kind from my mother's stories.

"Allow me," Benji said. His unusually light, high-pitched voice was almost comical compared to the gravity of his words. "Our club explores the power behind our gifts, delving into the origins of magic itself. We seek out secrets lost to the ages, whispers of ancient knowledge the Spirits left hidden among the elements."

"You mean Celestial magic?" Something felt off, maybe the contrast between his airy tone and the weight of his words, almost as if he was weaving a spell to distract me from the deeper meaning.

The mention of Celestial magic stirred memories of Ethan Weiss like a shadow lingering in my mind. I hadn't seen him since the last time outside the restroom, and suddenly, I wondered where he was or what he might be doing. My stomach fluttered, and I forced myself back to the conversation.

"Partly. Do you know the history of Celestial magic, Ashlyn?" Benji asked, pulling me back to the discussion.

"Yes. I know that magic was a gift to the ruling families from the Spirits."

"Ah, but do you know why Celestials are so rare?"

I looked around the room. A few students had started dancing, and the sight of it brought me back to reality, making our conversation seem even more surreal. I shook my head, wondering why this wasn't something we'd learned in class.

Howard leaned forward, his amber eyes glinting as they caught the soft gleam of the enchanted lights overhead. "Celestial was the ruling element when magic still existed on Earth. In those days, humanity wielded immense power, drawing directly from the primal forces of the universe. But that power came at a cost. They began to reshape the world in their image, ignoring the balance the Divine had set forth. Kingdoms rose and fell in flames. The earth cracked, the skies raged, and the Spirits watched as humanity's greed consumed the very magic they were entrusted to protect."

He paused, letting the weight of his words settle over the table before continuing, his voice lowering to a near whisper. "When it became clear that humanity could not be trusted, the Divine intervened. The Spirits, bound by their duty to maintain order, stripped Earth of its magic, leaving it a husk of what it once was. But magic cannot simply disappear—it is a living force, one that must be nurtured and used wisely."

Howard's gaze locked onto mine as if willing me to absorb every word. "So the Spirits sought a new home for this power—a parallel world, untouched by the corruption of humanity. Andis was chosen not because it was perfect but because it held promise. The Divine guided the first settlers, humans brought from Earth, who proved themselves worthy of the Spirits' trust. They were the ones who rebuilt a system of magic based on balance, binding each individual's gift to a contract to ensure responsibility."

His words stirred something within me, a sense of connection

I hadn't fully understood before. Andis wasn't just some isolated world. Its reflection of Earth was deliberate, the legacy of those first settlers. The traditions, the architecture, the way we marked the seasons—everything carried an undercurrent of Earth's influence, a subtle echo of a world that no longer held magic.

Howard spread his hands, his voice steady and filled with quiet authority. "Your family, Ashlyn, was among those first settlers, chosen to safeguard the contracts and uphold the balance, chosen because of your pure lineage. Over generations, they became the stewards of Elementum, ensuring that no one would ever again wield more power than they could control. Just as the rest of us here descend from bloodlines entrusted with protecting magic's legacy."

Carla, who had remained silent until now, spoke for the first time. Her voice was sharp and clear, cutting through the moment like a blade. "But balance is delicate, and even here, the old greed lingers. That is why the League exists. We seek to ensure that the mistakes of Earth are not repeated on Andis."

Her words felt like a warning, reverberating in the quiet room.

Pure...

The word clung to me like the echo of Cole's father's speeches at every event, wielded as though it elevated him above everyone else. Howard's explanation of magical history might have been accurate, but his use of "pure" stirred an unease within me, its supremacist undertone hard to ignore.

"So, you're a professor here, sir? What do you teach?" I asked, hoping to steer the conversation away.

"Yes, I teach Magical Theory, and please, call me Howard. No need for formalities," he replied smoothly, amber eyes gleaming under the enchanted lights. "I'm sure you'll be in my class next year."

"Shouldn't I take the class first before I join the club?" I asked, still puzzled that Jenny had been recruited before school had even started.

Howard dismissed the question with a casual wave of his

hand. "Our numbers are limited, and we are very selective of the company we keep. By that, I mean we look for those who share a common thread—be it intellect, potential, or simply curiosity about the deeper truths of our world."

Oh, I understood. He was laying it on thick, a charm offensive meant to rope me in, and I couldn't help wondering if he'd done the same to Jenny. She didn't strike me as naive, yet she'd fallen for it.

"So, would you like to join us, Ashlyn?" Carla's sharp green eyes gleamed with amusement.

"Do I have a choice?" I asked, keeping my tone light but wary.

Her smile was too knowing, like I'd stumbled into some unseen web. "Of course you do. But I urge you to ensure it isn't a decision you'll come to regret later."

The glance she exchanged with Howard sent a chill prickling across my skin, though I couldn't pinpoint why.

Howard leaned forward, his voice like velvet. "So, what do you say?"

"Please say yes," Jenny said, her eyes wide with hope.

When Jenny first mentioned the club, I'd asked her what they actually did. She'd sidestepped the question, and now I was starting to understand why. My gaze shifted between the three older students, their perfectly poised exteriors, and Jenny, who didn't seem to notice the tension. Why hadn't she asked Emma to join, too?

Standing abruptly, I smiled tightly. "I'm grateful for the offer, but I need time to think about it. We've only been here a week, and I'm still adjusting to school life." I stopped myself before they could detect the excuse in my tone. "I'm going to grab a glass of punch and hit the dance floor. Are you coming, Jenny?"

Jenny hesitated, her brow furrowing as she avoided my gaze. "I'll catch up with you."

I didn't want to leave her with them, but she clearly wanted to stay. Perhaps I was wrong—first impressions could be deceiving, and Jenny knew them better than I did—but I needed to step away to sort through my thoughts.

I hurried to the punch bowl, head down, so distracted by the strange exchange that I collided with someone. Red liquid splattered into the air, narrowly missing my outfit.

"Oh." I gasped, looking up to find Shane Aster standing before me. His unbuttoned shirt revealed a glimpse of his chest, now speckled with stray drops of punch.

"Sorry," I stammered.

"I'm sorry, too." He wiped at his shirt with a napkin, his green eyes scanning me from head to toe. "You look... different tonight. Beautiful."

I froze at the compliment, the warmth in his tone catching me off guard. It felt insincere, as though he could erase the years of silence and distance with a single word.

"Maybe that's because I've grown up," I replied, brushing past him to leave the room.

Outside, the cool air hit me like a balm, and I tilted my head back, staring at the twin moons casting their ethereal glow over the courtyard. One moon hovered like a guardian, its smaller sister clinging close to its side. I breathed deeply, forcing my thoughts to settle.

The conversation with the League swirled in my mind. Howard's tale of humanity's greed on Earth and the Spirits' decision to move magic to Andis had been compelling, but there was something unsettling about the way he'd spoken about lineage and purity. It felt like a thread pulled too tight, ready to snap.

"Tired of the party?" the voice came from behind me, low and familiar.

I turned to see Ethan Weiss, most of his face cloaked in shadow, his green eyes catching the faint glow of the moons. For a moment, the world seemed to still, the chirping of night birds the only sound.

"What do you want, Ethan?" I asked, my tone sharper than intended. "Why are you even here?"

"I have my reasons," he said, falling into step beside me. His casual hum felt intrusive, as though he belonged here when he clearly didn't. "Are you having any difficulties? I heard about the heirs."

"Everyone has heard about them," I said curtly. "What do you want?"

He stopped abruptly, forcing me to do the same. His gaze pinned me in place. "You shouldn't be out here alone."

"Aurora is safe," I shot back, annoyed that he'd followed me. "Why are you out here in the dark?"

Ethan sighed, his breath visible in the cold air. "You're stubborn, do you know that? You don't want my help, yet you're angry when I don't offer it." His laugh cut through the silence like a blade.

"Tell me the truth," I demanded. "Why are you here?"

He hesitated, then leaned closer, his voice dropping to a whisper. "Has your family told you everything about Aurora?"

His question lingered in the air, heavy and strange. What could there be to tell? My father barely acknowledged my presence, let alone shared secrets about the university.

"What do you know, Ethan?" I asked warily, unsure whether to trust him or dismiss him entirely.

He stepped back, a faint smirk curling his lips. "More than you think, Ashlyn. But I'll let you figure it out on your own. For now."

Without waiting for a response, he turned and disappeared into the shadows, leaving me with more questions than answers.

Chapter Eleven

Cole

"Harpe left me partnered with Ashlyn on purpose," Jase grumbled.

We'd been at Aurora a month, and I was starting to think every conversation revolved around Ashlyn when I wasn't in the room. Jase had barely waited for me to go into the kitchen to grab coffee before launching into his usual complaints about their biology project. My dad should've gotten me into Aurora a year early like he'd promised. Then, I wouldn't be stuck babysitting these three, clinging to their nostalgic dreams of childhood while ignoring the political realities of the industries. I often wondered what they'd do without me.

I placed a hand on Jase's shoulder—it was usually enough to bring him back to reality. Physically, he was the strongest of us, but emotionally? He was years behind. If he wasn't careful, Ashlyn and her power-hungry father would sniff out that weakness and make a play for his industry.

I set my coffee down on the desk and pulled the chair around so that I faced them, stuffing a pastry into my mouth. "You're looking at this all wrong. You should've used the project as an opportunity to make her work hard to keep up with you." At

Jase's vacant stare, I added, "Let me guess: you're letting her do all the work, so you don't have to spend any time with her."

Jase slumped back in his seat. "I don't want to spend any time with her. She's different to how she used to be."

"She's two years older," I snapped. "And so are you."

"Besides, her little friend Jenny Webster gives me the creeps. I don't trust her."

"Webber," I corrected him. "Her name is Jenny Webber. Don't you remember her from Terrace?"

"Hey, I can't remember the name of every girl who follows me around." Cole shrugged.

Kris threw a pastry at him, crumbs flying across my comforter. "Climb down off the pedestal, dude. I don't think she's interested in your muscles."

"What do you think she's interested in?" I asked him. I'd been debating kicking them out so that I could have some alone time before my next class—my roommate spent most of his time in the common room, so there was no chance of him coming back until later—but the conversation was about to take the kind of turn I might enjoy.

Kris was sitting on the floor, his back against the wall, tossing a small, squishy ball into the air. He dropped it and tried to stop it from rolling away from him. "I don't know. All I meant was, I don't think Jase is her type."

I could tell Kris was holding back his true thoughts; he always did. Like my father always said, if you want something done right, do it yourself.

"Her uncle works for my father," I said casually, letting the weight of the information hang in the air. "I used to talk to her cousin, her uncle's son, but I stopped."

"Why?" Shane glanced up from his assignment; I knew that he'd been following the conversation because he hadn't typed a word on his MagiScreen since I came back into the room.

"Weird vibes. He's always poking into business that doesn't

concern him." I sipped my coffee. "I think the whole family is bitter about the heirs."

Shane took a deep breath. I could always rely on him getting his hackles up whenever the conversation veered toward the subject of Ashlyn and her new friend. "Why would they be bitter about the heirs? The industries have always belonged to our respective families."

"He always mentioned the superiority of magic users a lot," I said, studying my embossed initials on the side of my cup.

"I've heard Jenny doing that too," Jase said, eyes narrowing. "She always tosses in these comments about how precious we'll *all* be when we unlock our gifts, but the way she says it is like her gift might somehow be better than mine. She's also always talking about how the heirs are nothing special."

"Jealousy. Sounds like she wants to be an heir," Kris said. "She's fawning over Ashlyn... popularity by association." He reached into his satchel and pulled out his MagiScreen.

"What are you doing?" Shane asked.

I kept quiet.

"Just checking out her background." Kris didn't even glance up from his MagiScreen.

"Her mom is a guidance counselor here, and Cole just said her uncle works for his dad. What else do you need to know?" There was an edge to Shane's voice, like he was already panicking about what Kris might discover.

"Yes." Jase's eyes widened as he scrunched up an empty packet of pastries and peered over Kris's shoulder. "Let's see what she's all about."

"And then what?" Shane asked. "You'll run to Ashlyn with this? What's that going to achieve?"

"Relax, Aster." I rolled my eyes. "Ashlyn has a right to know if there's something shady about her new best friend."

Shane shook his head at me. "Yes," he said, "only Kris isn't prying into that girl's personal history because he cares about Ashlyn."

That could've been taken two ways, but this wasn't a discussion about whether any of us did or did not have feelings for Ashlyn. "So, what if he isn't? We're all heirs in this room, and I, for one, want to know what we're up against here."

Shane's shoulders slumped. He knew when he was beaten.

Kris's face was a picture of concentration. Finally, he said, "So, I'm diving into the systems where all the magical contracts statuses are listed."

"Wait." Shane was alert again. "That can't be legal. How can you—"

"No system is impenetrable," I interjected. "Three guesses whose family created the system in the first place."

Kris looked up and grinned at no one in particular. "There's always a way in, a crack that no one knows about until it appears."

"Doesn't make it right, though," Shane said.

"If you don't like it, you don't have to stick around." I gestured to the door. As predicted, Shane didn't leave. I would have to keep an eye on him in case he decided to go blabbing to Ashlyn with whatever dirt we managed to find on her little friend.

"Yes!" Kris said, his face tinted silver with the glow from the screen. Shane slumped back, defeated. Kris's face was lit by the soft glow of his MagiScreen. Finally, he grinned. "Born Jennifer Sarita Webber. December 14. Magical contract: unknown."

"Obviously she hasn't unlocked it yet," I said. "Anything else?"

Kris frowned. "Her brother was Harvey Webber."

The name hung heavy in the air.

"Harvey Webber?" Shane said, sitting up straighter. "The guy who was killed last year?"

"By a non-user," I added. "It happened in Drayvarn, the closest town to Aurora. Attacked from behind. The murderer slit his throat and then took his own life. Investigations revealed no obvious connection between the killer and Harvey Webber, which means the police have no motive to go on either."

"And you knew this all along," Shane said, his gaze accusing.

I shrugged. "Kris just jogged my memory."

"That's brutal." Jase's gaze was fixated on the information on the screen.

"It explains why she's so anti-non-users," Shane said. "Imagine someone you're close to gets murdered in cold blood. Maybe she feels like she should use her magic for the greater good of all magic users. I think we should back off."

"I think you should stop giving her the benefit of the doubt." I kept my tone level and my eyes fixed on Shane, using the Bevair glare that my dad perfected long ago. "Or," I said smoothly, "her whole family's a bunch of zealots who want to wipe out non-users."

"You say this like you're horrified by the idea," Shane muttered.

"Get a grip, Aster. What, do you think I set her up for this? Relax."

Jase snickered at Shane and tossed a balled-up sheet of paper at his head. "So serious, Aster."

"You guys can be so annoying, you know that?" Shane dodged the paper ball and rolled his eyes.

"Guys," Kris said, interrupting them before the goofing around took over. "There's an encrypted file attached to Jenny Webber's contract."

I sat forward, my pulse picking up speed. This was more like it. "Can you open it?"

"Well," Kris said, his fingers flying across the keys, "I'll have to whip out the hardcore hacking skills."

"Do it," I said.

"It's encrypted for a reason." There was no mistaking the panic in Shane's voice now.

"Why would Jenny Webber have an encrypted file attached to her records?" Jase asked, picking up the squishy ball and tossing it from one hand to the other; he always thought better when his hands were kept busy. "It's not like her family is important or anything."

"It probably has something to do with her brother's death," I suggested. "I still say Reeve should hack into it. The more we know about her, the better prepared we'll be to handle whatever she's plotting with Ashlyn."

"I don't like it," Shane said. "It's wrong."

He glanced at each of us in turn and, realizing that Kris was paying no attention—the encrypted file a challenge he couldn't refuse—started packing up his MagiScreen and assignment notes.

"Hey, it's not that deep," Jase said.

"It's an encrypted file attached to a magical contract. I'd call that pretty deep." Shane rose, hoisting his bag over his shoulder.

I wasn't going to stop him. Protected or not, I wanted to know what was in that file, and I wasn't going to let my friend's morals stand in my way.

CHAPTER TWELVE

Shane

Cole could be overbearing most of the time, but this was seriously low, even by his standards. Ashlyn's parents looked after the magical contracts. If they discovered that we'd hacked into a protected file, the consequences would not be good... for any of us. I wanted no part of it. I was surprised that Kris was willing to go ahead with hacking into it, but he'd probably already convinced himself that it was research and that decoding the file would provide his family with the incentive to increase cyber security surrounding the magical contracts. Win-win in his eyes.

None of them had considered what this meant to Jenny... or to Ashlyn and her family. I didn't know anything about Jenny Webber, but the girl deserved some privacy, especially considering what her family had been through. The news about her brother's murder kind of shed a different light on Ash's new friend, and rather than trying to find some information that we could use against her, it would've been kinder if we'd altered our attitudes to be a little more lenient toward her. None of us could say with any degree of certainty how we would react under the same circumstances.

I cut through the Student Commons on my way to the sports

complex. I needed to be outside, somewhere I could sit on the grass without feeling contained by four walls. I was so wrapped up in imagining Kris probing the encrypted file like a surgeon trying to slice open its chest and examine its beating heart that I almost collided headfirst with Bellis Reeve. Kris's cousin.

"Shane Aster?" She took a step backward, appraising me as though she were an aging auntie I hadn't seen since I was a baby. "It *is* you. Fancy bumping into you here."

I glanced around. She must've just left Dean Bask's office. If I'd been paying attention, I could've turned around and avoided her—she might not have recognized me from behind—but now I had no choice but to speak to her because anything else would make me appear rude. Not the impression I wanted to give a TruthForger, even if she was Kris's cousin.

"Hey, Bellis," I said, hauling my bag higher onto my shoulder.

Bellis graduated from Aurora last year, but she seemed years older than the last time we met. Perhaps it was the clothes. She wore a smart pantsuit with a gold scarf fastened loosely around her neck. Her once-unruly hair was now glossy, the sun highlighting the hint of red, making it glow. Unlike her cousin, Bellis craved attention. If she hadn't gone into Truthforging, she'd have made a great performer.

"What are you doing here?" I asked. I wondered if Kris knew that she was here or whether she was hoping to surprise him later.

"Just visiting Dean Bask." She glanced behind her at the door to the dean's office. "I have some time on my hands, so I'll probably catch up with my favorite counselor, Madam Webber."

I swallowed. Was that name going to follow us around the whole time we were here? "I haven't had the pleasure yet."

Bellis's eyebrows shot up. "You might know her daughter, though. Jenny? She's a first-year student." I must've hesitated a beat too long because before I could respond that I didn't know her, Bellis asked what I thought of her.

I shrugged, thinking of Bellis's cousin sitting in Cole's dorm room right now, hacking into Jenny Webber's magical contract.

Heat flooded my cheeks. What did Bellis know about Jenny? Was she here because she knew about her friendship with Ashlyn? It was too much of a coincidence that she'd already maneuvered our brief conversation from the counselor to the counselor's daughter.

"I don't really know her that well," I said. "We've never spoken."

Bellis studied my expression with narrowed eyes before brightening suddenly and fixing a glossy red smile into place. "So, how are you all settling in? How's my cousin?"

"Kris is good," I said.

She ostentatiously peered around the Student Commons as though they might all be hiding from her. "Where are they then? You guys never do anything alone."

"Um, this is university. We're not all joined at the hip, you know. I'm heading to the Luminarium." I regretted the lie the moment it left my mouth. Bellis tilted her head, her lips twitching with suppressed amusement as her eyes darted to the path I'd been taking. The Luminarium was in the opposite direction, and she definitely knew that. Of course she did—she'd probably spent half her time there when she was a student here. I could practically feel her filing the information away for later.

It was obvious that she knew I was lying. "I bet Kris is holed up in one of the tech labs teaching the professor a thing or two, huh?"

"Something like that." I smiled at her. "I'd best get going."

I didn't know why she made me feel so uncomfortable. Perhaps it had something to do with the fact that she'd always been nosey. At our preparatory academy, she'd set up a Nodesite on the AndisNet, designed to keep students apprised of all the latest news. No one ever figured out how she got hold of some of the stories she posted; a lot of students spent Bellis's final year praying they wouldn't end up as the subject of her next exposé. Or perhaps it was because if anyone was going to find out what Kris was up to, it would be Bellis.

I walked away, feeling Bellis's eyes drilling holes in the back of my skull.

Maybe I was wrong. Perhaps it was a sheer fluke that Bellis happened to be in Aurora today. I only hoped the encrypted file would turn out to be nothing more than a note about Jenny's brother Harvey.

Even as I made my way around the sports complex and back into the building for my first class of the afternoon, my brain was reminding me that, according to Cole, the motive behind Harvey Webber's death was still a mystery.

I wondered if Ashlyn knew about Jenny's brother. It didn't exactly make lighthearted conversation, but then again, they were supposed to be friends.

CHAPTER THIRTEEN

Ashlyn

I woke early on the day of our initiation ceremony. I swear my heart stopped when I received my EchoMail confirming the date, but now that the day had finally arrived, I could hardly keep still. It was lucky that we didn't have to attend classes because there was no way I would've been able to concentrate. Today was the day that I would finally unlock my magical contract.

Jenny and I were part of the first group to attend the ceremony, and, of course, so were the other heirs. With birthdays so close together, it was inevitable. Twelve students total, and five of them were heirs.

We met our guide outside the administration building. Jenny and I arrived first because I had practically dragged her there. I couldn't sit around in the dorm any longer, nerves thrumming too wildly to even eat breakfast—a rarity for me. Jenny, however, was calm and composed, grinning at me like I was a restless spark ready to ignite.

"Just our luck," Jenny muttered, nudging me in the ribs as Shane, Kris, and Jase approached the group. Cole wasn't with them. Of course, it would be just like him to show up late, making a grand entrance so the ceremony could revolve around him.

I turned away. Nothing was going to ruin today for me. This was the first day of the rest of our lives, and I was determined to savor every moment so that, one day, I could tell my own children all about unlocking my gift.

Madame Fiona Wickets, our guide, had a commanding presence despite her small stature. Her attire shimmered with an iridescent glow that shifted hues as she moved, making it difficult to discern where her cloak ended, and the air around her began. A crescent-shaped charm floated near her shoulder, its glow pulsing softly like a heartbeat. She carried a staff that hummed faintly with energy, its tip resembling a shard of raw crystal. She clapped her hands sharply, the sound resonating with an echo that silenced the group. "Follow me."

I exchanged a wide-eyed look with Jenny, who was finally catching my excitement.

We followed Madame Wickets and her assistant, Professor Kellar, beyond Aurora's protective wards and into the vibrant heart of the Eldergreen Forest. The shimmering barrier we crossed rippled like water, its glow briefly enveloping us in warmth before letting us pass. On the other side, the air was alive with magic. The towering, silver-barked trees seemed to stretch endlessly upward, their faintly glowing leaves catching the sunlight filtering through the dense canopy. Around us, the forest thrummed with life—the rustle of unseen creatures, the melodic calls of enchanted fauna, and the steady, ever-present hum of magic woven into the land.

The Eldergreen Forest was said to be a place of wonder, a living reminder of Andis's legacy as a world chosen by the Spirits to protect and nurture magic. Here, the colors of the land were more vibrant, the air itself seemingly charged with the energy of the ancient magic that pulsed through its roots and streams. I couldn't help but think about the first settlers from Earth, those chosen by the Spirits to rebuild magic's legacy after humanity's greed had nearly destroyed it. This forest had been their sanctuary, a place where they'd forged the balance that sustained our world today.

Jenny peered up at the diamonds of sunshine winking through the branches. "Harvey and I used to sneak out here sometimes," she whispered. "Mom never knew, of course. Harvey would've gotten into trouble for it, but I think he was only trying to impress me. He was an aeromancer." She smiled wistfully at me as we kept walking. "He would sweep me off my feet and swoop me up into the treetops, and no matter how high we went, I felt safe because I knew that he would always be there to catch me."

There were tears in her eyes, and I reached for her hand to squeeze it. She'd told me about Harvey before. They were close—like twins, she said—but he'd been killed a year ago by a non-user. I didn't know all the details. Jenny always grew quiet when she spoke of him, and I didn't like to press her on something so painful. It amazed me how she carried herself with such confidence and joy despite her loss. I couldn't imagine how I'd handle something so devastating.

"All five heirs in one year group," Madame Wickets mused as she slowed her pace, falling into step beside Jenny and me. "And to witness them all unlock their gifts on the same day—what an honor." She clutched a charm that hung near her shoulder, its soft light pulsing briefly as though responding to her emotions.

"Does this mean they get special treatment?" Jenny asked, leaning forward to catch Madame Wickets's reaction.

"Oh, not at all!" The guide's tone was firm but kind. "Like anyone else, they must follow the rules and learn to understand their element." I was grateful for her response, even as I tried not to dwell on how our inheritances already set us apart. I didn't want anything else to make me feel like I didn't belong.

"That should be simple enough," I said, though my voice betrayed my unease. Madame Wickets's attention already felt too focused on me, and I wished she would leave us to walk in peace.

"You'd think so, wouldn't you?" she replied. "But many

students have nearly lost their lives sneaking off to practice magic alone. Power without understanding is always a dangerous thing."

"You might need to repeat this to the other heirs then, Madame Wickets," Jenny said, smirking at me. "I have a feeling they'll be the first to break the rules."

I didn't know what she was playing at, but it wasn't something that I'd put past Cole. I wondered if he'd finally made it, but I forced myself to keep my gaze fixed ahead and not turn around to see if he had joined the group.

"We'll hope for the best," Professor Kellar chimed in, his soft voice oddly calming. He'd fallen into step beside us, his slender frame moving with the grace of someone more at home among the trees than in the halls of Aurora. "As the heirs, I would expect you all to set a good example."

I bit back a sharp retort, reminding myself that this was neither the time nor place to argue. "I'm sure we will, Professor," I said, keeping my tone polite.

Professor Kellar spoke of the forest then, of its historical significance to magical history and the first settlers who had built Andis into the world it was. His words reminded me that this was the reason Aurora had been built here, in the heart of the Elder-green Forest.

"It's why Aurora is the most famous of all the magical academies," Madame Wickets added. "But you will learn all about it in History of Andis class."

As she spoke, we entered a clearing, and I forgot my irritation in an instant. The space was magical. Twelve ancient tree stumps formed a perfect circle around an unlit bonfire. On the far side of the clearing stood a two-story log cabin, its wraparound porch blending seamlessly with the surrounding trees. It looked as if the forest itself had grown the cabin into existence, its branches sheltering it protectively. It was breathtaking, a perfect blend of nature and magic.

Jenny squeezed my hand, her eyes wide as she gestured toward the corked potion bottles filled with a glowing blue liquid atop each stump. My chest tightened with excitement. This was it. The moment I'd dreamed of my entire life.

Madame Wickets clapped her hands again. "Everyone, I want you to choose a stump and stand behind it."

Jenny and I walked around to the far side of the clearing and chose a stump, excitement gurgling inside my chest. I peered around the group. Only one student separated me from Shane. Kris and Jase were next, but when my eyes finally settled on Cole, I realized that he had chosen a position diagonally to me, almost as if he wanted the best view of me unlocking my gift. Or rather, he wanted *me* to have the best view of *him* unlocking his gift.

A smug grin appeared on his face. He nudged the girl standing next to him and said, "Well, isn't this perfect?" his eyes were on me the entire time.

Of course, Cole had to turn even a ceremony like this into a performance. He never did or said anything unless it provoked a reaction or benefited him in some way, and the way he was staring at me now left no doubt that he wanted me to notice him. Typical Cole. Always seeking the spotlight, always angling for the upper hand.

I tore my gaze away, refusing to let him get under my skin. Today wasn't about him—it was about all of us stepping into our futures. I wasn't going to let him ruin it.

I studied his face, the classically handsome features that I'd once found so attractive but which now made my pulse race for all the wrong reasons. Something had happened to Cole. Sure, he'd grown into his looks over the past two years—we all had— but his features were slowly twisting into something unrecogniz- able... I swallowed as it dawned on me that he looked more like his father than he ever had.

"Welcome to the ritual grounds." Madame Wickets circled the group slowly, hands clasped behind her back as though she were talking to herself, and I dragged my eyes away from Cole so that I could concentrate. I noticed that Professor Kellar had wandered over to the log cabin and was perched on the porch stairs. Was he keeping a safe distance between him and the students as though his presence might interfere with the ceremony?

"The bottle in front of each of you contains the unlocking potion," Madame Wickets continued. "I understand that you are excited, but let me remind you of what it means to possess a magical gift. Magic is for conventional use only. It is a wonderful gift, but also a dangerous one, and misuse comes with its own consequences." She kept walking, every student in the circle hanging onto her every word. "Your contract begins once you have unlocked your ability. Any misuse of magic will see the contract removed and ripped up before you can say, '*You never told us that would happen, Madame Wickets.*' Do I make myself clear?"

Her eyes met mine briefly, and then Madame Wickets stepped away from the circle.

"When I call your name, I want you to pick up your potion bottle."

I glanced around at the other students once more. Everyone was wide-eyed with excitement and a little fear following Madame Wickets' words. Our lives would never be the same after today. It was a strange and exciting thought, and my heart rate gathered speed.

Madame Wickets pulled a clipboard from the sack on her hip, cleared her throat, and said, "Jase Branson."

All eyes went to Jase, including mine.

Jase reached down and picked up the potion bottle in front of him.

"Now, you get to do the honors and show your classmates how it's done," Madame Wickets said. "Grab the neck of the bottle firmly and smash it as hard as you can into the bonfire."

Jase looked confused. The pit in front of us was still unlit, still cold, a fine layer of ash and leaves blown into the clearing on the breeze, the only indication that it might once have contained flames. I watched Madame Wickets raise her right hand as flames roared to life, spitting and crackling as the heat spread outwards.

Jase hesitated a moment. Then, remembering that he was setting an example for the rest of us to follow, he raised the bottle above his head, pausing dramatically, before sending it hurtling into the fire.

We all gasped.

Across the circle, a girl covered her face with her hands as Jase jumped backward. He would've lost his footing if Kris hadn't grabbed his arm to keep him upright.

The flames had turned blue, dancing and hissing higher until they were taller even than Jase, but it was what was in the middle of them that caught everyone's attention. A wisp of silver-gray light rose from the flames like a fairy without wings, trailing a tail of sparkling silver behind it. The Spirit-like creature spun toward Jase, hovering in front of his mouth. The instant his lips parted, the magical creature slipped inside his mouth and down into his throat.

Jase clutched his chest, coughing. Hunched over, he struggled to breathe, fingers clawing at his throat while Kris and Shane patted his back. I watched, frozen, uncertain if this was what should've happened. It all seemed so … painful.

"Breathe, Master Branson," Madame Wickets said. "You only swallowed air."

"Air?" Jase turned watery eyes toward her. "It felt… like it went… down the wrong pipe," he managed to choke out. He stopped when he noticed that his hands were glowing silver like the wisp that had leaped from the flames, clouds of sparkles swirling around them. "What's happening?" he asked. "What does that mean?"

"Congratulations, Jase Branson. You have been chosen to practice metallurgy."

Jase continued to examine his hands, a tentative smile on his face, as Kris and Shane slapped his back, and everyone else in the group began to clap... apart from Cole. What was his problem? Jase was the first heir to receive his gift, and he couldn't even celebrate with him? I glared at him as Jase, oblivious, punched the air with a glowing fist.

"Now, moving on," Madame Wickets announced. "Marilyn Danvers."

Marilyn, a girl with pale, freckled skin, was standing on the other side of Jenny. Her cheeks turned pink as Madame Wickets explained that, to avoid choking, she should allow the element to make its own way inside her rather than inhaling to speed up the process. Jase grinned at her.

Marilyn stepped forward, clutching her vial with trembling hands. She threw it into the flames, and they roared blue again. Another wisp emerged, this one rippling like water. It entered her chest in a smooth motion, and her hands began to glow with a faint blue aura.

"Congratulations, Marilyn Danvers," Madame Wickets said. "You are an aquamancer."

By now, we knew what to expect, but even so, it still took me by surprise when Cole's name was announced next. Confident as always, he stepped around the stump and smashed his bottle into the fire without even flinching as the flames roared above our heads.

"Psycho," Jenny whispered, and I ignored her. Cole had lived for this day almost since he was born, and despite his attitude, I was curious to find out what gift he would receive.

He stepped backward as a blue Spirit revealed itself from the flames, the same color as Marilyn's. I frowned. I'd expected Cole to get fire at the very least, although I knew that he expected to get Celestial. Could I have been wrong?

He shared a similar confused expression, his gaze following the wisp drifting toward him. He braced himself for the element to slip into his mouth, barely causing him to clear his throat, his eyebrows lowering further when he raised his hands in front of his face. They were shimmering with a brilliant blue fog.

"Congratulations, Cole Bevair," Madame Wickets said. "You will now practice aquamancy."

Cole's bottom lip twitched. He resumed his position without acknowledging the claps and cheers, and I noticed that the other heirs didn't rush to congratulate him. He was unhappy with his gift. As heir to the Mercantyl industry, he'd clearly expected more. We might not have been friends now, but I still felt bad for him—he would have to explain this to his father, and I could imagine exactly how that conversation would go.

"Jenny Webber!"

My heart skipped a beat. I was as excited for Jenny to unlock her gift as I was to receive my own. Like Cole, Jenny grabbed her potion bottle and approached the flames confidently, turning back to give me a thumbs-up before hurling it into the fire.

The flames roared angrily, forcing us all to step away as the fire reared taller than it had before, like a crazed animal trying to escape. Jenny returned to my side and grabbed my arm. I wanted to cover my ears against the terrible hissing and spitting, but I clung to Jenny instead.

Madame Wickets strode purposefully into the circle of stumps, positioning herself close to the raging fire. She raised her hands, palms facing the crackling flames, and began to chant in a steady, low voice. I blinked in surprise as the fire responded immediately to her words. The fierce, chaotic blaze began to calm, the flames shrinking and flickering less wildly with each passing moment. Her voice resonated through the clearing, steady and commanding, until the fire's brilliant intensity faded entirely, leaving behind its familiar, steady orange glow.

"W-what happened?" Jenny asked.

"Jenny, please come with me." Madame Wickets gestured for Jenny to follow her to Professor Kellar, who was now standing, watching the proceedings, his face even paler than before, if that were at all possible. Professor Kellar led Jenny up the stairs and inside the log cabin, the door closing softly behind them.

The other students whispered among themselves, everyone

confused about what had happened to Jenny. Did this mean that she wasn't going to receive a gift? Could that happen to any one of us? Like the other heirs, I'd always taken it for granted that I would unlock my gift when I turned eighteen—what if I, too, didn't get one?

Madame Wickets came back to the circle and cleared her throat. "Let us continue."

"What happened?" I blurted out. "Is Jenny okay?"

"She is absolutely fine." Madame Wickets eyed me from beneath her hat. "A fluke in the test. It happens on rare occasions."

"What does that mean?" I asked.

"Jenny Webber will require a separate test, nothing for you to worry about. Now. Ashlyn Grove!"

My heart was still skipping from what had happened with Jenny, and I wasn't mentally prepared for it to be my turn. Still, I reached down mechanically and grabbed the neck of my bottle, walked around the stump, and tossed it into the flames before my anxiety got the better of me. I sighed with relief, knees trembling, when I saw the dancing blue flames appear among the orange. It had worked. I couldn't imagine having to go through this again, and poor Jenny would probably have to do it alone next time.

But nothing happened.

Puzzled, I waited, wondering why my Spirit was taking so long to reveal itself. Was there another problem? If so, was it possible that the potion bottles had been tampered with? It would explain why Cole had received the water element when he'd clearly been expecting more. For several moments, the flames remained blue, and then, to my utter horror, they reverted to orange.

I couldn't look at the other heirs. I knew exactly what they must be thinking, that I'd gotten everything I deserved, and tears prickled my eyes.

Madame Wickets approached the fire. "Odd," she mumbled, staring at the flames, "two flukes in a row."

"Madame Wickets!" One of the other students was pointing above our heads, and we all turned to follow his gaze.

Above the clearing danced a glowing, white Spirit with a long, shimmering tail. But as I watched, other Spirits joined in, appearing from nowhere, wisps of every color imaginable, twirling and spinning and swooping around the clearing, long glittering tails brushing the tops of our heads and demanding our full attention. I was smitten—it was the most magical performance I'd ever seen, and I'd seen plenty in my lifetime.

I glanced at Madame Wickets, who had one hand pressed to her throat.

When I turned back to the Spirits, they'd come together to create one shimmering luminescent light that hovered closer and closer to my face. I closed my eyes and parted my lips.

Warm air flowed down my throat, filling me with an instant, overwhelming tenderness like being hugged. I felt it come to rest inside my chest and shuddered, a flood of warmth traveling from my core through to every part of my body until I was tingling from head to toe.

I released a gasping breath, opened my eyes, and stared at my hands. They shimmered with an opal luminescence that reminded me of the full moons lighting up the sky. My arms glowed, too, I realized. I was a walking rainbow, a reflection of the sun's rays, every movement creating an iridescent arc that lingered behind me. I couldn't help smiling. It felt so good, like I was light as a feather.

"The heavens..." Madame Wickets murmured, bringing me back down to reality.

Everyone was staring at me. It was only when my feet touched grassy soil that I realized I'd been floating about a foot above the ground. I stared at my feet and then at Madame Wickets. "What just happened? What ... element is this?"

She hesitated, removing her hat and rubbing her forehead with one hand while she regained her composure. Hat clasped to her chest, she smiled at me. "My dear, this is no ordinary element..."

My heart lurched sickeningly. I sensed the glow inside me, and although I still had no idea which gift I'd been given, I could feel the power emanating from my pores.

"Ashlyn Grove," she said, her voice rising a notch, "you have acquired Celestial."

CHAPTER FOURTEEN

Cole

elestial?

Ashlyn Grove had unlocked Celestial magic?

I could see it with my own eyes, but I refused to accept it. If anyone deserved Celestial, it was me. She didn't even care about what gift she would get—*she'd have been happy with aquamancy*—so why did she get the one gift that I'd been waiting for my entire life? How did the Spirits believe this was acceptable?

The cheers and congratulations and the squealy, girly hugs faded into the background as I tried to reassemble my thoughts. What if... What if the Spirits didn't believe that Ashlyn Grove was worthy of Celestial, but she'd somehow found a way to manipulate our potion bottles so that our gifts swapped. That had to be it. I had no idea how she'd done it or what kind of magic would even be powerful enough to affect the results this way, but I was going to get to the bottom of it, even if it was the last thing I did. Ashlyn Grove wasn't getting away with this. She had my gift, and I wanted it back.

I swallowed, my thoughts settling as my pulse regulated, and the clearing came back into focus. Madame Wickets was standing there with her hands clasped to her chest like she was afraid she might explode with excitement. Jase and Kris hovered either side of me, more from concern about how I would react than any strong sense of loyalty, and Shane... There he was, waiting in line to congratulate Ashlyn as expected.

Finally, I allowed my gaze to settle on Ashlyn, the new Celestial, one of only four in known existence. It made my throat constrict to see the way her skin glowed, to watch the wisps pirouetting above her head, to see her eyes so wide with feigned surprise. My only consolation was that Jenny Webber's potion had misfired, and the girl was in the log cabin where she couldn't witness the celebrations firsthand. If she was here, she'd be all over Ashlyn. Come to think of it, didn't anyone else find it suspicious that Webber's potion drew a blank, and then, miraculously, out comes a Celestial? As if we didn't need more reason not to trust the girl...

I felt the weight of eyes on me. The other students had taken a step back, leaving just me, Jase, and Kris to supposedly get all excited over the new Celestial in our midst. I could almost hear their thoughts buzzing in the air. *A Celestial—right here in our midst. And Cole Bevair only got aquamancy? He's going to be livid.*

Everyone knew the heirs didn't exactly get along, and this twist was sure to stir the pot.

I forced a smile and walked toward her. Behind me, Jase said, "Cole? Are you okay?" I ignored him. Kris's hand brushed my arm, reacting a beat too late to stop me.

Ashlyn's glow was fading, the shimmering halo surrounding her body slowly evaporating as she turned to face me. She couldn't keep the excitement from her eyes. I hadn't been this close to her in two years, and it would've been easy to get drawn back into those wide eyes, just like in the past, if I hadn't reminded myself that the girl had had plenty of time to improve her acting skills.

"Congratulations, Grove," I said. No emotion. Something I'd learned from my father. I wanted to add that it was an honor to be awarded Celestial, but I wasn't about to give her anything to twist around and pin on me later when she and Webber were discussing the day's events.

Her eyes narrowed for a split second as if expecting more, but then she nodded, still smiling, and said, "Thanks, Bevair."

Sure, I'd used her last name, but it stung when she turned it back on me. It felt like the final confirmation that our friendship was over. I didn't react. It's what she was hoping for—a reaction—something to dissect in her dorm room, proof that I was the one keeping her separated from the other heirs.

Turning, I retraced my steps back to my stump and gestured to Kris and Jase, who still hadn't moved, to do the right thing and offer their congratulations, too. It was what we were good at, doing the right thing. It had been drummed into us since we were old enough to speak, our parents knowing that the whole of Andis was watching our every move.

I caught Shane's eye. He was watching me carefully, too, like he knew I'd offered a token gesture, no more and no less than was expected of me. I raised my eyebrows. I was in no mood for his diplomatic responses. He gave me one anyways. "Now will you agree that Ashlyn is more special than we ever gave her credit for?"

I let out a huff. "You're naive, Aster. Something is going on here, and I will find out what it is."

Shane rolled his eyes and let out a sharp breath, his shoulders visibly tense. "You're just bitter, Cole. You wanted Celestial, and now you can't stand the idea of Ashlyn having what you thought should be yours. Admit it—the only thing happening here is your jealousy getting the better of you."

I rotated my shoulders and ran my fingers through my hair. Maybe it was time to cut ties with a second heir. Kris and Jase returned to their stumps, Kris's gaze flitting between me and Shane. "How close are you to cracking that file, Reeve?" I kept my voice low so no one else would hear.

Kris hesitated, peering around at the others, who were all still apparently fascinated by the new Celestial. "Still working on it.

It's tough, must be magically infused. I've never had this much trouble decrypting a file before."

"Magically infused?" Jase frowned. "What, like fusing magic with tech?"

"Yeah," Kris said. "It's above my skills, though; only a metal practitioner can do it."

Jase grinned and thumped his chest with his thumb. "And you're looking at one of those right here. Let me at it."

"You haven't even begun using your gift." Shane shook his head, watching me like this was all my fault.

"I don't care how you do it. Just figure it out," I said to Kris. "And while you're at it, find out why Webber's test backfired. I suspect we're going to find out that this is all connected somehow."

"As you command." Kris gave me a mocking salute as Madame Wickets called for everyone's attention.

I saw Ashlyn's back disappear into the log cabin and pictured Webber gushing over her when she heard the good news.

"We still have more testing to complete." Madame Wickets clapped her hands excitedly. "You'll have to forgive me if I don't seem quite myself. I've been doing this job for twenty-five years, and I've never seen anyone acquire Celestial magic."

I kept my expression serene as I eyed the rest of the group, all nodding in agreement.

Madame Wickets glanced at her clipboard, having seemingly composed herself, and said, "Kristopher Reeve. You're next."

I watched, stiff-spined—another trait inherited from my father—as Kris acquired geomancy and Shane was given pyromancy. As if this day couldn't get any worse. Why did he get fire when I was stuck with water? Whatever Ashlyn and that girl Webber had done to manipulate the Spirits, they'd not only cheated me out of Celestial but out of my second-choice gift, too.

I was glad when it was finally over. Madame Wickets led us back to school while Ashlyn remained in the log cabin with Webber and Professor Kellar. Why? Why did Webber get to find out what happened next for Ashlyn while the rest of us were kept in the dark? I didn't speak on the way back. I needed to stay focused and figure out my next move: I had to find out exactly how Celestial was acquired and what Ashlyn had done to make it happen. If she could do it, there was nothing stopping me from doing it, too, because I refused to sit back and watch her brandish her gift like a golden sword. I refused to let her be more powerful than me.

I marched straight back to the dorms, bypassing the Dining Pavilion and the other students milling about—my appetite had vanished this morning. Kris and Jase followed me to my dorm, although I barely noticed them. We lost Shane somewhere along the way. Not that I cared. More and more frequently, the dynamics were shifting when Shane was in our company, and not for the better.

Thankfully, my roommate Winston wasn't around when we got back to my room. I removed my jacket and tossed it onto the bed, taking a seat at my desk. Waking my MagiScreen from its slumber, I opened the NodeNavigator and searched for relevant NodeSites. I needed to do more research on Celestial as an element. There must've been something I'd missed, something that Ashlyn had somehow discovered and worked to her advantage.

"What's the plan, guys?" Jase flopped onto my bed, arms folded behind his head. It must've been great to be him, satisfied with his gift because he'd entered the ritual with zero expectations. I guessed that was the difference between me and the other heirs.

"We need to crack that file," I said. "And figure out how Ashlyn was chosen."

Kris hovered, peering at the MagiScreen over my shoulder. "I'm honestly not sure what you think you're going to find Cole," he said. "Celestial chooses the person, not the other way around. The best you can hope for is to find out that it chooses people with a particular trait."

I glared at him, and he backed away, but not far enough. "Trait?"

"Sure, maybe something like compassion or an affinity for magical creatures. I know I'm grasping at threads here, but if that were the case, it wouldn't be Ashlyn's fault that she has it and you don't."

I ignored him. I thought I knew all there was to know about Celestial magic, and never in my wildest imagination would I have believed Ashlyn Grove worthy of it. According to myth, Celestial wasn't meant to be revived for mortals to use, although there had been three cases already where it had slipped through the magical cracks. Four if you counted Ashlyn. And I wanted to know how and why.

"I think we should focus on cracking the code and getting into the file attached to Jenny Webber's contract," Kris said. "Something happened today to make her potion faulty when everyone else's worked just fine. Maybe it's connected to whatever is in that file. It's too much of a coincidence that it happened to Ashlyn's best friend right before Ashlyn got Celestial."

"Yeah, what he said." Jase raised his knees to his chest, ready to spring off my bed, as I glimpsed my roommate standing in the doorway, fastening the zip of his pants.

He froze. His gaze hopped between the three of us like we'd suddenly grown two heads, and then he swallowed, his Adam's apple bobbing uncomfortably above the neckline of his shirt. He must've been in the bathroom. He was so quiet I didn't bother to check, and now I had no idea how long he'd been standing there or how much of the conversation he'd heard. I quickly replayed in my head what we'd been discussing. He must've heard us discussing Webber's encrypted file and Ashlyn getting Celestial.

"Hey, Cole," Winston said. Was it my imagination, or did I hear a tremor in his voice? "What's up, guys?" He'd met the guys before, and although he was quiet around them, he'd never appeared to be outwardly intimidated before. Now, he stood on the threshold of the bedroom like he was debating whether to run or stay.

"Winston." I forced a smile. "Don't stand there, come in. We were discussing our ritual, which was, let's just say, eventful." I waved him into the bedroom, and he obeyed, his legs moving on autopilot. I needed to find out how much he'd heard. I didn't want it getting all around the university that we were trying to hack into encrypted files. I particularly didn't want it to get back to Ashlyn.

"E-eventful?" His eyes blinked slowly behind his glasses, and he shoved them further up his nose with his index finger.

"I'll let you into a secret," I said, drawing him in. He stepped closer. As if he actually believed I'd share my secrets with him. "Our friend Ashlyn Grove got Celestial today." Everyone in Aurora would know by this evening anyway, but I needed to find out if he heard us talking about Webber.

He blinked faster now, his eyes all over the place until they finally settled on the open MagiScreen on my desk. He'd heard our conversation. There wasn't even a hint of surprise at the news there was a Celestial in the building. It must've dawned on him then that we were expecting a reaction because he said, "Celestial, wow," with zero emotion.

Something was going on with him. He was a nerdy kid who only became animated when he was discussing the latest games with Kris, and I wondered if he was figuring out who to tell first about our plans to hack into a secret file.

"You won't tell anyone, will you?" I held his gaze, making it clear that I wouldn't be happy if he did.

Jase sat up on the bed and opened his mouth to speak. I shut him down with a warning glance.

Winston blinked again. "No... I... I won't say anything. They won't hear it from me."

He almost seemed afraid of me, and I know I can come across as a little intimidating sometimes—it's necessary for the future heir of the Mercantyl industry to be recognized as a strong-willed and determined character—but this was unusual even by Winston's standards. Was it because we were discussing Webber? Was he friends with the girl? He stared at my wardrobe and refused to make eye contact.

"That's good to hear," I said.

Winston still didn't move.

"Perhaps we should go," Kris said, gesturing at Jase to get up. I held out an arm to make him stay where he was.

"Was there something else, Winston?"

"Well... I..." He swallowed again like he had an apple core stuck in his throat, his eyes still fixated on the wardrobe. I followed his gaze. Nope, I hadn't left my underwear hanging on the back of the door.

"If you have something to say, you can say it in front of the guys," I snapped. This was becoming painful. "We're all friends here."

"I know." He shook his head. "I know, you've been nothing but kind to me..." I wouldn't have gone that far, but hey, I'd take it. "And I'm so sorry. I really am. She paid me to do it and promised me that it was for a good reason. I don't even know if she's heard anything, but—"

"Wait! What?" I balled my fists and stood up, causing Winston to flinch. "What the hell are you talking about? Who paid you to do what?"

"B-Bellis R-Reeve." He was still shaking his head. "She promised me that nothing bad would happen, that I was doing the right thing by keeping quiet. But I can't do it any longer. It keeps me awake at night. I can't even eat."

That was a lie—I'd seen him stuffing chocolate-dusted moonberry pastries into his mouth only last night after curfew—but that wasn't important right now. If Bellis Reeve was involved, this wouldn't be good.

"What's going on, Winston?" I lowered my voice. "Tell me now before I go to Dean Bask."

"It's inside your wardrobe," he said.

Kris yanked open the doors and started rummaging through my clothes, crumpling the fabric and knocking a few items off their hangers.

"Leave it!" I snapped, shoving his hands away. "Winston! What am I looking for?"

"At the back," Winston's voice came, steady but tense.

I carefully parted the layers of garments. There, in the bottom right-hand corner, I spotted it—a tiny black orb, barely the size of a button, pulsing faintly with a silvery-blue light. It was fixed to the back of the wardrobe with adhesive sigils that dissolved the moment I touched it. I pried it free and held it up. "What is this?"

"It's an Eavesdrop Crystal," Kris muttered, avoiding my gaze.

I turned the small device over in my hands, its smooth surface faintly humming with residual magic. "Why would Bellis Reeve, *your cousin*, plant a magical Eavesdrop Crystal in my wardrobe?" My mind raced with possibilities, each worse than the last.

If I knew Bellis—and unfortunately, I did—she was chasing a story. One that would bring her fame while leaving me with the kind of bad reputation that my father would have to swoop in and fix.

"I don't know." Kris shook his head.

"Find out now, Reeve, or I'll get my father involved." It was the threat that always worked, not that I had any intention of my father finding out. I turned to Winston. "Who else knows about this?"

"N-no one, I swear."

I believed him. If he'd told anyone else, it would've spread through the university faster than an uncontained spell in a novice's hands: *an heir being spied on!* Whatever Bellis Reeve was up to, she'd picked on the wrong person, and I would see to it that her career ended before it even got started.

Chapter Fifteen

Ashlyn

Everything happened in a blur.

Inside the log cabin, I listened to Professor Kellar telling me what a huge responsibility it was to have been given Celestial magic. "It's a combination of every magical power in existence, Ms. Grove. We believe that it can control the weather and make use of cosmic energy, and by this, I mean all the Celestial bodies in the universe."

I nodded along. It was too much information to process all at once. How could I possibly have that much power inside me after smashing a bottle of potion into a bonfire? I was still me, wasn't I? I stared at my hands, his words floating around me as I realized that there was a tingling warmth inside me that hadn't been there before. Or was it my imagination?

"I can't believe it! You got Celestial, Ashlyn. You did it!" Jenny kept her distance, as if she were afraid to touch me, and it slowly dawned on me that her potion bottle hadn't worked.

"Jenny, I-I don't know what to say. What about your gift?"

"What about it?" She shrugged, grinning at me like she, too, was still trying to process the new *Celestial* me, trying to figure out what had changed. "It'll work next time."

She seemed so certain of her gift, so unconcerned that her

potion had misfired this time, that I kept my worry to myself. What if it didn't work? How would she handle having no gift while sharing a room with someone who'd been given Celestial magic? She was like Cole in that respect—they believed in their Divine right to the gift awarded to them at birth, and I didn't want this to spoil our friendship.

Cole's reaction to my gift snuck back into my head. It had taken all his willpower to congratulate me, and I was certain that he only did it because it was expected of him. He needed to save face. But I also knew that he'd have been devastated that I'd gotten Celestial instead of him. Would he accept it quietly? No. But there was nothing he could do to change it, which meant that he would probably make my life even more difficult going forward.

Great!

I'd come to Aurora hoping to blend in, make new friends, and create new contacts, and now, as if being an heir didn't already set me apart from everyone else, I'd been given the gift of the most powerful magic there was. Cole was bound to turn this around somehow. He'd probably try to make it seem that I'd planned all along to outshine the other heirs, even though it was impossible to know which gift we'd be granted until we turned eighteen.

When we got back to the dorm, I still felt numb. Jenny talked all the way back about how different my life would be now, the kind of doors my gift would open for me, not to mention the other heirs having to acknowledge that my power was greater than theirs. I kept quiet. It didn't feel right thinking that way. I didn't want to be *better* than the other heirs; I simply wanted to prove that I was worthy of taking over my industry when the time came.

Emma came running into our room, squealing as she threw her arms around me and gave me a big, warm hug. News traveled fast. "I can't believe it!" she said. "How do you feel? Do you feel different now that you're so powerful?" She studied my face, looking for signs.

I couldn't help smiling at her. "I feel exactly the same, just overwhelmed."

"Typical Ashlyn," Jenny said, sitting on the edge of her bed, watching us. "What do you think your parents will say?"

"I'm sure they already know." I sat down on my bed facing Jenny, and Emma sat next to me, too excited to go anywhere right now. "Professor Kellar said I would need to be registered immediately. I'll have to meet with the Council soon, too." Celestial was so rare that my parents had never mentioned the process for handling the contract attached to it. Would I have to go to the Council, or would they come to Aurora? Would I require special lessons on how to manage my gift? The list of official requirements that I would have to fulfill now stretched endlessly in front of me. I wanted to curl up on my bed, sleep for a whole day, and give my brain a chance to catch up.

"Madame Wickets was fluttering around like a sprite on festival day," Jenny said to Emma. "You'd think she'd unlocked Celestial herself. And Bevair? Pompous, as usual."

I swallowed, picturing Cole coming over to congratulate me, his charming smile fixed in place. Everyone else would've heard him say, "Congratulations, Grove," and moved on. I was the only one who would've noticed the clenched jaw and heard the strain in his voice. Then it hit me: Jenny wasn't even there. She was in the log cabin with Professor Kellar, so why was she saying stuff about Cole? And why hadn't she mentioned her own test going wrong? Unless she was more embarrassed than she was letting on and was using me as the topic of conversation to divert attention away from herself.

We were catching up on assignments in our room later, Jenny laying on her stomach on her bed, MagiScreen glowing softly in front of her, while I sat at my desk, mostly staring at the wall and reliving the moment I received my gift when I heard her gasp. She'd been quiet since Emma left. I wanted to ask her why she hadn't mentioned her own failed test, but I didn't want to embarrass her further. Professor Kellar had said she would need to retake it another time and that they did malfunction occasionally, but he'd been vague about why, and I wondered if it was because he didn't know the answer.

"News travels fast." Jenny's doll-like eyes were even wider when I looked at her. "Howard wants to go ahead and formally initiate you into the club!"

"The club?" I repeated, my brain cells still lingering back in the clearing in the woods.

"The League of Magical Theory?" Jenny grinned at me. "Professor Kellar must've told him. They're good friends. And now he wants to make it official and initiate you."

I know I'd relented after the welcome party and told Jenny that I would join the club, but now all my original misgivings came rushing back, flooding my face with heat. Was it because I felt protective of my new powers? After all, I knew so little about my gift, and the weight of what it represented was overwhelming. Maybe I wasn't ready to take on something as significant as joining their club just yet. Or was it just the same uneasiness creeping back in, the one I'd felt when I first met the other members of the club? They'd accepted Jenny without a gift. So, why didn't it sit right with me that they'd heard I was Celestial and immediately wanted to initiate me?

Initiation? Wasn't that for cults? I was certain that there'd been no mention of it before now.

"No one said anything about an initiation," I mumbled.

"We did, I'm sure we did," Jenny said. "I had one. It's nothing to worry about."

I was even more sure now that they hadn't mentioned an initiation into the club. I'd have remembered.

Jenny was still staring at her Echo Panel. "Howard wants to conduct it on the next full moon."

"Next full moon?" It was an interesting choice of words. Ancient magic had conducted rituals around the full moon, and connecting it to an initiation—*my initiation*—made it sound even more cult-like. "What exactly do I have to do, Jenny?"

"It's only a ceremony," she said, her curls bouncing around her face. "Preferably done when our moons are full because that's when the planet's energy is strongest."

"What kind of ceremony?" I prompted her because it felt like she was avoiding giving me a direct answer.

"When both moons come together, we can combine our elements with you since you're Celestial." Her eyes were distant, as if she were witnessing another ceremony that had already taken place. "Harvey was part of the club; that's why they inducted me early, but imagine the magic in the air now that we have you, Ash. The first female Celestial and the first Celestial to join our club."

She paused, realizing that I wasn't gushing along with her. Her smile faded. I was still trying to process what she'd said: *We can combine our elements with you since you're Celestial*. What did that even mean? Would my gift make their elements stronger? Jenny didn't even have her element yet.

"What's wrong?" she asked, sitting up. "I feel like I'm getting excited alone over here."

"Sorry." I shook my head. Why was I apologizing? "It's a lot to process."

"What is there to process?" Her eyes narrowed. "Why haven't you called your parents yet to give them the good news?"

Good question.

Was it because I knew how they would react, and I didn't want them quelling my excitement before I'd even gotten used to thinking about being Celestial? My father might not see it as a powerful gift, one that I could use to help me rule our industry, but rather as a dowry to convince one of the other heirs to marry me. My stomach twisted. What if they'd already started planning an alliance with Cole Bevair... Or even worse, with the other Celestial, Ethan Weiss?

"Look, I know your dad still treats you like a little girl rather than the heir to his industry," Jenny said, her voice softening, "but this must change everything. Celestial chose you, Ashlyn Grove."

I nodded. I worked so hard in preparatory academy to prove my worth, and now I was the first female Celestial, the first Divine heir. My magic was that of the Spirits and the rarest of all. Maybe now my father would finally see me.

"You're right." I reached for my Echo Panel. "I'll call them."

Jenny leaped off her bed and clapped her hands. "Yes! And I'll let Howard know to begin preparations for the ceremony."

"No, wait, slow down." My pulse was racing. One thing at a time. I would speak to my parents first and then think about the ceremony. But Jenny was already sending the message, her tongue poking from the corner of her mouth in concentration. "I need details of the ceremony first before I agree to it."

My Echo Panel vibrated in my hand: my mom was calling me.

I swallowed, fumbling with the device as I raised it to my ear, turning away from Jenny. "Mother?"

"Ashlyn, sweetie."

I could hear the excitement in my mom's voice and glanced at Jenny, who mouthed something from the doorway about giving me privacy before she disappeared.

"I was about to call you, Mother," I said, giving her my full attention. "I wanted to tell you that—"

"You're Celestial! I just got off the Echo Panel with Madame Wickets. Ashlyn, I can't believe it."

"Me neither." I paused. "It's not what I expected."

"No one could've expected this, honey. Your father and I are so happy."

"Father is happy?"

"Of course he is! You have no idea how proud I am."

"You are?" My heart flipped with excitement. "Is Father proud, too?"

She paused a beat too long, a beat in which my head fought with my heart and came back certain that this wouldn't change anything between me and my father. I left my seat and crossed the room to my bed, slumping on the edge.

"He is proud, Ashlyn," she said. "I know you think he's too busy to pay attention to you, but he is proud of you."

So proud, she had to repeat it twice?

"This goes way beyond anything your father and I expected," she continued.

"So, what does this mean? Is there something I need to do moving forward?"

"Nothing imminent. You will meet with the Council at some point; I'm sure they'll put in place programs to help you hone your magic to its fullest potential—Oh, and you should probably speak to Ethan Weiss. He must be ecstatic to have another Celestial around."

I doubted that, but I didn't say it out loud. I especially doubted he wouldn't immediately decide I was his competition. Would he become another Cole? Threatened by me and my powers? My heart quaked for a second. I didn't need more complications.

"Celestial magic is so rare that your father and I will have to revisit your contract with the Council's guidance, but it's nothing you need to worry about. Just promise me you will listen to the Council—they'll be here to help you all the way."

"Thank you, Mother. I will listen to them."

"Are you okay, sweetie? I imagine this is overwhelming, but just give yourself some time to adjust. One step at a time. You can't go rushing into anything with magic like Celestial; there's still so much that we don't understand."

I knew she meant well, and she was only thinking about the practicalities of my new gift, but she was making me feel anxious. There was so much to think about, and I felt as though I'd barely been able to string a few coherent thoughts together since the ritual this morning.

"I'll let you get some rest then," my mother said, as if she could sense my energy waning. "I just wanted you to know that we are in your corner, okay?" She paused, and I could hear the muffled sounds of her speaking to someone else, the Echo Panel pressed against her chest so that I couldn't hear. "Sweetheart, your father wants to speak to you."

I sat up straighter, the fogginess in my brain evaporating almost immediately. I hadn't spoken to my father since I came to Aurora, and we hadn't exactly parted on the best terms. My stomach lurched when I recalled our last conversation over dinner the night before I left for university.

There was a rustling sound, followed by my father's gruff voice. "Ashlyn?"

"Good evening, Father." I wondered briefly if Jenny addressed her father the same way and quickly dismissed it.

"I heard about your gift."

I rolled my eyes. *How are you feeling, Ashlyn? How are you enjoying Aurora?* Nope, straight into the conversation that was most important to him.

"Yes, Father. Madame Wickets has informed me that there will be a meeting with the Council to advise me on which programs I'll need to attend."

"Celestial magic comes with a tremendous responsibility. I don't want you falling behind with your studies."

Tears stung my eyes. He couldn't simply come on the Echo Panel and give me some words of encouragement. Instead, he was already focusing on the negatives: the gift being too much for me to handle. In the past, I would've said exactly what he wanted to hear and finished the call feeling disheartened and unworthy, but I was done allowing my father and the heirs to make me feel like I wasn't good enough. I was. I was Ashlyn Grove, the first female heir and one of only four Celestials in the history of Andis.

"Father, I can and will manage both my studies and learning about my powers. You don't have to worry about me."

I pictured my father's grip tightening around the Echo Panel. "Then perhaps you might also manage to mend your relationship with the other heirs."

I took a deep breath. No backing down now. "It was my choice to leave that circle of friends, and it will be my choice to mend those relationships when I am ready. I assure you that you will be the first to know when and if it happens."

I sensed his anger brewing on the other end of the Echo Panel. I didn't want to argue with him, not today, not when I should be celebrating, but I needed him to understand that I was eighteen now, and I was determined to run the Elementum industry one day, with or without his blessing.

"Why are you so against giving me a chance to prove myself, Father? Now that I've gotten my powers, I will learn to use them for the good of the Elementum industry. You refuse to acknowledge the fact that I might actually be capable of running it properly, with no justification to back up your beliefs. When have I ever let you down? When have I not worked hard, harder even than the other heirs, because I understand that you and the other Lords frown upon a female in control of an industry? I know you will view this conversation as me being defiant, but that is not the case. I'm taking control of my life, Father, and I will prove you all wrong. I love you."

I ended the call before he could respond, letting the Echo Panel dim as I slumped backward onto my bed, my heart racing. The conversation played on a loop in my mind. I hadn't said anything wrong. I hadn't been rude or disrespectful—though in his eyes, it might have come across that way. All I'd done was stand my ground, firmly and unapologetically, declaring that I would not step aside for a male heir to take what was rightfully mine.

I suddenly remembered that I hadn't said goodbye to my mother. Sitting up, I called her back, praying that my father wouldn't answer, and almost cried with relief when I heard her voice.

"Ashlyn, what did you say to your father?"

I pictured him, red-faced and narrow-eyed, silently fuming as he handed the Echo Panel back to her after I ended the call. The thought unsettled me, but I needed her to understand. I needed to hear that at least one of my parents believed in me.

"I told him," I said, my voice steadier than I felt, "that I'm going to run the Elementum industry one day, Mother."

There was silence on the other end of the line, heavy and suffocating.

"Please don't tell me you agree with him," I said, my voice trembling with frustration. "That you think he's right—that I'm incapable of taking over from him just because I'm a girl. He hasn't even given me a chance! And, you know what? Even if I fail, isn't it his job as a parent to encourage me? To support me? Not to crush my confidence every time I try to prove myself?"

My chest heaved as I waited for her response, my emotions crackling like unspent energy in the air.

"Ashlyn, I—"

"I wish you would stand up to him, Mother. You said you have my corner, yet Father gets on the Echo Panel and immediately tells me to reconcile with the other heirs. I want to learn about our industry, even if Father refuses to teach me, and I won't let him dictate my future. Celestial chose me, Mother."

The words echoed in the quiet room, and it struck me that I was quoting Jenny. But she had a point—one I couldn't ignore. Celestial had chosen *me*.

My mother sighed. When she spoke, her voice was low, meant only for my ears. "I want you to know that I'm proud of you, Ashlyn. Don't ever stop believing in yourself, and I know you will prove them all wrong. I'm beginning to realize that Aurora is good for you, sweetheart."

I smiled even though she couldn't see me. "Thank you, Mother. I'm kind of happy you called.

"Only kind of?"

"Okay, I'm really happy you called. I love you, Mother."

"I love you too, Ashlyn."

I ended the call, lay back on my bed, my Echo Panel clutched to my heart, and waited for my breathing to regulate. Now, I could allow myself to celebrate my gift.

Squealing with excitement, two words scrolled through my brain on repeat: *I'm Celestial. I'm Celestial. I'm Celestial.*

———

I SLID OFF MY BED, unable to sit still any longer, and began pacing the room. The rush of emotions from earlier still swirled within me, a tangled mix of excitement and uncertainty. I folded my arms, trying to contain the giddy energy threatening to spill out. I'd always been careful not to show too much, even in front of Jenny, but tonight felt different. Everything felt different.

Jenny's voice broke through my thoughts. "You're practically buzzing, you know that?" She was sprawled across her bed, her MagiScreen glowing faintly as she looked up at me with a knowing smile.

I paused mid-step, forcing myself to act calm. "Am I? I guess I'm still trying to process everything."

She chuckled, closing her MagiScreen and sitting up. "You've been processing ever since we got back, Ashlyn. How about we take a walk? Clear your head. You're going to wear a groove in the floor at this rate."

I hesitated, glancing out the window. The moons were already high, casting a pale glow over the campus. "It's late."

Jenny hopped off her bed, grabbing her coat. "And? A walk might help settle that storm in your chest. Besides, you've been grinning at your bookshelf like it just told you the meaning of life."

Heat rose to my cheeks, and I turned away, grabbing my own coat to distract myself. Jenny had a way of reading me that made me uncomfortable at times, but I appreciated her efforts to draw me out. "Fine," I said, slipping into my coat. "But just a quick walk. I don't want to be up all night."

We stepped out into the cool night air, the soft glow of

enchanted lamps lining the pathways. The Eldergreen Forest loomed in the distance, its towering trees swaying gently in the breeze. The campus felt alive in the quiet, magic humming faintly in the background like a living heartbeat.

Jenny kicked at a pile of leaves, her steps carefree. "Do you think anything will change now?"

I glanced at her, surprised by the question. "What do you mean?"

"You have Celestial now." She shrugged. "It's a big deal. Do you think it'll change how people treat you?"

I exhaled softly, my breath visible in the cool air. "I don't know. Maybe. Probably." I shoved my hands into my pockets. "I just want to figure it out—what it means, what it'll require of me. I wasn't expecting all this attention."

Jenny smiled knowingly. "You'll get used to it. Besides, it's not like you're going to let a little extra attention stop you from being you, right?"

I gave her a faint smile, unsure how to answer. The truth was, I didn't know what being "me" meant anymore. Everything felt like it was shifting beneath my feet.

We stopped beneath a cluster of trees, the moonlight filtering through the branches. I tilted my head back, letting the stillness of the moment wash over me.

The sound of approaching footsteps shattered the quiet. Jenny stiffened beside me as Ethan Weiss stepped into the clearing, his dark coat blending with the shadows.

"What are you doing here?" My voice was sharp, more from surprise than anger.

"I heard," he said, his tone even, as if his presence here were the most natural thing in the world.

Jenny moved closer, her posture defensive. "And what exactly did you hear, Weiss?"

Ethan's eyes flicked to hers, then back to me. "Can we talk? Alone?"

Jenny folded her arms, her jaw tightening. "Whatever you have to say, you can say it to both of us."

"Jenny," I said softly, placing a hand on her arm. "It's okay. Just give us a moment."

She hesitated, her gaze locked on mine. Finally, she stepped back, but not before shooting Ethan a glare that could have frozen water.

"What do you want?" I asked, my voice low.

Ethan studied me for a moment, his expression unreadable. "How does it feel?"

I frowned. "How does what feel?"

"Celestial," he said simply.

I crossed my arms, meeting his gaze. "It feels... overwhelming. Like it's bigger than I am."

He nodded, as if that were the answer he'd expected. "It is. And you need to be ready for that. People will want things from you, Ashlyn. They'll see what you have and wonder how they can use it to benefit themselves."

His words were calm, but they carried an edge that made me uneasy. "What are you trying to say?"

"Be careful," he said, his voice dropping lower. "Don't trust too easily. Not everyone who smiles at you has your best interests at heart."

I stared at him, the weight of his warning settling uncomfortably in my chest. "Thanks for the advice," I said, my tone colder than I intended. "But I think I can figure this out on my own."

He stepped back, his expression softening slightly. "I hope so."

Without another word, he turned and disappeared into the shadows, leaving me standing there, unsure whether to feel grateful or insulted.

Jenny was by my side in an instant, her eyes narrowing as she glanced in the direction Ethan had gone. "What did he want?" she asked, her voice sharper than I expected.

"Nothing important," I lied, brushing past her and heading back toward the dorms.

Jenny fell into step beside me, her arms crossed tightly over her chest. "Don't let him get into your head, Ashlyn. And don't forget—you can trust me."

The comment struck me as odd. I didn't think Jenny had interacted with Ethan before—at least, not that I'd known—but the way she spoke about him, so certain and dismissive, made it seem like she already knew him. My thoughts swirled, questions bubbling to the surface: How does she know what Ethan's like? Have they spoken before?

I glanced at her out of the corner of my eye. Jenny's expression was guarded, her lips pressed into a thin line, and for a moment, I wondered if I should ask her outright.

But then I caught the tension in her posture, the way she kept glancing back over her shoulder as if to make sure Ethan was really gone. She wasn't just annoyed—she was on edge, and I couldn't tell if it was because of him or something else entirely.

I swallowed my questions, deciding to wait. If Jenny was hiding something, now wasn't the time to confront her. After all, tonight wasn't about Ethan or even Jenny—it was about my gift. I needed to focus on figuring out what Celestial meant for me and what would come next.

"Let's just go," I said softly, tightening my coat around myself as we walked.

Jenny's gaze lingered on me for a second longer before she nodded, her expression softening. "Yeah. Let's get back."

We made the rest of the walk in silence, but my mind churned with unease. Jenny had always been so open with me—why did it feel like there was something unspoken between us now?

By the time we reached our room, I'd convinced myself that I'd bring it up another time. Tonight, I needed to sleep and sort out my own feelings before I could handle anyone else's secrets. Jenny crawled into bed without another word, and I followed suit, though it was a long time before sleep finally claimed me."

Chapter Sixteen

Ashlyn

I felt like even more of a celebrity, though not in a way I enjoyed. This was different from the attention of being an heir. Everywhere I went on campus, students stopped to congratulate me, shake my hand, or simply stare as if they could see the magic radiating from me in shimmering waves. I'd never blushed so much or fiddled with my hair so often in my life.

It was the next afternoon, and I was on my way back to my dorm to meet Jase—even Celestials had assignments to complete —when someone called my name. I turned, and my stomach dropped. Bellis Reeve, Kris's cousin, stood there, looking polished in a tailored crimson suit, a glowing emblem pinned to her lapel marking her as part of a TruthForger guild. Beside her was a tall, dark-haired man holding an IllumaLens—its crystal orb shimmering faintly as it hovered above his hand, capturing every detail of its surroundings. Seeing Bellis now, as a professional Truth-Forger, was surreal.

"Ashlyn!" she gushed, rushing toward me with outstretched arms. She air-kissed my cheeks before stepping back, her hands immediately fussing with my hair. "Spirits, it's so good to see you again. And you look stunning! Aurora must be working wonders for you."

I could feel the heat rising to my cheeks again—at this rate, they'd be permanently red. "Thank you, Bellis," I said awkwardly.

"I had to find you," she said, adjusting her glasses. "Congratulations on your gift!" Her smile widened, and her attention shifted momentarily to the IllumaLens, its orb tilting slightly to capture my face.

"Thank you," I mumbled, acutely aware of the hovering device now aimed at me.

"Meet Rocco," Bellis said, motioning to the man, who gave me a small nod. "He's my IllumaCaster. Isn't this exciting? I'd love to interview you, Ashlyn—get your thoughts, your feelings, your plans for the future. Oh, and maybe a few images, too."

My heart skipped a beat. I stared at her, then at Rocco, then back at her again. "Um..." I twirled a strand of hair nervously. Should I run back to my room and change into something more appropriate? But then, what about Jase and our project? He'd be livid if I showed up late because of this. Then again, if he wanted to complain, he could take it up with Bellis.

Bellis gasped dramatically. "Don't tell me someone else has already interviewed you!"

"No, no," I stammered, laughing nervously. "You're the first."

She clapped her hands, her grin triumphant. "Perfect! Don't be nervous—you'll be great." Reaching into Rocco's satchel, she pulled out a wireless EchoMic.

"Um, I..." My words trailed off as Bellis whisked my bag off my shoulder and began adjusting my hair and tilting my chin like a professional stylist.

"Do you have lip balm?" she asked.

"Yes." Automatically, I reached into my satchel, retrieved it, and applied it while she fussed with my hair again.

"Perfect," she declared. She stepped back, gesturing for Rocco to start. The IllumaLens hovered closer, its faint hum blending with the quiet murmur of nearby students. My pulse quickened.

Bellis raised her chin, her polished smile beaming into the lens. "Three... Two... One."

"I'm Bellis Reeve, TruthForger and chronicler of extraordinary stories," she announced, her voice smooth and confident, "and I'm here at Aurora University with the extraordinary Ashlyn Grove. Yesterday, during the first round of magic reveals, Ashlyn Grove became the first female Celestial and only the fourth in existence in the recorded history of Andis." She turned to me, her eyes sparkling. "Thank you so much for joining us, Ashlyn. You must still be in shock."

She held the EchoMic out to me. My mind blanked for a moment before I forced a laugh. "Yes, definitely still in shock." My giggle slipped out unbidden. "It's... a lot to take in."

"I can only imagine," Bellis said with practiced ease. "Not only have you been gifted the rarest magic in our world, but you're officially part of Andis history. Future generations will study your story. How does that make you feel?"

"Oh, wow..." My voice faltered as I tried to process her words. "Flattered, I guess." I hadn't even considered the historical weight of it all until now. Glancing around, I noticed our growing audience. I shouldn't have looked—I knew better—but the number of curious faces made my heart race even faster. I turned my focus back to Bellis, hoping she couldn't see how much I wished the ground would swallow me whole.

Bellis's smile remained fixed, her enthusiasm undimmed. "Tell us what it was like, Ashlyn. How did you feel when you realized you'd been given Celestial magic?"

"Um..."

I hesitated as Cole and Kris emerged from the Dining Pavilion, their presence immediately pulling my focus. Cole's sharp eyes zeroed in on Bellis and Rocco, his expression darkening when he spotted the hovering IllumaLens. He smacked Kris's arm and gestured for him to keep moving. I watched them stride away until Bellis gently tilted the EchoMic closer to me, pulling me back into the moment.

I forced a bright smile, grateful my cheeks were already pink. "The only way I can describe it is that I felt as light as air, like I might drift right off the ground. Actually, I did float without realizing it." I paused, finding my rhythm. "The Spirits were breathtaking—every color you can imagine. It was surreal, like stepping into a dream. And the energy..." I trailed off, remembering the tingling warmth spreading through me. "It was like they were tickling me, playful and warm, making it impossible not to smile. So, I did."

"Wow," Bellis said, her voice soft with awe. "I'm comparing your experience to my own. When I unlocked aeromancy, it wasn't nearly as heavenly. The flames nearly scared me out of my skin, and I practically choked when the Spirit entered." She laughed, and I couldn't help laughing with her.

"I was lucky to have watched the others before me," I said, still smiling. "It helped to know what to expect, so I held my breath."

Bellis winked at me and turned back to the IllumaLens, her voice rising with practiced ease. "This moment is one for the books, folks. Ashlyn Grove, heir to the Elementum industry, has just made history. At only eighteen years old, she's become the first female Celestial in recorded history. We all wish her the very best of luck as she embarks on this incredible journey. Stay tuned for more of this story. Bellis Reeve, signing out."

"And scene," Rocco said, slicing a flat palm across his neck to signal the end of the recording. He lowered the IllumaLens, and the faint hum from the device ceased.

Bellis beamed at me, clapping her hands as a small crowd of students around us applauded. "You were phenomenal, Ashlyn!" she squealed. "You nailed it. I owe you big time."

I couldn't help smiling, even as I brushed a lock of hair behind my ear nervously. "What happens now?"

"I'll craft the story and send it to you for approval before we share it." She switched off the EchoMic and slid it back into her bag. I adjusted my satchel, ready to leave, when Bellis leaned in conspiratorially.

"Are you still roommates with Jenny Webber?" she asked casually.

My brow furrowed. "Yes… Why do you ask?"

Her smile didn't falter. "Just curious. Her mom was my guidance counselor when I was here." She glanced at Rocco, who gave a small nod, signaling he was ready. "Thanks again, Ash. We'll catch up soon."

I watched her and Rocco head off toward the Student Commons, her red suit standing out against the soft tones of the campus. As they disappeared, my Echo Panel buzzed in my pocket. My heart sank as I remembered Jase—I'd completely forgotten about meeting him. Groaning inwardly, I fished out the device and hurried toward my dorm.

———

"You're late." Jase was leaning casually against the wall outside my dorm room when I arrived, breathless from running. His posture was relaxed, but his tone carried an edge, one that told me he'd been waiting longer than he liked.

"Sorry, I got held up," I said, fishing my key from my pocket.

"Interviews are more important than school projects now, huh?" He straightened and stepped closer, his presence a little too much in the small hallway. The faint scent of his shampoo reached me.

Cole must've told him about Bellis.

I unlocked the door, keeping my response measured. "Not everything is about you, Jase."

He followed me into the room, his steps deliberate, the silence heavy. "Don't act like you're not enjoying all the attention," he pressed, his voice baiting.

I turned slowly, tossing my satchel onto the floor near my bed. "What's that supposed to mean?"

Jase shrugged, his grip tightening on the straps of his satchel.

"You've always tried to be different—standing out just because you were the only girl."

I blinked, taken aback by the sheer immaturity of his comment. "Seriously? That's what you're going with?" My voice was quieter than I expected but no less sharp. "You think my entire life revolved around being the only girl in the group? That I was just... what? Acting differently to get attention?"

He shifted uncomfortably, but his bravado didn't falter. "It's what it felt like. Back then, anyway."

I felt a flicker of sadness, quickly doused by frustration. "Grow up, Branson." My fists clenched at my sides. "I wasn't trying to be different. I was trying to keep up with you. With all of you. I thought we were friends."

His jaw tightened. "Friends don't do what you did. You played us against each other."

I stared at him, the weight of his accusation heavy in the room. "Is that what Cole told you?" My tone was soft and controlled, and for a moment, it silenced him. "Of course, it is. You've always let him think for you."

Jase looked like he wanted to argue, but I didn't give him the chance. The words spilled out, steady and firm, words I'd held in for too long. "You blamed me for what happened because none of you had the guts to stand up to him and admit that you initiated it. You all turned on me, cut me off, and named me the guilty one. And you know what? I let you. I let you because I cared about all of you, and I thought you'd come around." I took a deep breath, my voice softening but losing none of its edge. "But I'm done. I'm done letting you use me as your excuse."

"Don't get dramatic, Ashlyn," he muttered, but his confidence wavered, his eyes darting away.

I let out a bitter laugh. "Dramatic? You brought up the past. If you can't work on the project without dredging up old wounds, then go. I'll finish it myself and tell Professor Harpe that you didn't pull your weight."

Jase's shoulders tensed. "Come on, it's not that serious, Ash. Let's just finish the project. I need the grade."

I crossed my arms, my tone turning icy. "You need the grade, but you can't even respect me enough to leave the past where it belongs even when, deep down, you know you're all wrong. Figure it out, Jase. Or better yet, ask Cole for help. You seem to rely on him for everything else."

"That's a bit harsh," he snapped, his face hardening. "But why am I not surprised?"

"Get. Out." My voice cut through the tension like a blade, each word deliberate and sharp. I pointed at the door, my hand trembling ever so slightly—not with fear, but with the effort of holding back the storm brewing inside me. Jase stared at me for a moment, his mouth twitching as if he wanted to retort, but he seemed to think better of it.

The air between us felt taut, a silent standoff where neither of us would back down. Finally, he turned on his heel, his jaw set, and stormed out, slamming the door with a force that rattled the walls. I flinched at the noise, the echo lingering longer than I expected. My gaze stayed fixed on the door long after he'd gone, my chest rising and falling with the effort of controlling my emotions.

The room was silent now, save for the faint creak of the floorboards beneath my feet, but the charged energy lingered, thick as smoke. I let out a long, shaky breath and dropped my arm, the weight of everything that had just unfolded settling on my shoulders. Yet, for the first time in a long while, I didn't feel powerless. I had drawn a line, and this time, I wasn't going to let anyone cross it.

They couldn't hurt me anymore. I wouldn't let them.

Chapter Seventeen

Kristopher

My cousin was avoiding me. I'd seen her interviewing Ashlyn, and Shane mentioned that she'd spoken to him, but whenever I tried to track her down, she seemed to vanish. I needed to know why she'd planted an Eavesdrop Crystal in Cole's room. More importantly, I wanted to ask her about Jenny Webber—what she knew about her brother Harvey and, most importantly, the encrypted file attached to Jenny's magical contract.

No one knew that I'd cracked the file the night before. One of the older metallurgy students had been intrigued enough by the challenge of breaking into a fused file to help, asking no questions —just how I preferred it. I hadn't opened it yet, but just knowing I could was weighing heavily on me, especially with Cole breathing down my neck to uncover its contents. The whole Jenny Webber situation was suspicious. A sealed file was one thing, but paired with the malfunction at her ritual? Even I had to admit it seemed deliberate. Cole swore it was all part of some grand scheme—some malicious design that explained why Ashlyn had been gifted Celestial. I didn't know how much of that I believed, but it was hard to ignore the pattern. Jenny's brother was murdered last year. A malfunction at her ritual. A hidden file. It felt like something bigger, and that's why I needed Bellis.

I messaged her to meet me in Drayvarn, the nearby town, away from prying eyes—and, more importantly, away from Cole. I told her I had news she might find interesting. I ordered a Terra-Ride to take me to town, and now I sat in the main courtyard with my MagiScreen resting on my lap, its weight a constant reminder of the secrets it held. I couldn't shake the thought of why Bellis was even hanging around Aurora. She wasn't one to linger without purpose. Planting an Eavesdrop Crystal in Cole's room wasn't just idle curiosity, and she wasn't probing Shane about Jenny because she liked her. Bellis was investigating something, and I intended to find out what. The encrypted file was my bargaining chip. An information swap—that was Bellis's language.

A hum drew my attention, and I spotted the enchanted Terra-Ride approaching the school gates. The self-navigating vehicle glided across the shimmering moat and slowed to a stop in the cul-de-sac drop-off area. Its polished, sleek exterior caught the glow of the courtyard lights, its runes softly pulsating to indicate it was ready for its passenger. I approached, tapping the panel by the door to open it, and climbed into the cushioned interior.

"Drayvarn Diner," I said aloud.

The TerraRide acknowledged with a soft chime and began its smooth journey toward the town. I leaned back, the MagiScreen warm against my lap, the encrypted file heavy on my mind. The silence of the ride gave me too much time to think.

Ashlyn's face kept appearing in my thoughts. As one of only four Celestials, she was already known all over Andis. Part of me hoped she would grab this opportunity and prove her father wrong, showing him she could lead the Elementum industry as effectively as any male heir. That night at the Bevair mansion, though, still haunted me. If only I could rewind the clock, erase everything that happened, and go back to the way things were:

friends laughing, supporting each other, the silk threads of our bond unbroken.

But I wasn't naive. I wasn't even sure if Ashlyn would want to repair the past. I couldn't blame her if she didn't.

Drayvarn came into view after about fifteen minutes, nestled in the woods like a well-kept secret. It was a magic town, its aura unmistakable, and none of its fifteen-hundred inhabitants were non-users. The cobbled streets wound between homes that seemed plucked from a storybook—some tall with spired roofs, others squat and cheerful with round windows that seemed to smile.

The TerraRide slowed as we reached the sunny yellow facade of the Drayvarn Diner. The shutters were open, spilling warm light onto the cobblestones. I tapped the ride's panel, thanking it with another soft chime as I stepped out. Before it departed, I scheduled its return for nine-thirty to ensure I'd make the ten o'clock curfew.

The diner was larger than its exterior suggested, opening into a cozy tavern with low wooden beams and a crackling hearth. Booths made of polished oak lined the walls, each offering a sense of privacy, while waitresses in frilly aprons wove between tables with trays of steaming food and sparkling drinks.

I spotted Bellis immediately. She was in a corner booth, her satchel beside her, her sharp eyes scanning the room. When she saw me, she raised a hand, a faint smirk tugging at her lips. Whatever this was, she was enjoying it already.

"Well, well." Bellis's sharp, appraising gaze flicked to the Magi-Screen in my hand as I slid into the booth. Her curiosity was palpable, like a taut string ready to snap, though she tried to mask it behind a lazy smile. "Look who decided to find me tonight."

"You're looking well, Bellis," I replied, setting the MagiScreen down on the polished wooden table. Her eyes lingered on it, calculating, before returning to meet mine. It wasn't just an object to her—it was an opportunity, a tantalizing key to knowledge she didn't yet possess.

"What's new, Kris?" she asked, her tone light but with an edge of knowing. "Been keeping yourself busy with your usual group?" The smile that accompanied her words was sly, nearly predatory.

Before I could respond, a waitress approached, her movements as smooth as the enchanted tray that hovered just above her hand. "Water and magebrew, please," I said, trying to sound casual. Bellis gestured for another refill of her steaming black brew, not bothering to look up as she did so.

"How are you?" I asked once the waitress left, leaning back against the smooth wooden panel of the booth. Bellis wasn't one for idle chatter, but the question gave me a moment to compose myself to gauge her mood before diving into the questions that burned at the back of my mind.

"Exhausted," she said with a sigh, slipping her delicate glasses from her face and rubbing the bridge of her nose with crimson-painted fingertips. "You're fortunate I care enough to show up. I was planning on turning in early tonight."

"You've been hard to find," I said, more pointedly this time. "If you hadn't been avoiding me at Aurora, this wouldn't have been necessary."

Bellis tilted her head, a trace of amusement softening her sharp expression. "Avoiding you? Don't be dramatic. I've been busy." Her gaze flicked once more to the MagiScreen on the table, this time openly intrigued. "But let's not waste time. What's on your mind?"

The waitress returned, her tray hovering for just a moment before she slid my drinks onto the table. Bellis waited until she'd walked away before leaning forward, her hands loosely clasped in front of her.

"Why did you plant an Eavesdrop Crystal in Cole's room?" I asked, keeping my tone steady and my expression neutral. This wasn't about emotion; it was about answers.

Bellis didn't flinch. "I figured that's what this was about." She leaned back, her lips quirking into a faint smirk. "I knew Cole's roommate would report it. He's so predictable."

"At least you're not denying it," I said, studying her for any signs of guilt or hesitation.

She sighed, her demeanor sharpening like a blade. "I had my reasons. I don't trust Bevair, and I wanted to know if he had any… plans that might harm you or the other heirs." Her voice dropped lower, drawing me closer as though the weight of her words demanded it. "But that's not all I uncovered. I overheard enough about Jenny Webber to make me curious. What's your connection to her?"

I frowned, the question throwing me off balance. "Why are you interested in Jenny?"

Bellis leaned forward slightly, her eyes narrowing as though she were weighing how much to reveal. "There's something off about her story," she said, her voice barely above a whisper. "I overheard enough to make me wonder if the suspicions are warranted or if she's just a convenient distraction."

"Back up," I said, trying to regain control of the conversation. "Why don't you trust Cole? You've known him as long as I have."

Bellis tilted her head, her silver earrings catching the light. "Regalis Bevair," she said simply. "As a TruthForger, I spend my days listening to whispers from the industry leaders, and his are the most dangerous. He's ruthless, Kris. His ambition knows no bounds."

She outlined the intricate web Regalis had spun, his rivalry with Kenneth Grove, and the way he viewed Ashlyn as both a threat and an opportunity. "Regalis sees Ashlyn as a disruption to his plans," she continued, her voice gaining a sharper edge. "And Cole? He's caught in his father's web."

The pieces of the puzzle shifted uneasily in my mind, but instead of clarity, I found more questions. "What's this got to do with Jenny Webber?"

Bellis leaned back, her hands resting lightly on the table. "That, little cousin, is where you come in. I need your help." Her gaze dropped once again to the MagiScreen. "The encrypted file on Jenny's magical contract—what have you found?"

My fingers brushed the edges of the MagiScreen, its smooth surface cool against my skin. I hadn't told anyone that I'd cracked the file the night before, and now, with Bellis staring at me like a hawk circling its prey, I wondered if I'd made a mistake.

"I unlocked it last night," I admitted, my voice quieter than I intended. "I haven't looked at it yet."

Bellis's eyes lit up, and without waiting for an invitation, she slid around the booth to sit beside me. Her focus was so sharp it felt as though it could cut through the screen itself. "Then let's see it," she urged her tone light but with an undercurrent of command. "You trust me, don't you?"

Her words settled over me like a heavy cloak, making the air feel thinner. Bellis wasn't cruel, but she was relentless. Once the secrets in that file were out, there'd be no going back.

I hesitated, my mind racing through the possible repercussions. If the file contained something damning, could I keep it from Cole? Could I shield Jenny or even Ashlyn? Would this help, or would it unravel the fragile threads holding everything together?

With a deep breath, I tapped the file to open it. The glow from the MagiScreen seemed to intensify, casting long shadows across the table as the contents began to unfold.

Bellis leaned closer, her breath quiet but audible. The weight of her expectation was nearly suffocating.

As the words on the screen took shape, the atmosphere in the booth shifted. It was as though the air itself had thickened, pressing down on my chest. My throat tightened, my pulse quickened, and I suddenly wished I hadn't opened the file at all.

Bellis's voice was low but insistent. "Now do you see why I'm here?"

I couldn't answer. The implications of what I was reading were staggering. My hands trembled slightly as I stared at the screen. I'd stepped into something far larger than I could have imagined.

And now, I knew too much.

Chapter Eighteen

Ashlyn

Jenny wasn't in her bed when I woke up. I'd had my gift for a couple of weeks, and she'd been more excited about me being Celestial than I had, if that were at all possible, or maybe she was simply more vocal about it than I was. But she still refused to talk about her own misfired potion, even with Emma. I hadn't had a chance to speak to Emma alone, but I wondered if Jenny was embarrassed or perhaps concerned that the League of Magical Theory would no longer want her as a member. It was odd that they'd initiated her before she joined Aurora. But it was entirely possible that they might rethink their hastiness if there was a chance Jenny's gift might not materialize. Harsh, I know, but I didn't know them well enough to believe otherwise.

Jenny came bounding through the door to our room as I was about to head to the Dining Pavilion for breakfast. "I got aero-mancy!" she squealed. She was practically jumping up and down on the spot, her entire body fidgety.

"Wait! What?" I stood in the middle of our bedroom while realization sank in. "How... I mean, when did you...?"

"This morning. I got up and went out to the clearing early with Professor Kellar and Madame Wickets. Can you believe it?"

Her eyes sparkled behind her glasses, and her voice caught in her throat.

I could believe the gift, but I was confused that Jenny hadn't told me she was doing her retest this morning. "Why didn't you say anything?"

"It was all planned last-minute." Jenny flopped onto her bed, her excitement bubbling over as she kicked her legs up and down on top of the comforter like a child on Solstice morning. "I only found out last night! I didn't even know Wickets would be there until she was waiting for us in the clearing this morning."

I frowned and quickly smoothed my expression into a smile—I didn't want to dampen her excitement. "You thought Professor Kellar was going to do the retest alone?" I asked, trying to keep the concern from my voice. I knew Professor Kellar and Howard were friends, so maybe I was overreacting, but it almost seemed like the club might've had some influence over Jenny's gift.

Jenny didn't appear to notice. "All they needed was a different potion." She shrugged. "Simple. I have the same gift as Harvey, Ash. Isn't that the best coincidence ever?"

Her eyes were large with tears, and I felt instantly contrite. No wonder she was so excited. She'd already told me how Harvey would use his gift to fly her into the treetops in the woods and for her to have received the same gift... I couldn't begin to imagine how she must feel.

I sat beside her on the bed and squeezed her hand. "I'm happy for you, Jen."

She smiled and wiped the tears from her cheeks with her fingertips. "Whenever I use my gift, I'll be thinking of him," she whispered.

"I know."

We sat for several moments, shoulders touching, and then Jenny pulled away. "The best bit is," she said, "I got my gift just in time for your initiation."

"My initiation?" My heart lurched at the mention of it, my hands and face growing pink and sweaty. My stomach twisted whenever I thought about joining the club, even when the initiation ceremony was some vague possibility in the near-distant future, but now, Jenny had suddenly made it a reality. And I wasn't sure I was ready for it.

"Full moons tomorrow," she said, grinning at me. "I'm so excited, Ash. Forty-eight hours, and you'll be one of us."

She made it sound like I'd be different after the ceremony, as if becoming a fully-fledged member of the League of Magical Theory would set me apart from everyone else, even without the gift of Celestial. My palms tingled.

"I-I don't know," I mumbled. "I have my meeting with Dean Bask and the Council tomorrow."

My parents were coming to Aurora for the meeting, too. I hadn't seen them since I started university, and the last time I spoke to my father, the conversation hadn't exactly ended on the best terms. In fact, I would never admit this to anyone, but I was worried about how my father would react to seeing me. A few nights earlier, I dreamed that he told the Council he was canceling my contract and removing my Celestial gift because I didn't deserve it. I'd woken in a cold sweat, reminding myself over and over that it was only a dream. He wouldn't dare cancel his own daughter's contract. Would he?

"That's okay. It will all be over before the ceremony." She said it so matter-of-factly, like she couldn't understand the problem, that it made me question why I was panicking. "Don't tell your mom about it, though."

I stood so abruptly that tiny stars spiraled in front of my eyes. "Why not?"

"Technically, we're breaking club rules. You're meant to be part of the club for a couple of years before initiation, but Howard is so keen for you to join he's prepared to overlook procedures."

"You joined early, too." Jenny had mentioned on several occasions that she was accepted into the League early because of her brother, so I didn't understand the need for secrecy.

"Because of Harvey," she said patiently.

"Did your mom know about it?"

"Yes. I couldn't keep it a secret from her, not after what happened to my brother." Her smile faded, and I felt bad for questioning her motives.

"I still don't understand why I can't tell my mom or why it has to be tomorrow."

"If not tomorrow, then we'll have to wait for the next full moon to come around," Jenny said. "The League can help you so much with your gift. Don't you want them to help? If it was me, I'd want to learn everything I could about being Celestial. I'd be knocking on Howard's door every day until he got fed up with me." She grinned, and I couldn't help grinning with her.

She was right. I did want to learn about my gift. I'd waited two weeks for my meeting with the Council, and I had no idea how much longer it would take them to devise a special program of education to accommodate my rare powers. I knew it had to be strictly regulated and monitored because of how little was known about it, but I guessed the League of Magical Theory would have some answers. Still, my gift made me twitchy every time I thought about the club, and that wasn't a good sign—it was almost as if it was warning me to wait.

My Echo Panel vibrated on my desk. I crossed the room, unlocked it, and found a message from a number I didn't recognize. I opened it anyways, my pulse racing when I read the first line:

Ashlyn, it's Ethan Weiss. After our talk in the forest, I couldn't stop thinking about what you said. Celestial is overwhelming—it is bigger than you are. I know what that feels like, and I also know how lonely it can be trying to navigate it all.

You have a lot ahead of you, and people will try to pull you in different directions. If you want someone who understands, who's been there, I'm willing to help. No pressure—I just thought you should know you're not alone in this. Let me know if you'd like to meet. It's a lot to take on alone.

I read the message three times, my emotions swaying between annoyance and unease. *It's a lot to take on alone.* Did he think I was so helpless that I couldn't manage without his wisdom? And yet, I couldn't ignore the strange flutter of curiosity beneath my irritation. What exactly did he think he could offer me that I couldn't figure out on my own?

"What's going on?" Jenny asked from across the room, her brow furrowed.

"It's Ethan Weiss," I said, clutching the Echo Panel against my chest as if to block the message from sight. "He messaged me. He says he wants to help me with my gift."

Jenny raised an eyebrow, her arms crossing over her chest. "That's convenient. He didn't seem all that eager to help in the forest."

I sighed, lowering the device. "Exactly. He's arrogant... and conceited... and just—ugh! He acts like he knows everything." My voice faltered as I tried to pin down what exactly bothered me about Ethan's message. "Why does he even care? If he wanted to help so badly, why not stay and actually give me advice then?"

Jenny's expression softened, though her tone remained skeptical. "Do you think he's up to something?"

I shrugged, a frown tugging at my lips. "I don't know. Maybe. Or maybe he just can't resist the chance to prove he's the better Celestial."

Still, a small part of me—the part that couldn't forget his warning in the forest—wondered if there was more to it. Ethan Weiss was frustratingly enigmatic, and while his message irritated me, I couldn't shake the feeling that he knew something I didn't.

"What are you going to do?" Jenny asked, her voice cautious.

I hesitated. "I haven't decided. But if he thinks I'm going to go chasing after his advice like I'm desperate, he's in for a surprise."

Jenny smirked, her arms still crossed. "Good. He doesn't deserve the satisfaction."

I nodded, but the truth was, I wasn't entirely sure what I

wanted to do. Ethan's words in the forest had stayed with me, and now his message seemed to echo them. As much as I didn't want to admit it, some part of me wanted to know what he knew.

"Whatever you do, don't tell him about the League of Magical Theory," Jenny said.

It was the second time since mentioning the initiation ceremony that she'd told me to keep it a secret, and my brain was kicking into overdrive.

Before I could ask why, she continued, "He'll want to join too —fear of missing out—and you don't want him taking your rightful place, do you?" She climbed off her bed and came over to me, holding my arms and looking me in the eye so I couldn't avoid her. "I'm only looking out for you, Ashlyn. I want everyone to know how special you are. And not because I want to gloat that you're my friend, but because it's what you deserve."

I relaxed, tears prickling my eyes. Jenny might've been a bit over-exuberant when it came to me joining the club, but her intentions were genuine. She believed they could help me, and she wanted me to prove that I was a worthy heir to my family's industry.

"You're right," I said. "I don't want to see him anyway." A small voice of dissent told me that wasn't true. I resolved immediately to ignore it. It didn't matter. I wasn't making any attempt to get involved with Ethan. He had been bad enough when I didn't have my gift; I couldn't imagine what it would be like now.

Jenny smiled. "I don't know about you, but I'm starving with all this morning's excitement."

She reached for her bag, and I grabbed my jacket off the back of the chair when my Echo Panel vibrated again. This time, it was a message from Jase:

Sorry about what I said before. Can we finish the project together? Please?

I shook my head. After our last conversation, I spoke to Professor Harpe, who informed me that Jase had asked to swap partners before we even started the project. She said she was surprised we'd lasted as long as we had and was happy for me to complete the assignment alone, especially when I told her that I'd done most of the work anyway. It made me even more determined to do well and show Jase what he was missing out on.

"Ethan Weiss again?" Jenny asked.

"No. Jase Branson wants us to complete our project together."

Jenny rolled her eyes, a wide smile on her face. "Funny that. I hope you've sent him a big fat no."

I typed the words "big fat no" into my Echo Panel and hit SEND. "Yes."

I knew Jase had always struggled academically and was probably panicking right now, but I had too many other things to think about and told myself that he was not my responsibility. He would have to figure this one out for himself.

———

LATER THAT AFTERNOON, I escaped to the library for some much-needed solitude and old-fashioned research. The second floor quickly became my favorite place, a haven steeped in history and quiet magic. Rows of Lexicons lined the walls, their spines etched with titles that shimmered faintly in the soft light, enchanted to preserve their lettering no matter the years. The air smelled of aged parchment, old ink, and the faint tang of protective spells. It was a place that seemed untouched by time, where even the whispers of the past felt alive.

The architecture itself felt steeped in enchantment. Dark, polished wood paneling gleamed like it had been freshly treated, though no hand had touched it in years. Ornate columns carved with intertwining vines and sigils seemed to shift subtly, almost imperceptibly, as though imbued with life. Above, crystal chandeliers hovered without visible support, their facets emitting a silvery glow that pulsed faintly in time with the ambient hum of magic.

Plush red-and-gold rugs muted my footsteps as I wandered

through the aisles, their intricate patterns appearing to shift when caught at the edge of my vision. Stained-glass windows lined one wall, casting dappled patterns of light onto the polished floors. Each pane depicted pivotal moments from Andis's history: the forging of the magical contracts, the founding of Aurora, and the rise of the industries. The colored light seemed to dance with purpose, lending an almost sacred quality to the space.

I trailed my fingers along the spines of the books as I passed, their faint warmth spreading up my fingertips as if they recognized a kindred Spirit. I selected a particularly heavy Lexicon embossed with silver runes and carried it to a secluded desk tucked into a quiet corner. The chair groaned softly as I sank into it, the wood cool against my hands. On the desk, an enchanted inkwell gleamed faintly, its ink swirling with an iridescent sheen as though it were waiting to be used.

For a while, I simply sat, letting the serenity of the library settle over me like a soothing balm.

Finally, I stood and made my way toward the back shelves, searching for the book I needed. I noticed that the books in the back didn't seem to be as preserved as the books in the front. I found the book I needed nestled between two massive tomes, titled *Compendium of Arcane Sciences*, its spine slightly cracked with age. Pulling it free, I blew a thin layer of dust from the cover and hugged it to my chest. As I turned to head back to my desk, I nearly stumbled over a book lying on the floor.

Frowning, I crouched to pick it up. It was old—so old, in fact, that the cover was tattered and flimsy, barely holding the pages together. "*Power in Divine Wielding*," I read aloud, brushing a layer of dust from its bronze surface. The title, embossed in faint black cursive, was difficult to make out against the worn background. I must've been too focused on the shelves to notice it before.

Glancing around, I half-expected someone to claim the book, but the library was still. The librarian remained at her desk, distracted by an unsteady stack of books. No one else appeared to be there.

Curiosity prickling at my skin, I carried the old book to a nearby table, setting my Lexicon aside. As I opened the cover, I noticed an inscription on the first page but skipped it, eager to see what the book held. My excitement was quickly replaced with confusion—the pages were blank.

I flipped through several more, each as empty as the last. But then I ran my fingers lightly across one page, and something extraordinary happened. Words began to appear, unfurling as though an invisible quill were at work. My breath caught as I watched the words spread across the surface like ink on water: *Chapter One: The History of Divine Magic.*

Flipping to the next page, I found it blank, but a touch of my fingertips summoned new lines of text. I gasped softly, glancing around to see if anyone else had noticed. I sensed the urge to be discrete. But the library remained silent.

Was it my Celestial magic that triggered the book's reaction? Or had the book simply been waiting for someone to find it? I tried again, brushing another page, and watched as it filled with more words written in elegant, magical script. Each page seemed alive, responding to me and me alone.

A faint chill crept up my spine. I suddenly felt exposed, as though someone was watching. I snapped the book shut and clutched it tightly, trying to shake off the feeling. But the sensation persisted, a prickling awareness at the back of my neck.

I stood, my pulse quickening, and glanced around. That's when I saw it—movement in the next aisle, just beyond the thick rows of books. My breath hitched. Someone was there.

"Hello?" My voice wavered, barely above a whisper. No response.

I stepped cautiously toward the end of the aisle, my heartbeat hammering in my ears. The space was empty. I pivoted, my eyes darting to the shadowy corners of the library. For a moment, I thought I caught a glimpse of a figure slipping out of view, but when I rushed to the next aisle, it was deserted.

The silence was oppressive now, the hum of magic no longer comforting. It felt charged, almost suffocating, as if the air itself was conspiring to keep me on edge. My palms were damp as I clutched the books tighter, forcing myself to move toward the front desk.

"Who else is here?" I demanded, my voice louder than I intended.

The librarian blinked at me, startled. "No one," she said, her tone uncertain.

"Are you sure?"

"Yes," she insisted, though her gaze darted nervously to the books in my arms. "Are you checking those out?"

I hesitated, then nodded. "Yes. Sorry."

She took the books and processed them, her hands lingering briefly on the old one. My heart pounded as I waited, half-expecting her to question its blank pages or its unusual weight, but she simply handed it back without comment.

As I stepped out into the cool evening air, the tension still coiled in my chest. Someone had been there watching me, of that I was certain. Clutching the book tightly to my chest, I quickened my pace toward the dorm. Whatever secrets this book held, I had no intention of letting anyone else find out—at least, not until I knew more.

Someone had seen me with this mysterious book—I was sure of it—but I didn't know who. All I knew was that I needed to get back to my dorm and stash it somewhere safe.

Chapter Nineteen

Ashlyn

I spent the rest of the afternoon propped up against the pillows on my bed, reading *Power in Divine Wielding*, the ancient book spread open in front of me. I was glad Jenny had other classes. I needed this quiet time to wrap my head around everything I was reading.

The book described Celestial magic as the ability to control the sky and weather. But it wasn't just about storms or sunshine—it went deeper than that. Celestials could harness light and energy from the sun, moons, and stars. Some of the explanations were tangled in old-fashioned language, making them hard to follow, but as I pieced it together, it began to make sense. The descriptions reminded me of my ceremony—the way the Spirits swirled together, their colors blending into a radiant rainbow before they merged with me.

I paused, staring at the words as doubt crept in. How was I supposed to handle a gift like this? I wasn't exactly the picture of strength or confidence. Ethan came to mind—his self-assurance and the way he carried himself, like his power was second nature. Me? I still felt like a little girl playing dress-up, trying to figure out how to stand on my own two feet. Maybe that's why I hadn't fully believed Madame Wickets when she hinted at the enormity of my gift. Her excitement at the time had felt exaggerated, like a teacher hyping up their star student.

Flipping the page, I gasped softly. A new section appeared: *Spells For Beginners*. My heart raced as I skimmed the list. There was one for combining weather conditions—creating a rainbow. I couldn't help the small smile that spread across my face. I'd loved rainbows since I was a child, and the thought of making one myself felt like pure magic. Another spell explained how to store energy from the sun and moons for later use.

I couldn't stop the ideas from forming in my head. If I could master this, maybe I could use it to help the Elementum industry. What if I could find a way to use my gift to increase energy production? Maybe then Father would finally look at me differently. Maybe then he'd see me as more than his daughter—as someone capable of leading one day.

When I heard the dorm door creak open, I instinctively slid the book under my pillow and picked up the heavy *Compendium of Arcane Sciences* I'd borrowed earlier for my project. Half-laying on my bed, legs crossed at the ankles, I pretended to be engrossed in a random chapter I hadn't actually read as Jenny walked in and dropped her bag onto the floor beside her bed.

"How do you even concentrate on lessons since you got Celestial?" she asked, sitting heavily on her bed. "I can't remember a single thing I learned today."

I smiled at her from behind the Compendium. "You get used to it," I lied.

I felt bad for hiding the magical book from her, but something deep in my gut told me to keep it to myself. If I told Jenny, she'd want to show the other members of the club, and they'd turn it into a group project. She'd already mentioned how Celestial magic could amplify their own gifts. I didn't want to be a tool for someone else's benefit—not this time. I needed to understand my power on my own terms.

Jenny pulled out her MagiScreen and started typing, her focus shifting to a history assignment. I glanced down at the Compendium in my lap, its pages a blur to my unseeing eyes. The book under my pillow practically vibrated with its presence. I could feel its pull, its promises. I'd already decided—I needed to try a spell. My gift had been sitting dormant inside me for too long, and the possibilities it held were endless. Tonight, I'd sneak out and try one of the simpler spells. A test run.

By eight o'clock, I'd made up my mind. Tugging on my Aurora hooded cloak, I stuffed the book into my satchel, taking care to act as casually as possible. Jenny barely glanced up when I told her I was meeting with Dean Bask to discuss my gift ahead of tomorrow's meeting.

"I can't believe he's making you give up your evening," she said, rolling her eyes. "Couldn't it wait until tomorrow?"

"Apparently not," I said with a shrug. "I'll be back before curfew."

Stepping out into the night, I felt a pang of guilt for lying, but I pushed it aside. This was my journey—something I needed to figure out alone.

Crossing the campus, I avoided the better-lit paths, heading toward the sports complex. Jenny had told me about a small exit behind the building that led to the woods surrounding Aurora. Students weren't supposed to use it, but according to Jenny, the woods were still protected by the academy's magic. If the professors didn't lock the gate, they probably didn't mind the occasional wanderer—so long as no one broke curfew or got into trouble.

The gate was exactly where Jenny said it would be—a rusty, wooden thing tucked between overgrown hedges, creaking as I pushed it open. Beyond it, the forest was dark, the moonlight casting eerie shadows that danced between the trees. I pulled out my Echo Panel, activating the flashlight, its golden beam slicing through the gloom.

My heart raced as I stepped onto a rickety bridge that spanned a narrow stream. The planks creaked beneath my weight, and I hesitated, gripping the strap of my satchel. Jenny and Harvey had crossed it countless times, I reminded myself. Still, I darted across, my breath catching until my feet hit solid ground on the other side.

The trail ahead was faint but navigable, branches and bushes trimmed just enough to make walking possible. The forest felt alive around me—the soft rustling of leaves, the distant call of a bird, and the hum of magic in the air. I followed the path to a small clearing surrounded by towering trees that seemed to stretch endlessly toward the stars.

Reaching into my satchel, I pulled out the book. My hands trembled slightly as I turned in a slow circle, scanning the clearing for movement. A faint rustle caught my attention, and I froze. My pulse thundered in my ears as I held my breath, waiting.

A flitfox darted up a nearby tree, its iridescent fur shimmering faintly in the moonlight, catching every fragment of glow. Tiny, feathered ears flicked sharply as it paused mid-climb, claws chiming against the bark in an unsettling rhythm. Its luminous eyes fixed on me, unblinking, their glow intensifying like a predator locking onto prey.

The air grew tense, heavy with the creature's judgment. My pulse quickened as I stood frozen, the ancient book clutched tightly to my chest. Tales of flitfoxes flashed through my mind— how they were guardians of the enchanted forests, harmless to the respectful but ferociously territorial against perceived threats.

The soft rustling of leaves in the wind seemed amplified, a hollow sound echoing my rising anxiety. The flitfox's long tail, tipped with a glowing blue tuft, swayed deliberately, its movements slow and measured as if weighing its options. It tilted its narrow head slightly, and the blue glow of its tail brightened, a warning signal I couldn't ignore.

I dared not move, not even to take a calming breath. Would it attack? A surge of panic bubbled beneath my calm exterior as I held its gaze, silently pleading for the creature to deem me harmless.

An eternity seemed to pass before the flitfox let out a soft chime-like trill, its luminous tail dimming slightly. Its sharp ears twitched again, and with one final, piercing look, it turned and scaled the tree with fluid grace, retreating to a higher branch where it melted into the shadows of its habitat.

Only when its glow disappeared completely did I dare to breathe. My knees felt weak as I sank against the nearest tree trunk, my heart pounding in my chest. Whatever magic lingered in this forest, it was alive and watching. I wasn't sure if I felt more awed or terrified.

My heart was still racing, and I clutched the book tighter, its weight against my chest both reassuring and foreboding. I hadn't thought about the possibility of encountering creatures like the flitfox—or worse—when I made the impulsive decision to come here alone at night.

What was I thinking?

A flicker of doubt crept into my mind as I glanced around the clearing, shadows stretching and twisting like silent watchers. Aurora's protective magic extended to the surrounding woods, but even that didn't mean I was invulnerable. If a creature like the flitfox had decided I was a threat, I wouldn't have stood a chance. My stomach tightened at the thought. For someone who prided herself on being prepared, I'd rushed into this without a single thing to protect myself. I didn't even know how to use my magic.

My legs felt rooted to the spot as I scanned the edges of the clearing for movement, half-expecting something else to emerge from the shadows. The soft glow of the moonlight did little to ease my nerves; it only made the darkness beyond seem deeper, more impenetrable.

I should've waited until morning, but...

I looked down at the book, its cover catching the faint light. The pull of it was undeniable, like a whisper in my mind urging me forward. There was something here—something I needed to understand, and the thought of returning to the dorm without taking the first step felt unbearable. This book had found its way to me for a reason. It had waited who-knows-how-long, hidden and forgotten until I picked it up. I wasn't going to turn my back on it now.

I exhaled slowly, clutching the book tightly. This was it. I was ready.

Chapter Twenty

Cole

I couldn't study. I was getting angry with myself for thinking about Ashlyn and her Celestial magic, and the angrier I got, the less I was able to focus. Of all people, why did *she* have to be the one to get *my* gift? Two years ago, my father's suspicions regarding her true intentions became a reality. Her father had used her as a pawn in his game to gain more power, and now he had the upper hand. What were the odds?

Yet, I could find no evidence to support the man's manipulation of his daughter's contract. I'd read endless books in the library when I should've been studying, asked countless professors, and even reached out to my father, and found a dead end at every turn. Someone must know how they did it, but no one was willing to talk. What hold did Kenneth Grove have over them? Even Kristopher claimed he couldn't find anything, but I didn't believe him. They were all on her side, all protecting poor little Ashlyn because she'd made them feel guilty for cutting her off. Kris, Shane, Jase, and even Bellis. Couldn't they see that they were playing right into her hands? Divide and conquer. Split us up and take us down one by one.

Well, not if I had anything to do with it.

I sighed, wishing I could shove away the thoughts endlessly

circulating around my brain. I'd hardly seen my roommate since he confessed to knowing about the Eavesdrop Crystal in the wardrobe. Suited me just fine.

9:15—too late to go outside and too early to turn in, not that I'd be able to sleep, anyways. I opened my MagiScreen, thinking I would utilize my time to do more research on Celestial magic, when something caught my eye through the window.

Alert now, I kept perfectly still and stared outside. The sky was midnight-dark, a veil of stars twinkling above the treetops, the forest stretching as far as I could see like a carpet of black. There it was again. A flash. Like lightning, only more contained and coming from the other side of the wall. Was someone out there?

Before I could talk myself out of it, I grabbed my jacket off the back of my chair and swiped my room key off the dresser before racing to the door. I slipped my feet into my shoes, which were lined up neatly against the wall, and headed down the hall, closing the door behind me with a gentle click.

Sitting at my desk, I often saw students sneaking back and forth between dorms and the tennis courts. I'd always assumed they were using the secret exit to make out in the woods, but I'd never seen anything like this. This was magical, I'd bet my best suit on it. Someone was practicing magic in the woods and had been careless enough to get themselves spotted, and I was going to take full advantage of it. The professors might look the other way when it came to students sneaking out, but practicing magic without supervision came with a penalty. And penalties made people vulnerable. It opened them up to endless potential for blackmail and bribery.

Winston, my roommate, was heading toward me with a pastry in hand. He went to say hi, and I shut him down without a second glance. He'd get over it. And if he didn't, it wasn't my problem.

I knew about the secret exit, but I'd never used it myself. With it being so close to curfew, I figured it would be the easiest way to get into the woods without being spotted; if I got caught out after ten, my grades would be docked, and as curious as I was, I wasn't about to go spoiling my perfect grades for anyone. Even someone worth blackmailing.

My shoes crushed damp grass as I cut off the well-lit paths and crossed the grounds behind the professors' dorms until voices made me freeze. I pressed my back against the wall and peered around the corner. A small group of girls were chatting and giggling. One mentioned Jase, who had apparently given her his Echo Panel link earlier in the day.

Groaning to myself, I stepped out from behind the wall—I didn't have time for this if I was going to make curfew. Slipping my hands into my pockets, I played it cool, acting like I was out for a stroll. "Good luck with that," I said. "You know he has a girlfriend back home." Then, I kept on walking until I was out of sight. I heard one girl say, "Ignore him. He's only jealous." Right. I had absolutely nothing to be jealous about.

Out of range of the lights surrounding the area, I broke into a jog, scanning the wall for a gap. There'd been no more flashes of light from beyond the wall—well, not that I'd seen anyway—and I hoped I wasn't too late, although anyone heading back into Aurora would have to pass me. I spotted another flash and sped up.

The gate was barely latched and swung open almost before I'd touched it. It was a miracle it was still clinging on to the hinges. Switching on the flashlight on my Echo Panel, I slipped through the exit and into the wooded area beyond the wall, the temperature dropping with the dense canopy of trees preventing the sun from warming the ground.

My heartbeat quickened. It was eerily dark and silent, penetrated only by the creatures breaking the surface of the moat beneath the bridge. A bird flapped somewhere nearby, making my heart lurch, and I swallowed, telling myself not to be a wimp. The flashlight picked up a bridge ahead. It didn't look safe, but it seemed to be the only way through the prickly foliage, so I had to trust that every other student who'd come this way before me had used it. One step. The bridge creaked but didn't move. Another step, and another, and then I heard another sound that caused me to sprint the rest of the way.

Feet planted firmly on the other side, I caught my breath, swinging the light around in an arc, refusing to look in the darkness it left behind. I waited, ears keened for more sounds. Maybe I imagined it because the silence was dense and cloying, and I almost turned around and went back to my room. It was only the thought that I might miss something worthwhile if I headed back now that kept me going.

I followed the manmade path deeper into the woods, the flashlight barely illuminating the foliage on either side of me. More noises. Nocturnal creatures waking up and examining this strange human in their midst. "I'm bigger than them," I told myself. "They're more afraid of me than I am of them." One foot in front of the other.

Then I saw it. Another light ahead, shimmering, swinging like a lantern. I pressed my Echo Panel against my thigh and squinted. Whatever it was, it was almost twinkling like a star. I killed the flashlight and slipped my Echo Panel back into my pants pocket, treading carefully into the bushes on my right, careful not to make a sound. I didn't want them to know I was there. Not yet. I needed to find out what they were doing first.

There was a lump in my throat as I inched closer, brambles and nettles snagging my clothes and making it difficult for me to move. The light grew brighter. Still, I stuck to the bushes, not wanting to be seen until I knew what I was up against.

Then, the foliage ended abruptly, and I stepped into the edge of a small clearing, my breath catching in my throat. The sight before me stopped me cold. Lights—dozens of them—twirled and danced above a still form lying on the ground. They moved like glowflies, their luminescent trails cutting through the dark, casting an eerie glow over the scene.

A gasp escaped me before I could stop it, loud in the otherwise silent night. The lights flickered briefly as if they sensed my presence, but didn't stop their ghostly dance.

Then I saw the hair—dark brunette, splayed out like a fan against the damp earth. Recognition hit me like a physical blow, my knees threatening to give out.

Ashlyn.

I dashed into the clearing, my heart thumping like crazy. The floating balls of light dispersed the instant I arrived as if frightened off by a predator, but not before I noticed that they resembled the Spirits we swallowed when we received our gifts. I was right. Someone had been playing with their magic unsupervised. Not someone. Ashlyn. And of all the gifts to go messing around with, she had Celestial.

All this zipped in and out of my head in a flash while my brain kickstarted my body into action. I covered the distance between us in three strides and crouched beside her. "Ashlyn?" I whispered. Nothing. She was lying on her side, her pale face smothered by her hair as if she'd been knocked over. Her fingertips were touching the cover of a book that was spread facedown on the ground.

I pulled my Echo Panel back out of my pocket, my fingers trembling so badly I almost dropped it, and switched on the flashlight. Ashlyn's eyes were closed. Smoothing her hair away from her face, I pressed my fingers to the pulsing vein in her neck—she was still alive.

I slid the book away from her hand and checked out the title. The cover was ancient, and the leather skin stretched almost to breaking point. I didn't know where she'd gotten it from, but for some reason, she'd brought it out here alone, in the dark, to practice her magic. When I opened the book, though, the pages were empty. I flipped from cover to cover and found nothing. *What in the name of the Spirits...?*

The sound of a twig snapping made me freeze. "Who's there?" I asked, pleased that my voice sounded stronger than I felt. I aimed the flashlight into the bushes surrounding the clearing, swinging it around in an arc, a shiver running down my spine at how eerie the forest looked at night with the beam bouncing off creeping vines and tangled nettles. The hairs on the back of my neck stood on end.

Nothing. It felt as though the forest was holding its breath, waiting for me to make a move. The instant I lowered my Echo Panel, I heard it again. This time, I was on my feet, pacing the perimeter of the clearing, shining the light into the foliage, but whoever or whatever it was, they weren't visible. Was Ashlyn out here with someone, or was it a wild animal, inquisitive of the light? If she was here with someone, they clearly didn't want to get caught. The first person who popped into my head was Jenny Webber. Part of me hoped I was right—what kind of friend would leave someone unconscious in the woods? It would mean I'd been right about her all along.

I went back to Ashlyn. Gently, one hand on her shoulder and the other cradling her head, I rolled her onto her back. The left side of her face was covered in dirt, but when I touched it, my finger came away sprinkled with soot. Had something exploded? There was no sign of a fire, but it could've been a spell gone wrong. Then I noticed the gash on the side of her head, blood dripping from her temple and into her hairline. Idiot! Did she know nothing about her powers?

"Ashlyn." I shook her shoulder, trying to rouse her, but she didn't even flinch. "Ashlyn!"

Nothing.

I couldn't leave her there, which meant I would have to carry her. We might not have been friends for a while, but despite what people thought of me, I wasn't the kind of person who would run off and leave someone who was injured.

The toe of my shoe brushed the spine of the book. Something about the empty pages was bugging me. It meant enough to Ashlyn for her to bring it out here, and I wanted to know what secrets it was hiding; scooting around the clearing, I spotted a boulder pushed up against a thick tree trunk and slid it into the gap between them. It would do for now.

I went back to Ashlyn, slung her bag onto my back, and hoisted her up, her head resting on my left elbow and her legs dangling over my right arm. She wasn't heavy, but the walk back along the trail and across the bridge to the university grounds was slower with her in my arms.

Chapter Twenty-One

Cole

I waited in the Vitalis wing located within the Student Commons while Nurse Lebowski, a petite, round-faced woman, ran some tests on Ashlyn. When she came back out and told me that Ashlyn must've fallen and banged her head, causing the concussion, I realized how tense my shoulders and spine were. Despite our differences, I didn't want to think of Ashlyn being hurt.

I nodded. "Thank you."

Standing up to leave, I was halted by Dean Bask and Officer Nite, who'd obviously been alerted to the incident by Nurse Lebowski.

"We need to ask you a few questions before you head back to your dorm," Officer Nite said as I sank back into my seat. "Can you tell us exactly where you found Ashlyn Grove?" He pulled out a slim, rectangular device made of smooth obsidian-like material, its surface gleaming faintly under the room's bright lights. A soft hum emanated from it as he tapped the side, and the top edge glowed briefly, indicating it was recording.

He settled next to me on one of the rigid wooden chairs. What was it with Vitalis rooms and these chairs? The polished seats were so slick you had to grip the edges with your thighs just to keep from sliding off. As if sitting here answering questions wasn't uncomfortable enough.

I might've known I'd get the third degree. Two heirs involved in an incident, one with a wound to her head and concussion. I crossed my arms and kept my voice steady. I wasn't the one practicing magic when I should've been in my dorm behaving myself.

I told them about the rickety bridge and the small clearing, making it clear that all the students used it.

Dean Bask, a tall man with bushy brows and tawny skin, was an ex-officer of Magical Law Enforcement and took the student body's safety seriously. He watched me carefully, his expression unfathomable.

"What exactly were you doing out there?" Officer Nite asked. He was in his mid-twenties, a good-looking guy who knew it.

"Jogging," I said. "I always jog before bed. I saw a flash of light over the wall, went to investigate, and found Ashlyn unconscious. I couldn't wake her, so I carried her straight back." It was true enough.

"What do you think your classmate was doing in the forest?" Officer Nite asked.

Another nurse walked past, glanced our way, and kept her head down.

"Maybe she was practicing her Celestial skills," I said. "The flash of light. The soot on her face." I wasn't about to do his job for him, but the focus should've been on Ashlyn, not me. I was the good guy in all this.

"Do you think she was in some kind of danger?"

"Danger?"

"Were there any signs that she'd been with someone else in the forest? Or do you believe that she was alone?"

I recalled the snapping twig and the prickling sensation that I was being watched, but there was no point in mentioning it. I could imagine how that would go down: *Yes, Officer, I heard a sound, but I can't give you a description because it was dark.*

"She was alone," I said.

Officer Nite nodded. "Okay, go ahead and get some rest, Cole. We'll speak to Ashlyn when she wakes up."

It was past curfew, so there was no one around when I headed back to the boys' dorm. In the morning, I would go back and confront Ashlyn, remind her that she'd gotten lucky when I spotted her. For once, I wasn't chasing glory. She was an heir, and as such, she had a reputation to uphold that would affect all of us.

Also, I wanted to know about the book.

————

I ATE breakfast early the following morning and went to the Vitalis room before class.

"Welcome back, Cole," Nurse Lebowski greeted me from behind the front desk. "She's awake."

"How's she doing?" I wanted to know if she'd spoken about what happened.

"Why don't you go find out for yourself?" The woman smiled and gestured for me to head on through.

Pausing outside her room, I knocked lightly before opening the door and peeking inside. Ashlyn was sitting up in the bed, wearing an ugly, green gown, gauze wrapped around her skull like a mummy. She was pale, with dark smudges under her eyes as if she hadn't slept for days.

"Ashlyn?" I whispered, stepping inside and closing the door behind me. "How are you feeling?"

As expected, her eyes flew open, and she instinctively shuffled back along the bed when she saw me, trying to put as much distance between us as possible. I guess I couldn't blame her, although she might at least show some gratitude for saving her last night. She tugged the comforter up higher, her gaze flitting between me and the door.

"I'm okay," she said. "Headache, but the herbs are kicking in."

It showed. The newly acquired sass had dropped for now. "Why are you here, Cole?"

I dropped my satchel behind the door and slid my hands into my pockets. No point in getting comfortable. "Just checking you're okay. I found you last night."

"Nurse Lebowski said." She paused, her eyes all over the place like she was finding it hard to concentrate. "Did you follow me?"

"Don't flatter yourself." I regretted the words the instant they left my mouth. She'd tell me nothing if I got her rattled before I'd even begun. "I saw a flash of light from my dorm. My window faces the back of the school in case you think I was spying on you." I moved closer to the bed. "Did you forget what happened?"

"No... I..." Her eyes met mine. "The last thing I remember is the light. Why did you come looking for me?"

"I didn't," I said truthfully. "I followed the light. I didn't expect to find you unconscious in the middle of the forest. What were you doing out there?"

She chewed her bottom lip the way she always did when she was thinking. Some things never changed. When she spoke, her voice was barely more than a whisper. "I was practicing my spell work."

"Alone?" I asked. "Without guidance?"

"Yes, without guidance. I needed to try it for myself." It was like a switch had been flipped, and the new, mistrustful Ashlyn came flooding back. "Where is my book?"

If that's how she wants to play it. "What book?"

"Don't play dumb, Cole. I know the doctors don't have it because I asked Nurse Lebowski, and you were the one who found me."

"Maybe there was someone else in the forest. Have you thought of that?" I asked.

"I was alone."

I shrugged, sat in the seat next to the bed, and stretched my legs. "What you did was stupid, Ashlyn. Whatever is in that book, you clearly didn't understand how dangerous it could be. What kind of Celestial magic were you even attempting?"

"Nothing is in the book. Just tell me where it is."

She clearly didn't remember which one of us had broken the rules here. "If there's nothing in it, why do you want it back so badly? I could go straight to Dean Bask and tell him what you were doing."

Ashlyn took a deep breath and shook her head. "I thought it was too good to be true that you would save me without wanting something in return."

"Hey, I didn't see anyone else rushing to help you."

"Please, just give me the book, Cole, and leave me alone." Tears welled in her eyes and spilled over her lashes, and a lump formed in my throat, making it hard to swallow. "You owe me that much. Did you ever tell the others that you instigated the whole thing that night? That I was on my way to find you first before I bumped into them? I know you've been vocal about me not being good enough to take over my industry, Cole. How do you think that made me feel? While you're all getting on with life like nothing happened, I have to work a hundred times harder just to get a chance to prove myself." Her voice trailed off, and she rested her head back against the pillows.

Her words cut through me, sharp and unrelenting. Memories I'd buried clawed their way to the surface: that night at the party, my father's cold commands ringing in my ears—*keep Ashlyn at a distance, sever the bond, make her life harder if you must.* But I didn't hate her. I'd lied to myself, told myself she didn't matter, that she was just another heir with no claim on my heart. Yet here she was in my mind, just as vivid as ever.

She was still Ash. The one who patched us up when we cut our knees or got splinters in our fingers. The one who could navigate the forest like it was part of her, who recognized danger in the glint of a toxic berry or the curl of a venomous leaf. The one who cried when hearing tragic tales and loved all creatures.

"I hid the book in the forest," I said softly. "I'll bring it back to you during lunch break."

Tears continued to spill down her cheeks, and she swiped them away with the back of her hand. "Thank you," she said, sliding under the covers. "Please leave."

I rose, grabbed my satchel, and went to the door, the lump still stuck in my throat.

CHAPTER TWENTY-TWO

Ashlyn

Jenny visited shortly after Cole left, bounding through the door and wrapping her arms around me carefully because of my bandages. "What happened?" she asked, perching on the edge of the bed. "I got such a fright when I woke up this morning, and you weren't back."

I was surprised that she hadn't realized I was gone sooner, but I didn't say this out loud. "I didn't go to see Dean Bask last night," I said.

"You don't say." Her eyebrows slid upward, and she pursed her lips in fake annoyance.

"I didn't want you to worry, and I wanted to do it alone." I took a deep breath and waited for my brain cells to settle. "I went to the forest to practice my magic."

Jenny shook her head, but I could tell that she got it. Maybe if the roles were reversed, she'd have done the same. "You know it could've been a lot worse."

"I know, *Mom*." I forced a smile.

"Howard said we can postpone the initiation ceremony tonight," Jenny said, her tone edged with disappointment. "Although he doesn't really want to wait for the next full moons."

Her words hung in the air, and I found myself battling

conflicting feelings. A part of me was relieved. I still wasn't entirely sure I wanted to go through with the ceremony.

Yet another part of me—a louder, more insistent part—felt frustrated by the delay. My failed attempt in the forest the night before still burned in my mind, a reminder of how little I knew about my magic and how unprepared I was to wield it. The thought of learning more, of finally making sense of what I could do, was tempting. Wasn't this what I wanted? To take control, to prove to everyone, including myself, that I was worthy of the gift I'd been given?

I sighed, tentatively running a hand over my bandages. "I don't know," I said slowly. "Maybe postponing isn't the worst idea."

Jenny frowned. "Sure, but the sooner you go through it, the sooner you can start learning. Isn't that what you want?"

Her words hit home, stirring the impatience that had been simmering beneath the surface. I did want to learn. Desperately. But I also couldn't ignore the nagging feeling that I wasn't ready. Still, the idea of waiting another month, of delaying my chance to take the next step, felt unbearable.

"I guess," I said finally, trying to sound casual. "It's just... a lot. I need to think about it."

Jenny's gaze softened. "I get it. But you don't have to do this alone, Ash. We're here to help you."

I nodded, forcing a small smile. "Thanks. I think we can go ahead and do it."

She squeezed my hand. "You're making the right decision, Ash. This is only going to help you. I'll let Howard know," she said as she hurried out the door.

As she walked away, I couldn't shake the feeling that I might have been making a mistake.

———

Cole returned the book during lunch break as promised. He came into the room, handed it over without a word, and left again. Something had shifted between us, and I couldn't put my finger on what exactly.

He'd always been naturally colder toward me than the others simply because that was his way. But after what happened two years ago, it had become personal. I'd felt as if our friendship had degenerated into something akin to hatred, and I certainly wouldn't have expected Cole to rescue me in the woods. I couldn't believe it when Nurse Lebowski told me he was the one who brought me in. I believed it even less when he agreed to give me back the book. Why? He'd obviously hidden it with the intention of using it against me in some way, so why did our conversation convince him otherwise?

Was Cole Bevair finally experiencing feelings of guilt?

Or was I missing something? I didn't like that my go-to reaction around him was wariness, but it was a tough habit to break.

Shortly after Cole left, Dean Bask and Officer Nite came to question me about what happened. I confessed to practicing my Celestial magic against school rules. Dean Bask's eyebrows twitched as he mentioned potential punishment, although he didn't push the point, maybe because my magic is so rare, and the Council had urged him to nurture it rather than contain it. He'd already spoken to my parents—the meeting with the Council was scheduled for today and had to be postponed due to my concussion. He almost seemed guilty when he broke the news that my parents wouldn't be coming to see me.

I didn't tell him that my father was the last person I wanted to talk to right now. I didn't need a lecture on rule-breaking and responsibilities and the dangers of misusing my gift—my head hurt too much for that.

Finally, before they left, Officer Nite cleared his throat and asked, "Did Cole Bevair hurt you, Ashlyn?"

"W-what?" I spluttered, the pain in my head knocking against my skull. "No. Why would you ask that?"

"We have to ask," Dean Bask interjected. "With the reputation... It's common knowledge that there's a rift between the heirs." His gaze hopped to Officer Nite.

"You would tell us if he'd threatened you to keep quiet, wouldn't you?"

"I... Yes. I would. But he hasn't." I squeezed my eyes shut, trying to contain the pain. "This was nothing to do with Cole Bevair."

I must've closed my eyes and drifted off to sleep because when I opened them again, they were gone.

Between Nurse Lebowski pottering about the room, checking my blood pressure and temperature, and administering herbs, I continued reading the book, sliding it under the covers whenever she came in. She'd already confirmed that I'd be kept in for observation for another twenty-four hours.

In the second chapter of the book, *Power in Divine Wielding*, I found a passage that mentioned the League of Magical Theory. I had to reread it to make sure it was the same club I was about to join—I hadn't realized it had been around for so long. The book claimed that the League had played a heavy role in the philosophy and usage of Celestial magic and its connection to the Spirits. It might've encouraged me further to go through with the initiation ceremony, but my magic started tingling while I was reading the passage, the sensation making me feel lightheaded and queasy. It was a warning sign; I was certain of it. I'd also read that Celestial magic went to those who were pure of heart—not sure how Ethan Weiss managed to get it—so whenever the user came within reach of something harmful or dangerous, the magic reacted accordingly.

It had been my original reaction to the initiation ceremony. Only now, I was torn. While I knew I shouldn't ignore the signs, I wanted to see for myself what the club was all about. Something was telling me they knew more about Celestial magic than most people, and they knew more about me than they were letting on. The League being mentioned in the book was too much of a coincidence. I had to find out what the ceremony was all about; I could always back out if things got so serious that my magic didn't like it.

"There you go," Nurse Lebowski said once she'd changed the dressing on my head wound. It was five-thirty in the evening. The herbal medication I'd been taking had dulled my headache to a steady throb, not helped by reading the book all afternoon and panicking every time the door opened. "Have you gotten plenty of sleep today?"

On cue, I fake yawned, making her smile. "I think so."

"If you sleep well tonight, I'll probably release you in the morning, but you'll have to take it easy for the next week or so."

Nodding still made me dizzy, so I smiled and settled back against the pillows. I was too anxious to sleep right now, and I wanted her to leave me alone so that I could think about the initiation ceremony. Why did I tell Jenny it should still go ahead tonight? Why could I not make a simple decision and stick to it? Even the thought of it looming over me was making my magic fizz inside the palms of my hands, and I didn't want Nurse Lebowski to notice—she didn't usually miss a thing.

The instant the door closed behind her, I whipped the book out from under the covers. I wanted to see if I could find anything else about the League of Magical Theory before Jenny came back.

I was concentrating so hard on the book that I didn't hear the door open. I jumped when Ethan Weiss appeared at the end of the bed, my hand instinctively flying to my bandaged head, knocking the book onto the floor. What was he doing here?

He wrapped his hand around the bed frame, watching me with those still eyes. "Sorry," he said. "I didn't mean to startle you."

"Maybe you should've messaged me to say that you were coming." My brain cells were swimming, and I waited for them to settle. "What are you doing here?"

"Visiting you." He walked around the bed, reached down for the book, and inspected the empty pages before handing it back to me. "I see it found you. The book," he added at my vacant expression.

What was he talking about? I had found the book, not the other way around.

"I have one too. Jumped out at me at my university's library one day. Almost took my head off." He went back to the end of the bed as if afraid I might press the buzzer for help if he came too close. My breathing settled a bit.

I don't know why, but I was disappointed to find that he had the same book. It kind of felt tarnished knowing there were two copies. Less special. Had he felt the same way? I wouldn't be surprised if he had.

"You could've asked me, you know," he said. "Instead of going out in the dark and almost killing yourself." His eyes lingered on my face, rolling over my bandaged head, an expression filling those depths that I couldn't understand.

"I didn't almost kill myself," I said. "I'm fine." Why did he unnerve me the moment I saw him? A shiver prickled along my skin, a deep instinctual warning that had nothing to do with my magic. It was as though the air around him carried a charge, one that set every fiber of my being on edge.

"The bandage around your head says otherwise." He tapped his own temple with his index finger, and I couldn't tell if he was making fun of me or not. "What were you trying to do?"

I rolled my eyes, pursing my lips. "How do you know I was trying to do anything?"

His lips tightened, too, and those green eyes flashed fire. "Ashlyn, I'm not here to play games."

"Why are you here then?" I snapped.

"I already said: I came to see you. Look..." He peered at the window, his face in profile as if he might find the right words. "It isn't easy, being Celestial. No one fully understands what we're capable of, and it worries me that, without the right guidance, we'll never unlock our full potential. We should stick together, me and you. Help one another."

Jenny's comment that Ethan wanted to join the League and claim my space for himself popped into my head, and I wondered if he'd somehow heard about the initiation ceremony tonight. Was that the real reason he was here? To bring down my guard so he'd take my place somehow?

"I don't need your help," I said. I didn't want his help either. I was doing just fine on my own. I had the book now.

He swallowed, a look of irritation passing across his eyes. "Don't write me off, Ashlyn. I can—"

"Help me," I interrupted him. "Yes, thank you, I get it. But the last thing I need is your help. I'm fine."

I couldn't believe his nerve, coming to find me in the Vitalis unit while I was vulnerable and weak, to convince me that I needed him on my side. All I wanted was for people to leave me alone to make my own decisions and give me a chance to prove myself. I bet my father asked him to come here. It wouldn't surprise me if the moment he walked outside, he was on the Echo Panel to my father, telling him how difficult I was being. Well, I had news for him...

"I'll manage quite well on my own," I said.

His eyes jumped to my bandaged head, a look of judgment flashing there that made me clench my fists. He was still the arrogant guy from the party. Nothing had changed. "Not that well."

I cut my eyes at his words. I wasn't surprised he was bringing up my injuries to convince me. It was just the sort of thing he'd do. "It might surprise you to know that I have friends who know all about Celestial magic." I hadn't meant to say it out loud, but he was making me feel like I needed him when I was done being told what to do. I flexed my fists, trying to control my rising temper. I wasn't going to give him the satisfaction of knowing he had gotten to me. Not on my life or his.

Now I had his attention. He straightened, a nervous tic appearing in his jaw. "Yeah, about that. Ashlyn, I really think you should—"

He didn't finish because Jenny appeared in the doorway then, her bulging satchel slung over one shoulder. Her gaze skipped between me and Ethan. Then she came in, lowered her bag onto the floor, and came and stood beside the bed, claiming me as her friend. "Everything okay?" she asked, concern in her voice.

"Yes," I said. "Ethan was just leaving." I wanted him gone. I was done letting anyone put me down.

Ethan didn't seem pleased to see Jenny. Without a glance in her direction, he said to me, "Be careful, Ashlyn, and trust your magic," before turning around and walking out, closing the door behind him with a click.

"What did he want, now?" Jenny asked.

"Nothing."

"Felt way too intense to be nothing." She watched me, arms folded across her chest, like she wasn't letting me get away with this one.

"He said we should stick together." I couldn't look at her.

For some reason, I didn't want to talk to her about Ethan. I was trying to process the conversation and figure out his real motives for coming to see me because it felt like he was trying to warn me about something when Jenny walked in. I tried dialing down my curiosity, but I couldn't help the thoughts twirling in my head. Did he know about the League of Magical Theory? Had they reached out to him when he got his gifts, too? Or was it a coincidence that he happened to be in Aurora when the moons were full?

"I bet he did," Jenny said. "He's always wanted to be somebody, and what better way to do it than being linked to another Celestial? I don't trust him."

I didn't trust him either, but what Jenny said didn't sit right with me. It didn't feel like he wanted to use me for his own gain. He was proud, arrogant, and sometimes downright mean, but he wasn't evil. My gift would have recognized that, but despite my reaction to him, none of it had been fear.

My head hurt, tiredness washed through me in waves, and all I wanted to do was sleep.

CHAPTER TWENTY-TWO

"Anyway," Jenny said brightly. "I have a plan."

"A plan?"

"Bailing you out of here tonight for the initiation." Her brow furrowed. "If you're still up for it. We don't want to push you, not with your concussion and everything."

I swallowed. As much as they wanted to get me initiated, they were more concerned about my health, and my chest swelled with a sense of belonging. "I'll only be standing, right?"

Jenny laughed. "Mostly, yes. We'll all be there to look out for you, remember."

I nodded. "What's the plan?"

"Well, Nurse Lebowski swaps shifts at curfew with the night nurse. We can sneak out while they're switching."

"You'll have to help me dress." We'd be breaking more rules going outside after curfew, but Howard was a professor, so the faculty must've known about the ceremony—another thing they turned a blind eye to, perhaps, unless the students got caught.

Jenny nodded. "I'll choose a dress from your closet. It's a formal affair, don't you know." She mimicked a posh accent, and we both giggled.

"What about when the night nurse comes in to check up on me?"

Jenny's face broke into a wide grin. "That's where the satchel comes in. We'll make a dummy of you under the covers so it looks like you're asleep. She won't disturb you because you need your rest. Then we'll meet the others in the forest."

My hands tingled, and I wriggled my fingers. Of course, it would be in the forest—under the full moons. How much more cultish could it get? My thoughts turned once more to Ethan. What had he been trying to warn me about?

"Just think, Ash," Jenny said. "By morning, you'll be one of us."

Chapter Twenty-Three

Kristopher

"I don't know, Bellis. I'm not comfortable with this."

I was perched on my bed, pillows piled awkwardly behind me, the Echo Panel balanced on my lap. Bellis's sharp gaze stared back at me from the screen, her expression unreadable but edged with impatience. I hadn't told the guys what I'd found in Jenny Webber's encrypted contract, and it was eating away at me like a secret too big to keep. It felt like holding the key to a locked door, knowing that whatever lay beyond it could shatter everything.

"You've already crossed the line, Kristopher," Bellis said coolly. "You cracked the file. You know what's in it. You can't just pretend it didn't happen."

"I'm not pretending," I shot back, leaning forward, the pillows tumbling sideways behind me. "But I don't know what to do with it. This isn't just some minor secret—it's huge. And dangerous."

Her brow arched, her glasses catching the light as she tilted her head. "Exactly. Which is why we can't afford to sit on it. Information like this doesn't just disappear because you're scared to act."

Scared. The word stung, probably because it wasn't entirely

wrong. I stared at the darkened sky beyond my window, searching for clarity that wouldn't come. "The file was hidden for a reason, Bellis. Magically sealed. We shouldn't have touched it."

"You mean *you* shouldn't have touched it," she corrected, her tone sharp. "But you did. So now the question is: what are you going to do about it?"

I pressed my hand against my forehead, the weight of the decision threatening to crush me. "I don't know," I admitted. "The authorities should handle it. This is way out of our league."

Bellis's laugh was dry, almost mocking. "Do you really think the authorities care? They're the ones who buried it in the first place. You think they'll thank you for digging it up?"

She wasn't wrong, but that didn't make me feel any better. "And what about the people involved? What if they're dangerous? What if this gets someone hurt?"

Her eyes narrowed. "It already has. Or did you forget about Harvey Webber? Do you think his death was an accident? You think Jenny ended up as Ashlyn's roommate by coincidence?"

My heart thudded painfully. "Are you saying Jenny manipulated the rooming assignments?"

Bellis's smirk was maddening. "I'm saying, what do *you* think?"

The weight in my chest grew heavier. If that was true—if Jenny had maneuvered her way into Ashlyn's life on purpose—it wasn't just unsettling. It was terrifying. And it made me realize how deeply Ashlyn might already be entangled in something none of us fully understood.

"I have to tell the others," I said suddenly, swinging my legs over the edge of the bed.

Bellis's face hardened. "You're making a mistake."

"They deserve to know," I argued. "This concerns all of us—especially Ashlyn."

Her lips pressed into a thin line. "Kristopher, you're not thinking this through. The more people you involve, the more dangerous this becomes. Do you trust them to handle this responsibly? To not make it worse?"

I hesitated, the question hitting harder than I expected. "I don't know," I admitted. "But I trust that they care about Ashlyn. That's enough."

For two years, we'd all pretended to cut Ashlyn out of our lives and acted like she didn't matter. But the truth was, you couldn't just erase someone like that—not someone who had been part of your life for so long. And despite everything, Ashlyn was still Ashlyn. I wasn't sure I could protect her, but I'd be damned if I didn't try.

"I'm done with secrets, Bellis," I said firmly. "This isn't just about me—or you. It's about Ashlyn's safety. And I won't let her face this alone."

Bellis sighed, her glasses catching the light as she leaned back. "Do what you want, Kris. But don't say I didn't warn you."

The call ended abruptly, the screen going dark. I groaned, running a hand through my hair. Every choice felt like the wrong one, but doing nothing wasn't an option. Not anymore.

Grabbing my Echo Panel, I opened the group chat with the other heirs and typed a short message:

We need to talk. Now. Common room.

It was quarter to nine. Plenty of time before curfew to lay everything on the table.

No more secrets. No more games. It was time to face the truth —together.

CHAPTER TWENTY-FOUR

Ashlyn

I opened my eyes and yawned sleepily when Nurse Lebowski came into my room with the night nurse. "Sorry to disturb you, Ashlyn," she said. "This is Nurse Cromer. She'll be taking the night shift, so if there's anything you need, don't hesitate to call for her."

Where Nurse Lebowski was round and sweet, Nurse Cromer was pinched and sour. Her smile didn't quite reach her eyes, and I instantly shrank beneath the covers. Her gaze darted around the room and finally settled on the chart hanging over the end of the bed. I had a feeling she wouldn't miss a thing and wondered if I should tell Jenny to cancel the ceremony tonight. Nurse Cromer might not be fooled by a dummy version of me with the covers pulled over its head.

"Ashlyn has a concussion," Nurse Lebowski continued, oblivious.

"I shan't be hearing from you until morning then." Nurse Cromer's lips formed a shape that was neither a smile nor a sign of her distaste, and I remained quiet. Perhaps Jenny was right, and she wouldn't even check up on me during the night.

After they left, I noticed that the lights in the hallway dimmed, the Vitalis wing settling down for the night. I felt the hush like a tangible thing, a gauze blanket smothering the entire area so that no sound could escape—it might work in our favor, but the only problem was Jenny still needed to sneak in to help me dress.

Maybe it was for the best if she couldn't get past the night nurse. Ethan's visit had unsettled me; I had no idea why he was here or what he knew about the League of Magical Theory, but I wouldn't put it past him to follow us and threaten to tell Dean Bask about the past curfew ceremony. Was he jealous that they'd chosen me over him? Was that why he'd tried to warn me away from them?

Was that why he was here, because he'd somehow heard about my initiation and was trying to destroy my chances of joining the club? Who would've told him, though? My pulse raced when I realized that I already knew the answer. The other heirs. Or perhaps I should narrow it down to one heir, the one who was bitter because I got Celestial, and he didn't.

Cole Bevair.

I was already sitting up in bed when the door to my room slid silently open, and I quickly ducked back beneath the covers. Jenny giggled, one hand smothering the sound so that Nurse Cromer wouldn't hear as she closed the door behind her.

"It's me," she said. "I brought your clothes."

Jenny looked sophisticated in a black, floor-length dress, black flats, crimson lip gloss, and smokey eyeshadow, completing the look.

"Wow," I said, wide-eyed. "You look amazing."

Jenny dismissed the compliment and handed me a similar knee-length black dress and my black flats. "We don't have much time," she whispered. "I managed to sneak in while the night nurse was checking out the patient across the corridor. Howard said that she'll go straight to the kitchen and eat before she takes over in reception, so we've got about ten minutes to get you out of here."

Her tone was matter-of-fact, and she worked efficiently, piling up the pillows and my regular clothes under the sheets to make it look like I was asleep while I tugged the dress over my head and slid my feet into my shoes. I felt clumsy and dowdy beside Jenny, who looked like she was dressed for an event at the Bevair mansion rather than an initiation ceremony in the forest. My movements were sluggish, a by-product of the herbs they were giving me for concussion.

She hesitated when she saw me standing there. "Hey, you look beautiful, Ash," she said, taking my hands in hers.

I frowned, the movement causing my headache to slide around inside my skull. "The bandages don't quite go with the outfit."

Jenny didn't waste a beat. She unwrapped the fabric around my head, bundled it into a messy pile, and tucked it under the end of the mattress. I flinched. *The Power of Divine Wielding* book was under there, too, but luckily, she didn't notice. Jenny straightened, gave me a once-over with narrowed eyes, and said, "That's better. You look good as new."

I forced a smile. The herbs were dulling my senses—probably exactly what they were meant to do—but it made my magic feel like it was bubbling just below the surface, trying to tell me something I couldn't quite grasp. It had stirred earlier when Ethan visited, but not like this. Now, it felt restless, as if the stronger dose I'd been given to help me sleep was smothering something important. Maybe I should've postponed the initiation until I was back to normal. I needed to be sharp for this. Everyone knew you didn't agree to something so big unless you had all the facts and a clear head to make the decision.

Jenny hesitated by the door and turned to face me. "Ready?"

"I... I don't know," I said. A rush of warmth flooded my veins —was it my magic trying to tell me not to go?

"You're not having second thoughts, are you?" Jenny's smile faltered, her brow knitting with concern as she leaned forward. "I'll be right there with you every step of the way. This is your moment, Ash." Her voice softened, but her conviction stayed firm. "I know you're still feeling a bit ill, but Howard can help you. We can all help you. After tonight..." Her eyes sparkled, her face lighting up as though she could already see the future. "There'll be no stopping you. You'll have the world at your fingertips."

I swallowed and unclenched my fists. She was right. This was what I'd always wanted—to belong—and if the League of Magical Theory could help me understand even a tiny portion of my gift, it would give me a head start on what I would learn from the Council.

"Ready," I said.

Howard had been right about Nurse Cromer, too. We closed the door silently behind us and tiptoed back through the Vitalis wing and out the door without even a glimpse of the night nurse. Seemed he had it all covered.

Excitement took over, and I followed Jenny back to the secret rickety fence that all the students used. It was already unlatched; had Howard and the others left it open for us, confident that Jenny would be able to sneak me out of the infirmary? I was suddenly overwhelmed with a sense of relief—how could this be wrong when it was being led by one of Aurora's own professors? All my fears were unfounded. Howard wouldn't let anything bad happen to me. Jenny was already initiated, and she was still just... Jenny.

We crossed the narrow, creaking bridge, and I kept my focus on the trail as Jenny led us deeper into the forest. The path veered right at one point, down a smaller trail I hadn't noticed before. The woods around us seemed alive, humming with sounds I couldn't place—the faint rustle of leaves, the soft call of creatures hidden in the shadows. Twin moons hung low in the sky, their glow casting silvery patterns across the trees. The air was cool but pleasant, the kind of cool that made me feel sharp, awake. I didn't even notice the ache from my injuries anymore; maybe it was the herbs, or maybe it was the excitement building in my chest.

The clearing we stepped into made me stop in my tracks.

Ground torches ringed the space, their flames steady and golden. The light danced across the clearing, illuminating a central fire pit filled with glowing embers that pulsed like a living heartbeat. Barrels sat scattered around the circle, inviting yet ominous. The air here felt different—charged, like something important was about to happen.

Jenny tugged me forward, pulling me between two torches and into the circle. My stomach tightened as I crossed the threshold. It wasn't fear, not exactly. It was more like... anticipation. Like I was stepping into something I couldn't quite take back.

"Ladies, welcome!" Howard's voice carried across the clearing, warm and confident. He stepped forward, his black suit crisp and immaculate. The flickering light of the torches played across his face, casting sharp shadows that made him look both familiar and foreign.

I barely noticed Jenny stepping away until I realized I was alone. My pulse quickened, and for a moment, I wanted to turn and grab her hand, to insist that she stay by my side. But I didn't. Instead, I swallowed the lump rising in my throat and stood still, trying to quiet the swirl of emotions inside me.

"Ashlyn," Howard said, his hands pressed together in what might've been a greeting or a gesture of reverence. His smile was calm, almost fatherly, but his eyes flickered in the torchlight, unreadable. "I'm so pleased you could join us tonight, especially given the challenges you've faced these past few days."

I nodded stiffly, clutching the edges of my dress. My heart beat fast, each thud reverberating in my ears. The flames of the torches seemed to grow brighter, their glow casting flickering patterns across the trees. I glanced around, searching for Jenny among the shadows, but I couldn't see her. All I could see was the circle of firelight and Howard standing at its center.

"Thank you," I murmured, gesturing around the clearing. The torches crackled softly, their light casting a golden glow. Despite the fog of the herbs and the haze of my lingering doubts, I couldn't help but feel a surge of gratitude. They had done all this for me. Now that I was here, surrounded by the club's warmth and camaraderie, it was easy to believe this was the right path.

Howard inclined his head, his movements fluid and deliberate. "I'm honored to induct you into our club."

His words carried a soothing weight, settling the faint unease I hadn't been able to shake. My eyes wandered to the other members of the circle. Carla and Benji's familiar faces offered some reassurance, but the rest were strangers cloaked in shadow. Twelve of us altogether. Twelve—a number steeped in magical significance. Had they come here specifically for my initiation? Why hadn't Jenny mentioned them before?

As if sensing my thoughts, Howard's deep voice cut through the quiet. "Everyone is here tonight for you, Ashlyn." His smile was warm and inviting, yet something about it made my stomach flutter. "Not only are you an industry heir, but you possess intelligence, generosity, and strength—qualities that make you worthy of this moment."

His words sent a flush of warmth through me, but they also unsettled me. His praise felt too pointed, almost calculated. Was this how he spoke to all initiates, or was there something different about me?

Howard stepped closer, his hands settling gently on my shoulders. The warmth of his touch spread quickly, softening the tension in my chest and filling me with a sense of calm I hadn't felt in weeks. "You've faced many challenges," he said, his voice low, almost hypnotic. "But tonight is the beginning of something extraordinary. Trust in us, and trust in yourself."

He stepped back, and I felt the loss of his touch like a physical ache. He clapped his hands once, and the group moved into position around the fire pit. The rustle of robes and the soft shuffle of feet were the only sounds in the clearing as the others formed a perfect circle. Howard gestured for me to follow, guiding me to a spot at the northernmost point.

"This is your place," he said, his tone steady.

I nodded, stepping into the position he indicated. The fire's heat brushed against my skin, but a cool breeze, laced with the sharp scent of impending rain, whispered through the clearing. Above us, storm clouds gathered, smothering the stars. Only the twin moons shone brightly, their silver light weaving between the trees and casting a spectral glow on the gathering.

My eyes sought out Jenny, who stood to my left, her face lit by the flickering glow of the flames. Like everyone else, she stood just outside the circle, her arms raised, palms turned toward the sky.

A pang of doubt struck me. Had she hidden more from me than I realized? But before I could dwell on it, my gaze snapped back to Howard, who stood across the fire pit. His dark pupils reflected the dancing flames, and when his eyes locked onto mine, I froze. There was an intensity in his stare, something that quieted my unease even as it pulled me deeper into the moment. I couldn't look away.

His voice rose above the crackling of the fire, smooth and commanding, as though the flames themselves carried his words. "Spirits, servants of the Divine. Please allow us to welcome Ashlyn Grove into our circle. We honor her with peace and gratitude under the protection of your light. Send us the energy of your gorgeous moons."

He lifted his hands, palms turned skyward, and flames erupted from them, spiraling upward in a serpentine dance. The fire seemed alive, responding to his call with perfect obedience.

I gasped, the brilliance of the fire illuminating his face in sharp relief.

Pyromancy.

I'd seen my mother wield fire before, her movements just as graceful, but this was different. There was a weight to the magic, a sense that it reached beyond mere control, extending into the very essence of the moment. The late hour, the heavy air of the clearing, and the fading effects of the herbs blurred my thoughts, leaving me enthralled.

"I ask that you embrace our energy," Howard said, his voice resonating through the clearing.

I glanced around the fire pit again, and the sight froze me in place.

"Rise, Spirits. Awaken the Celestial!"

Howard's voice rang out, a commanding presence that seemed to ripple through the clearing. The flames roared higher in response, their heat washing over me in waves. I jumped at their intensity, my breath catching as I took an involuntary step back.

Fear surged through my veins, cold and insistent, as I suddenly became aware of the spiritual light dancing in the palms of the other members' hands. Golden flickers, silver shimmers, emerald streaks—each element glowed in eerie harmony with the rising fire. What were they doing?

A vague recollection of Jenny mentioning how the club would benefit from my gift floated to the surface of my mind, only to be quickly drowned out by the mesmerizing sight of flames flickering in Howard's outstretched palms. They wouldn't try to harness my power for their own gain. Would they?

Howard was here to guide me toward my true potential. He had to be.

I glanced back at Jenny. Tendrils of wind danced across her palms, responding to her gift as though it had always been hers to command. She was calm, serene—completely at ease in this ritual, as if she'd done it countless times before.

How? Jenny had only just discovered her element. Her composure was unsettling, and a creeping doubt began to gnaw at the edges of my thoughts. I swallowed hard, the unease gurgling in the pit of my stomach, but I couldn't move.

I was rooted to the spot, compelled to stay. The pull was stronger than my fear.

These people wanted me—had wanted me even before I became Celestial. I was special to them, and I wanted to be a part of this.

"Ashlyn."

I jumped again, startled by Howard's sudden proximity. His hands came to rest lightly on my shoulders, the warmth of his touch radiating through me like sunlight breaking through storm clouds. A shiver traveled down my spine, but it wasn't entirely unpleasant.

"Please, allow me?" His voice was silk and honey, smooth and soothing, melting away my hesitation. My lips moved to agree before my mind could catch up.

He guided my hands upward, flattening my palms toward the heavens as he positioned his beneath mine. His fingers brushed against my skin, sending a ripple of energy through me, and then his eyes closed.

I couldn't have fought this if I'd wanted to. This was good. I could feel it in my core—a gentle, pulsing tingle like water rippling over stones in a quiet stream. If this was wrong, surely my magic would have warned me by now.

I gasped as Howard's energy surged through him. His veins glowed an unearthly red, like illuminated pathways mapped beneath his skin. I'd seen magic before—my mother had displayed her pyromancy countless times—but this was different. This was alive. This was power.

"Awaken the Celestial," he murmured, his voice meant only for me.

My palms began to glow. Gold at first, then shifting hues as the sensation climbed through me: toes tingling, knees trembling, shoulders alive with the same vibrant energy. I closed my eyes, letting the intoxicating feeling sweep me away.

The wind picked up, ruffling my hair and scattering embers from the fire into the night sky. The scent of smoke was heady, and I breathed it in like perfume.

When I opened my eyes, Howard was watching me, his own gaze molten red.

"Your eyes..." I whispered, unable to tear my gaze away.

"Focus on our energy," Howard urged, his voice as steady as the rhythm of my pulse.

And I did. My veins lit up with rainbow hues, a mesmerizing glow that pulsed in time with the rising wind and crackling fire.

This was it. This was the power I was meant to wield. It coursed through me, lighting me up from the inside, making me feel unstoppable.

"You have no idea how precious you are," Howard said, his words sinking deep into my chest. Butterflies danced in my stomach, a mix of nerves and exhilaration.

"I want you to repeat after me," he said.

I nodded, eager to hold on to this connection, this belonging.

"I am supreme," he intoned.

"I ... am supreme," I repeated, my voice trembling at first but gaining strength with each syllable.

"I am light."

"I am light."

"I am dark."

"I am dark."

My voice didn't sound like mine anymore. It was stronger, deeper, filled with the certainty of someone who had unlocked their destiny.

"Combined, I am a piece of the universe. By the Spirits, I command thee."

As I echoed his words, the wind howled through the clearing, bending the torches and whipping the flames into wild dances. Sparks scattered into the night, and the power inside me reached a crescendo.

"Very good," Howard said, releasing my hands.

The loss of contact was jarring, and I swayed slightly, bereft of his grounding presence. My veins still glowed, the rainbow colors mesmerizing and foreign. Would everyone see them once the ceremony ended?

"Before your membership can become official," Howard said, drawing my attention back to him, "you must complete one final task."

Task? Jenny hadn't mentioned a task.

"There is an item inside the log cabin," Howard continued,

his glowing eyes fixed on mine. "An opal carved into the shape of a feline. You must retrieve it and bring it back to me."

The other members stood motionless, their palms turned skyward, their elements still dancing in their hands. They were oblivious to the rising storm, their hair whipped by the wind but their focus unbroken.

Howard's energy lingered in my veins, urging me forward, but doubt crept in. Was this a test of loyalty? The opal was locked away for a reason.

"You want me to steal it," I said, the words slipping out before I could stop them.

Howard's smile was warm, his voice soothing. "You will be bringing it back home, Ashlyn."

The alarm bells in my head softened, smothered by the warmth of his presence. "Will you do it?"

"Yes," I said, the word escaping before I could think. I wanted to please him, to prove my worth to the group.

Howard nodded. "Very good. May the Spirits be with you, dear Ashlyn."

CHAPTER TWENTY-FIVE

Cole

Kris's message was urgent. He must've cracked the encrypted file and finally gotten the answers we needed about Jenny Webber. As if he thought we'd refuse to meet up with him. It had taken him long enough. It wouldn't even surprise me if he'd been sitting on the information for a while, keeping it close to his chest and worrying about what I would do with it. Lucky for him, I'd had other things on my mind. Like Ashlyn Grove.

The others were already gathered in the common room when I arrived. As usual, no one expected me to be on time. Kris looked annoyingly casual in his loose tunic and soft, dark pants. But it was the way he couldn't meet my gaze that gave him away—Kris had never been able to play it cool.

His fingers fidgeted with the glowing edge of his Echo Panel, the dim light catching the nervous twitch of his hands. It was clear he'd been sitting on this information, wrestling with whether to tell us, and that alone told me it was big. If he thought he could hide it from me, though, he was sorely mistaken.

"What's this about?" I asked, flopping into a comfortable armchair and sipping water from the bottle I'd brought with me.

Another student was reading under the glow of a table lamp

on the other side of the room, but he closed his book and left once I arrived. Good. Saved me the trouble of getting rid of him. Kris and Shane were sharing the couch opposite me, while Jase had his legs slung over the arm of a second couch, a pile of pillows stuffed under his head.

"You guys won't believe what I found out," Kris said, his voice trembling.

"Cut the dramatics," I said, leaning forward and resting my elbows on my thighs. He knew how desperate I'd been to hear this. "You cracked the file?"

"Finally." Kris still couldn't look me in the eye, and I knew I was right: he'd been hiding this for a while. "It wasn't easy."

I waited for him to elaborate; he was deliberately dragging this out, and I refused to play along by asking questions.

"You guys ever heard of Kaletha?" Kris asked.

"The demonic Spirit," Jase said. "She was banished by the other Spirits for doing something bad, wasn't she?"

Kris nodded. "So, there's this super cult of magical supremacists created by followers of Kaletha. The Council found out and disbanded them because, obviously, cults and magical supremacy... Not exactly what you want to hear in the same sentence when you're trying to maintain peace and harmony."

"What does this have to do with Webber?" I asked, although I could already hazard a guess.

"The encrypted file was a police report. The Magical Law Enforcement was investigating the Webbers."

"They belong to the cult?" The answer was obvious. "The cult who stole a bunch of stuff from my father before we came here. I heard him mention Kaletha. I don't think they were ever caught, though."

Shane's eyes widened, and he inhaled deeply. "Just because the MLE were investigating the Webbers, it doesn't mean that Jenny was involved."

"True," Kris conceded. "But the report claimed that her brother Harvey's death wasn't accidental."

Jase released a whistle. "That's not good."

That was an understatement. "So, you're saying the Webbers were allegedly part of a supremacist cult, and her brother was murdered?" I asked.

Kris folded his arms. "Crazy stuff, right?"

Shane glanced around the common room to make sure no one had come in while we'd been talking. When he spoke, he kept his voice low. "Why would someone encrypt a police file and attach it to Jenny Webber's contract? Why aren't they out there doing something about it?"

"I mean, if my family was part of a cult, I'd probably encrypt it too." Jase said, "I think it's true. Webber's been all over Ashlyn since she got here."

"That's just her personality," Shane said. "Doesn't mean she's in a cult."

"And her mom is a guidance counselor," Kris added.

"Maybe it was only Harvey who was involved in the cult," Jase suggested.

This had always been their problem—they gave people the benefit of the doubt and looked for the good in others instead of expecting the worst. They still had a lot to learn if they wanted to become successful Lords.

"Of course, it's true," I said, sitting back in the armchair as laughter erupted from one of the dorm rooms—at least someone was having fun. "Webber has been sniffing around Ashlyn since the moment we got here, trying to keep her away from us."

Shane shook his head. "We did a pretty good job of that before she came along."

"Webber hates us," I said, ignoring him. "She's up to something, and it isn't going to end well for any of us."

"Any of us?" Shane frowned. "Don't you mean this isn't going to end well for Ashlyn? What if her life is in danger, too?"

"I think we should warn her," Kris said. "Before someone gets hurt."

Too late for that, I thought. Whatever hold Webber had over

Ashlyn, it would take more than a chat to get her to believe us. "There's only one problem with that," I said. "Ashlyn is already in the Vitalis wing."

"What?" Jase blinked at me and furrowed his brow like I'd just informed him the sky was red.

The color drained from Shane's face. "What happened to her?"

"Are you asking me if I had something to do with it?" I clenched my fists. We'd been friends since we were old enough to walk, but it didn't give him the right to dish out accusations without any evidence.

"No," Shane said, "I'm asking what happened to her as you're the only one who seems to know about it."

I shrugged. I'd withheld this information from the guys because I was still trying to process why I'd returned the magic book back to Ashlyn. "I saw a flash from my room last night. I went to investigate and found Ashlyn unconscious in a clearing in the forest. She has a concussion and is still in the infirmary for observation."

"She was unconscious?" Shane was still pale. "Did someone attack her?"

"Maybe you should ask her yourself."

Shane rose abruptly. "Are you coming? We can tell her about Jenny at the same time."

Kris stood up next. "I think we should all go." This was aimed at me.

I grabbed my water bottle and joined them; I wasn't letting them do this without me.

"Um, question?" Jase sprung to his feet because he obviously hadn't burned off enough energy during the day. "You found Ashlyn Grove unconscious and what? You carried her back to the school?"

"No, I poured cold water over her and made her walk." I rolled my eyes. "I couldn't leave her out there, could I?"

I walked away, leaving them to their curious glances and their raised eyebrows behind my back. Any one of them would've done the same, so I didn't understand why this came as such a shock to them.

———

The lights were dimmed when we reached the Vitalis wing. The night nurse was dozing in the chair behind the reception desk, and we tiptoed past her, letting ourselves silently into Ashlyn's room.

It was dark. The only source of light was a soft, blue glow from a tiny lamp. We all congregated inside the doorway, hardly daring to breathe.

"Ash?" Shane whispered. "Ashlyn, are you awake?"

Ash didn't even stir under the covers. I spotted a glimpse of white fabric poking out from under the end of the mattress and wondered if she'd removed her bandages so that she could get comfortable. She'd obviously been given herbs to help her sleep.

I opened the door and gestured for the others to follow me back outside to the hallway. Still whispering, I said, "It's late. Ash will be safe for tonight. We should come back in the morning before class."

At the other end of the corridor, the infirmary door opened, and a figure darted through, the door swinging silently shut behind him.

"Who was that?" Kris asked.

The guy had kept his face hidden, but I'd seen him hanging around campus earlier. It had only been a matter of time before the other Celestial showed up and tried getting close to Ashlyn.

"That, my friends, was Ethan Weiss."

Chapter Twenty-Six

Ashlyn

Getting back through the woods back to Vitalis was a blur. My thoughts were spinning despite the energy still buzzing through my veins and the rainbow glow beneath my skin. Howard spoke privately to Jenny, and she grabbed my hand and led the way in the dark without even using her Echo Panel. It was almost as if the trees and foliage parted to allow us through.

Back in my room, Jenny pulled the covers and removed the pillows that she'd used to make it look like I was sleeping. "I'm so excited that you're going to be one of us now," she said, finding my pajamas and gesturing for me to get undressed.

I reacted mechanically, shimmying out of the dress and tugging the pajama top over my head. "Yeah, me too," I murmured, sitting on the edge of the bed.

The rainbow glow was fading, and I stared at my hands, trying to keep the glow in sight for as long as I could. My stomach twisted—my magic making a reappearance as the energy in my veins dissipated. I was uneasy about stealing the opal, but Howard wouldn't expect me to do something that would get me into trouble, would he? I'd come this far. I was so close to being a fully initiated member of the group that it would be silly to bail now.

But what if the Council found out and took my magic away? How would I cope with everyone in the land knowing that I'd been Celestial for a short while and blown it by doing something stupid? What would my father say?

I knew exactly what my father would say, but Howard had assured me the opal already belonged to the League.

"Does everyone have to steal something?" I asked Jenny.

She gestured for me to lie down and pulled the covers back over me. "Huh? Oh, yeah," she said, kicking off her shoes and settling into the chair by the side of the bed.

"What did you have to get?" I didn't want to lay down. I needed to release the energy that was still stored inside me, but for some reason, I obediently stayed where I was.

"Just some weird, old artifact. Nothing special." She grabbed a spare blanket from the bedside cabinet and covered herself with it, then gave an exaggerated yawn. "I'm exhausted."

The wind rattled the windowpanes, and I instinctively stared outside. "You'd better get back to our room before the nurse comes to check on me."

"I'll just sleep here," Jenny said, smiling. "I'll pretend I felt unwell or something."

I didn't know why, but I wanted Jenny to leave. We shared a room, so it wasn't like this was an unusual occurrence, but I wanted some space to clear my head and think about what Howard wanted me to do, and I didn't feel like I could do it with Jenny sleeping in the chair. Was it another warning from my magic?

"Tomorrow morning, we can make a plan for you to get the opal," she said, closing her eyes and resting her head on her folded arm. She looked uncomfortable, and I didn't understand why she didn't want to go back to our room and get a good night's sleep.

I lay on my back, staring at the gentle blue glow above my head until my eyes watered, listening to the sounds of Jenny's regular breathing. How could she sleep? I had so many questions about what had happened at the ceremony that I knew I wouldn't be able to switch off and close my eyes. How did Jenny know what to do with her magic? How did Howard always seem to get inside my head so that I couldn't refuse his suggestions? How did my veins glow with rainbow colors? Why did no one speak about the task associated with the initiation?

I rolled onto my side to look at Jenny. Her face was peaceful in slumber, even though her arm would be numb when she woke up. I didn't believe her when she said she was asked to steal something, too. The question was: *why did she lie to me?* Did Howard ask her to stay with me tonight? Was he worried that I would change my mind?

I tried to recall the words I'd spoken during the ceremony, the words I'd repeated after Howard, but they were proving to be elusive. Something about light and dark? I squeezed my eyes closed, and all I could see were Howard's glowing red eyes imprinted on the back of my eyelids.

Did Ethan Weiss know about the League of Magical Theory? Was that why he was here at Aurora, or had he been sent to kick-start my training? Now that the ceremony was behind me, and my head was buzzing with more questions than ever, I kind of wished I'd heard him out earlier. But Jenny had a habit of always showing up whenever I got close to someone else. Did she know that he was here? She hadn't been surprised to see him. I didn't like to question my friend's motives, but too many things were starting to not add up. Jenny's failed potion and then her retest carried out in secrecy. The way she handled her element in the clearing, like she knew exactly what she was doing. Her insistence that I join the club right from the get-go.

I was awake the rest of the night. I felt as though I'd shaken off Howard's energy, but that left my magic buzzing angrily inside me and making my head thump. I needed to get out of the room and walk, get some fresh air, and hopefully organize my thoughts into some kind of order.

Holding my breath, I located my Echo Panel in the bedside cabinet and checked the time. It was five in the morning, perfect timing as curfew had just lifted. I raised the covers and slid my legs over the side of the bed, pulling some clothes out of the cabinet. Getting dressed was the easy part. Pulling my shoes out from under the chair Jenny was sleeping in was a different matter, and I almost passed out when I bent over, evidence of my lingering concussion. I raised my knees and sat on the floor next to Jenny until the nausea subsided, praying that she wouldn't open her eyes and find me there.

She didn't.

I slid my Echo Panel into my pocket, tiptoed across the room with my shoes in my hand, and opened the door, checking Jenny was still asleep. My heart was thumping when I closed the door behind me and approached the front desk. Nurse Cromer was nowhere to be seen, and her absence lifted a weight from my shoulders—if Howard wanted to keep me inside, this wouldn't have been so easy.

Outside, it still looked and felt like it was midnight. The storm clouds were directly above Aurora, ominously black and heavy, thunder rumbling in the distance. I stepped out from under the cover of the building and pulled up my hood to protect me from the drizzle. Deep breath. Head down. I walked without paying attention to where I was going or the damp seeping through my clothes.

Before I knew it, I was deep in the woods, following the path that led to the log cabin near the potions clearing. I'd never walked in my sleep before or even talked in my sleep, but when I stood in front of the cabin, the ring of stumps and the sopping mess of the bonfire behind me, I couldn't even remember how I'd gotten there.

I turned back to the cabin, my curiosity outweighing my unease. Shielding my face with my hands, I peered through the small window, but the inside was pitch-black, offering no clues. My hand moved on its own to the door handle, but the moment my fingers brushed it, they bounced back, a sharp pulse shooting up my arm like I'd just touched a live wire. I frowned and tried again. The same thing happened—a magnetic force repelled my hand, invisible but undeniable.

A magical barrier.

The cabin was warded, its contents sealed off, and whatever was inside was clearly not meant to be disturbed. My chest tightened as realization dawned. The opal figurine was being protected, hidden away under layers of enchantments. Howard must have known this. He was a professor. He would've understood the weight of stealing from the university, yet he'd sent me here anyway.

He wanted the opal badly but not badly enough to risk taking it himself.

My magic fizzed and bubbled under my skin, no longer a comforting hum but a sharp, insistent warning. The unease that had been growing since the ceremony surged louder than ever, and I pressed a hand to my chest, trying to steady my breath. This was wrong. No club, no initiation, should require me to break through the university's magic and steal something that didn't belong to me. It wasn't a test of worth—it was a violation.

If they didn't want me as I was, then I didn't want them. I'd find another way to understand my magic, even if it meant disappointing Jenny.

I turned away from the cabin, determination hardening my resolve, but as my gaze swept across the clearing, I froze. Four figures were making their way toward me from the path, hoods up against the drizzle. Their movements were steady and purposeful, and though the storm-muted light obscured their faces, I could feel the weight of their attention.

The fizzing in my chest shifted, an odd sensation blooming at the base of my skull. It was faint at first, like the brush of a feather, but it grew, pushing against my thoughts until they felt distant and murky. I took a step back, my instincts screaming at me to leave, but my body wouldn't listen.

Instead, my pulse slowed, my breathing evened out, and a strange calm settled over me. My gaze returned to the cabin, my feet moving without my permission. My earlier doubts felt like whispers in the back of my mind, easy to ignore.

The opal. I needed to get the opal.

"Ashlyn," someone called out. They were here to stop me from fulfilling my task, and I wouldn't let them.

CHAPTER TWENTY-SEVEN

Shane

We met outside Kristopher's room at five in the morning, as agreed. I'd hardly slept all night worrying about Ashlyn and beating myself up for not waking her when we went to her room in the infirmary, but Jase looked even worse than I felt.

"Someone remind me why we had to speak to her so early?" he grumbled.

"We've already wasted enough time," I said. At Jase's blank expression, I added, "The Cult of Kaletha? The encrypted police file?"

"Let's get this over with," Cole said with his usual lack of warmth. "We'll tell her what we know, and then it's up to Ashlyn if she believes us or not."

By the time we reached the infirmary, we were all damp and shivering with the cold. We were about to enter when a voice behind us said, "Kristopher?"

It was Danielle—the girl Kristopher had been talking to—wearing running gear, rain dripping from her hair as she followed us inside.

"Where are you guys off to?" She addressed us all but only looked at Kris.

"Um, we're just on our way to, um…" Kris swallowed, his cheeks turning pink. Clearly, he didn't want her to know that we were going to see Ashlyn.

Cole had no such qualms. "We're here to talk to Ashlyn." He pushed the button to call the lift.

"She's not here," Danielle said, wringing water from her ponytail. "I've just seen her outside."

"Outside?" I glanced at the doorway, rain sliding down the glass. Cole said she was concussed. Maybe she was hallucinating and had wandered outside by mistake. "Where was she?"

"Heading toward the clearing, you know where we get our gifts." Danielle pointed over her shoulder.

The four of us exchanged a glance—there was no good reason for anyone to be out there in this weather and at this hour.

"Thanks, Danielle," Kris said, already walking back to the entrance. "I owe you one."

"Wait—" she called, but we were piling back outside and into the rain, pulling our hoods back up to shield our faces.

Was it me, or was the storm getting worse?

It only took a few minutes for us to cross the bridge and find the pathway into the woods.

"What's she doing out here?" Jase asked the question we were all thinking.

"No idea, but I've got a bad feeling," Kris said.

I did, too, but I kept quiet. We should've spoken to her sooner; if Ash was in some kind of trouble, I'd never forgive myself, and I had a feeling the others felt the same, too.

"Keep moving," Cole snapped.

I'd never seen him looking scared in any situation, but I was certain I could see fear in his eyes now. The ruthless persona was gone, and it almost felt like the old gang was back together again, all apart from Ashlyn.

The cabin appeared through the curtain of rain, dark and foreboding, as the storm raged around us. Lightning tore across the sky, a jagged line of white-hot fire that illuminated the clearing for a split second before plunging it back into darkness. Thunder crashed so loud that it felt like my ribs might crack under its weight. Every instinct I had screamed to get back to shelter, but then I saw her.

"Ashlyn," Cole said, his voice tight. Rain streamed down his face, but he didn't flinch.

She stood at the cabin door, her hood ripped back, her hair a wild mess in the storm. Even in the dim light, I could see something wasn't right. She was glowing—actually glowing, faint pulses of light radiating from beneath her skin like her magic was trying to claw its way out.

I barely had time to process it before she turned and saw us. Her steps faltered for just a moment, but then she started marching toward us, the storm bending around her, wind whipping at her cloak and hair like it was alive.

"What are you doing here?" Her voice cut through the chaos like a blade. She stopped a few feet away, hands on her hips, eyes like twin storms of their own. I wanted to believe this was still Ashlyn, but the intensity in her gaze made my stomach knot.

"What are you doing here?" she snapped, her voice slicing through the storm like a dagger. Her gaze darted between us, her lips pressed into a hard line. She looked ready to fight—or worse.

"Whoa, we just want to talk," Jase said, raising his hands in a gesture of surrender. His usual humor was nowhere to be found.

"Talk?" Ashlyn's laugh was sharp and bitter. "So, you followed me all the way out here? What gives you the right—" She stopped, shaking her head violently as if trying to dislodge a thought. Her glowing eyes locked on Cole. "And you? What do you want, Bevair?"

The anger in her voice was familiar, but there was something else beneath it—a strange detachment that sent a chill through me. This wasn't Ashlyn. Not entirely. Something was wrong.

"Ash, you're not okay," I said, my voice as steady as I could make it. "We're here to help."

Her sharp laugh cut through the storm, her expression

twisting with rage. "Help? You think you're here to help me?" She gestured wildly, and the storm seemed to surge in response, the wind howling louder, the rain slashing harder.

Cole stepped forward, blocking her path. "Ashlyn, what are you doing here?"

Her jaw clenched. "I don't owe you any explanations."

The glow beneath her skin pulsed, and for a moment, the storm seemed to ripple in response. My heart pounded as I took a cautious step closer. Whatever had happened to her, it wasn't just anger—it was something more, something we couldn't see.

"We need to talk to you about Jenny," Jase said, his voice careful but firm.

"Jenny?" Ashlyn's head whipped toward him, her expression sharp enough to draw blood. "What about her?"

Kris stepped in, hands raised in a calming gesture. "We think she's involved in something dangerous, Ash. Something you need to know about."

Her laugh was louder this time, carried on the wind like a taunt. She stared at each of us, her eyes flickering like dying embers. "You think you can just show up here and accuse my best friend of—what? Being dangerous? Jenny's the only one who's been there for me. Unlike you."

Her words cut deep, and I saw Kris flinch. I opened my mouth to say something, anything to defuse the situation, but the storm was a relentless distraction, blurring my thoughts. Another flash of lightning illuminated her face, and for a split second, I saw it. Fear. It was gone before I could process it, replaced by fury.

"You don't understand," Kris pressed. "We've seen her contract, Ash. There's a lot of dark stuff in there. It's serious."

Ashlyn's expression hardened, and orbs of light began forming around her, circling her like glowflies caught in a vortex. "You're lying," she said, but her voice faltered for a heartbeat.

"No, we're not," Cole said, his voice steady despite the chaos around us. "Jenny isn't who you think she is. She's dangerous."

Ashlyn's magic flared, and the orbs spun faster, their trails blurring into a glowing halo. "You've done nothing but tear me down since the day I got here," she spat. "Now you want me to believe you care? Spare me."

"Ashlyn, stop," I said, stepping closer despite the oppressive force of her magic. "We're not your enemies."

"Yes, you are!" she screamed, raising her hand and sending Cole flying backward. He hit the ground hard, the impact sending water splashing high into the air.

Jase rushed to Cole's side, but Ashlyn didn't even blink. She turned to face the rest of us, her chest heaving, her glowing eyes wild and untamed.

"This is what she's done to you, Ash," Kris said, his voice desperate. "Jenny's twisted you into something you're not."

Ashlyn hesitated. Her lips parted, her eyes flickering with a mix of confusion and anger. "I don't need you," she said, but her voice was softer now, less certain.

"Yes, you do," Kris pressed. "Please, listen to us. This isn't who you are."

Her magic wavered, the orbs slowing their frantic dance. Her hands dropped to her sides, and for the first time, I saw a flicker of the girl we used to know. "Just leave me alone."

"No," I said, taking a risk and stepping forward. The storm tore at my jacket, rain pelting against my face, but I didn't care. I wrapped my arms around her in a hug, grounding her as much as myself. "We'll never leave you alone again."

For a moment, I thought she'd shove me off like she had Cole, but instead, her shoulders sagged, and her head dipped slightly. The glow beneath her skin dimmed, though it didn't disappear entirely. I felt her pulse through the contact, her magic thrumming faintly against me like an engine idling. She didn't say anything, but she didn't pull away either.

Behind her, Cole groaned as he pushed himself upright, muttering something about how he was fine, no thanks to her. Jase shot him a glare, but I held Ashlyn tighter, murmuring, "We'll figure this out."

Finally, Ashlyn stepped back, her arms dropping limply to her sides. The fire in her eyes was gone, replaced by exhaustion. "I... I need to go," she mumbled, her voice barely audible above the storm.

None of us stopped her as she turned and trudged back through the rain, her steps slow and heavy, like she was wading through a dream she couldn't wake up from.

Chapter Twenty-Eight

Ashlyn

The morning light, faint and filtered through the infirmary windows, cast long shadows across the walls and amplified the throbbing in my head. I'd slept through yesterday and all last night after stumbling back here, exhausted beyond comprehension. The events in the forest felt distant now, dreamlike—fragments that skittered away when I tried to grasp them. I remembered deciding not to steal the opal and then that overwhelming compulsion that had gripped me...

"Here are your discharge papers, Ashlyn." Nurse Lebowski's voice pierced my foggy thoughts. She arranged herbal potions on the bedside table with methodical precision, the bottles clinking softly. "No strenuous activities, and make sure to stay warm. Stay out of trouble."

I nodded mechanically, not bothering to explain how unlikely "staying out of trouble" would be. My head still swam with disjointed images. Howard's hypnotic voice, Cole sprawled in the mud, those strange glowing orbs that had surrounded me like wayward stars. And the guys... showing up like they had any right to interfere in my life after two years of silence.

Part of me still burned with anger at their intervention, but another part—a quiet, stubborn voice I couldn't quite silence—whispered that without them, I might have actually gone through with it. Might have stolen the opal and sealed my fate with the club. The thought sent ice through my veins.

A heavy knot tightened in my chest as I spotted them waiting in the hallway. Of course they'd come back—probably to make sure their "intervention" had stuck. Cole leaned against the wall, arms crossed, wearing that mask of irritation I remembered so well. Kris couldn't seem to keep his hands still, fidgeting with his jacket. Jase balanced on the balls of his feet like he couldn't decide whether to flee or fight, while Shane stood apart from the others, gaze fixed on the floor until I emerged.

"Hey," Shane ventured, his voice carefully neutral. "How are you feeling?"

"Fine," I snapped, though the word came out slurred. The herbs they'd given me made everything feel slightly off-kilter, like walking on a shifting floor.

Cole's derisive snort echoed off the walls. "Yeah, right. You were glowing like a festival lantern yesterday morning."

"Cole," Kris warned, shooting him a sharp look.

"No, let him talk." I squared my shoulders despite the wave of dizziness the movement triggered. "If you've got something to say, Bevair, go ahead."

For a moment, something flickered across his face—concern maybe, or guilt. But then his jaw tightened, and he muttered, "Forget it," turning away.

I gripped the doorframe to steady myself, hating how weak I felt in front of them. "Why are you even here?"

"To stop you from doing something else stupid," Cole shot back, earning another glare from Kris.

"We're here because we care," Shane interjected, taking a careful step forward. Something in his eyes—regret maybe, or worry—made my chest ache. "Whatever's going on, you don't have to face it alone."

A bitter laugh escaped me. "That's rich, coming from you. All of you." The words tasted like ash in my mouth. "Two years of silence, and suddenly you care?"

"Because it's true," Kris said, his voice rising with unexpected intensity. "We're not here because of your magic or the industries. We're here because we care about you, Ashlyn."

"Funny how that caring only surfaced once I became Celestial." I let go of the doorframe, forcing myself to stand straight despite the lingering dizziness. "Where was all this concern before?"

"That's not fair." Jase stepped forward, his usually playful demeanor replaced by something raw and serious. "We've always cared, Ashlyn. We just... we messed up. And we're sorry."

"Are you?" I challenged them, my voice steadier now. Standing helped clear my head, making my thoughts sharper. "Are you really sorry? Or are you just trying to protect the industries?"

"Both," Cole said bluntly, earning shocked looks from the others. "But protecting you is part of protecting the industries. We need you, Ashlyn—not just because of your magic, but because you're part of this. Part of us."

His honesty caught me off guard. The silence stretched between us, broken only by the distant sounds of the infirmary. I studied their faces—really looked at them for the first time since they'd found me in the woods. The concern seemed genuine, but two years of silence had taught me to be wary.

"I'm not sure how much you remember about what we said yesterday since you didn't seem to be yourself. But, there's something you need to know," Kris said finally, his voice tight with anxiety. "About Jenny. And Howard."

My stomach knotted. "What about them?"

Cole's eyes locked onto mine. "That club isn't what it seems, Ashlyn. They're not helping you. They're using you."

"You don't know what you're talking about." I took a step back, bumping against the wall. The cool surface helped ground me.

"Don't I?" Cole stepped closer, his presence looming. "You

were willing to march through a storm yesterday, Ashlyn. For what? What could they possibly want from you that's worth putting yourself in danger like that?"

Heat crept up my neck. How much did they know? I glanced at Kris and Shane, but their expressions gave nothing away. "They're not asking me to do anything," I said, the lie bitter on my tongue. "You're making it sound like—"

"Like they're manipulating you?" Cole's voice cut through my protests like a blade. "Because they are. Howard—he's the worst of them all. He's the one calling the shots, isn't he?"

I swallowed hard against the truth in his words. "You don't understand. You don't know what it's like—having something inside you that you can't control. They said they could help me."

"By making you prove yourself?" Kris stepped forward, his face tight and concerned. "That's not how it works, Ashlyn. They're exploiting you, and you know it. Just tell us what they wanted."

My magic fizzed beneath my skin, caught between loyalty to the club and the growing cracks in their perfect facade. Four pairs of eyes watched me, waiting for answers I wasn't ready to give.

"Let me guess," Cole said, his voice razor-sharp. "They dangled promises in front of you—control, power, understanding—and all you had to do was jump through their hoops. Am I getting close?"

The accuracy of his words stung. How could I admit they'd asked me to steal? That I'd almost done it?

Kris shifted his weight, exchanging a look with the others before continuing. "Ashlyn, we're not making this up. We looked into Jenny's contract. There was an encrypted file attached to it— a police report. Her family has ties to the Cult of Kaletha."

The name hit me like a physical blow. "The what?"

"An extremist group," Shane explained, his calm voice at odds with the tension in his shoulders. "They believe in magical supremacy—pure bloodlines, ultimate power, no checks or balances. The Council disbanded them years ago, but they've been trying to rebuild in secret. Jenny's family was implicated in their activities." He paused, watching my reaction. "Her brother's death wasn't an accident."

I shook my head, memories of Jenny's warmth and friendship clashing with this new information. "That doesn't make sense. Jenny isn't like that. She's kind, she's..." But even as I spoke, doubts crept in. Her constant pushing about the initiation, her insistence that I complete the task, and her fierce protection of the club's secrets.

"Is she?" Cole's question was quiet but pointed. "Or has she been pushing you harder and harder, making sure you're loyal to the club?"

"And Howard?" Kris added. "What's his role in all this? Why is he so invested in you?"

"We should get you back to your dorm," Shane said, breaking the heavy silence that had fallen after their revelations.

I pushed away from the wall, determined to walk on my own. After being in bed for so long, my legs felt unsteady, but I refused to show weakness. The guys formed a loose circle around me as we made our way down the corridor, maintaining a careful distance that spoke volumes about our fractured relationship.

The morning light struck harsh and bright as we emerged from the infirmary. Students rushed past, some casting curious glances our way. Of course they would—five heirs walking together for the first time in two years would certainly fuel the gossip mill.

"People are staring," I muttered, more to myself than the others.

"Let them," Cole said from behind me. "We have bigger problems."

The walk to the dormitory building felt endless. Each step brought more questions and more doubts. If what they said about Jenny was true... I thought about all the times she'd encouraged me to prove myself to the club, how she always seemed to appear when I was with anyone else.

Jase cleared his throat. "Listen, Ash, about what happened two years ago—"

"Don't." I stopped abruptly, causing Kris to nearly collide with me. "I can't deal with that right now."

"Fair enough," Shane conceded. "But sooner or later—"

He broke off as two familiar figures rounded the corner ahead. Jenny and Emma approached us. Jenny's pink sweater was almost offensively cheerful in the morning light, its intricate embroidery shimmering with each step. Emma's attention remained fixed on her Echo Panel, but Jenny's eyes narrowed at the sight of our group.

"There you are!" Jenny rushed forward, her oversized pink sweater and matching beanie creating an image of calculated innocence. She shot a venomous glare at the guys before grabbing my hands. Her fingers felt ice-cold against my skin. "Are you discharged now? I've missed you."

I studied her face, searching for signs of the manipulation Cole had described. How had I never noticed the calculation behind her wide-eyed concern? "All better," I said carefully.

"I'd have come to meet you," she said, finally acknowledging the heirs with barely concealed contempt. "What are they doing here?"

The hatred in her voice was familiar, but now I heard something darker beneath it— something that made my magic stir uneasily. Before any of the guys could speak, I blurted out, "My parents asked them to escort me back. Officially. It's an heir thing."

The lie sounded ridiculous even to my ears. I caught Shane's frown from the corner of my eye, but Jenny didn't question it. Beside her, Emma finally looked up from her Echo Panel, her expression uncertain.

"Ladies." The silky voice slid over us like a storm serpent slithering across the floor.

Howard and Carla approached from the direction of the administrative offices, their movements unnaturally fluid. Emma quickly tucked away her Echo Panel, a blush creeping across her cheeks. The sight of someone else falling under Howard's charismatic spell made my stomach turn.

"Hey," Jenny greeted them with less enthusiasm than usual, and I wondered at the tension radiating off her. She linked her arm through mine, grip tightening like a shackle. "What are you guys doing here?"

"Professor Kellar is indisposed today," Howard said, his gaze never leaving my face. "So we'll be taking your class to the forest."

My magic flared in warning, sending electricity racing along my nerves. In my fog of sleep and recovery, I'd completely forgotten about our first practical magic lesson with Professor Kellar. The thought of demonstrating my powers under Howard's watchful gaze made my skin crawl. Had he manipulated this, too? Another chance to force me to retrieve the opal?

"Ashlyn?" Shane's touch on my arm startled me. Concern radiated from his expression.

I plastered on a smile that felt more like a grimace. "I'm fine. You guys don't need to hang around."

His gaze flickered between Howard and Carla before retreating. The heirs moved toward the Student Commons entrance, but I could feel them watching, a protective barrier I never thought I'd have again.

"They're pathetic," Jenny spat, her face twisting into an ugly sneer. "Just because they walked you back from the infirmary doesn't mean they can worm their way back into your life and destroy it all over again."

The venom in her voice startled me. How had I never noticed before? The way she'd worked to isolate me, to keep me dependent on her friendship? I could make my own choices about the guys—they hadn't destroyed me. I was still standing, still breathing. Still meant to be the first female Lord in Andis history.

Drawing strength from that thought, I straightened my spine

and fixed my gaze on Howard's lapel, careful to avoid his eyes. "I won't be joining your class this morning."

The air grew heavy with tension. Carla shifted her weight, a predator preparing to strike. "Must I remind you of your mission, Ashlyn?" Howard's honeyed voice carried a sharp edge. "You must complete the task before you're fully accepted into the club."

The warning in his tone was clear—had I looked into his eyes, I knew I'd be agreeing to anything he suggested. A movement caught my attention—Bellis Reeve near the administrative offices, raising some kind of device to her eye. She snapped a picture of our group before disappearing behind a column. The swell of magic in my chest told me that she knew about the cult, too.

Jenny detached her arm from mine and watched me, a curious expression on her face. "Are you not feeling well again?"

I dragged my gaze away from Bellis and back to the professors, disturbed to see that Carla was also looking in the direction of the column. Had she spotted Bellis, too?

"Ashlyn?" Jenny prompted again.

"Is something wrong?" Howard asked.

Bellis disappeared inside the building, and I could see her speaking to a man behind the glass door. I swallowed. Whatever she was up to, it concerned the cult, and my magic was bubbling beneath the surface, warning me to keep Howard and Carla away from her. "Um," I began. "Actually, there is something wrong. I don't think I can do this."

"Do what, Ashlyn?" There was a sharp edge penetrating Howard's smooth, honeyed voice. He knew what I was about to say, and he wasn't happy about it.

I checked that the guys were still watching. Cole's eyes were narrowed with mistrust. Kris and Shane were watching with blatant concern, their faces pale, and Jase's fists were clenched, his feet spread as if poised to pounce on Howard should it be necessary.

I took a deep breath. "I'm sorry, but I don't want to steal something to confirm my membership. In fact, any club that requires me to break the law isn't a club I want to join, so I think I'll pass."

There. I'd said it. My magic swelled inside me as if proud of my strength and resolve.

Jenny and Carla stared at me open-mouthed. Obviously, no one had ever refused them before.

"Well," Howard said, "this is most unexpected, Ashlyn. We've already completed the first stage of the initiation, so I suggest you rethink this decision." His voice was calm, but there was no mistaking the underlying threat in his words.

"I'm sorry," I said. "But I've made up my mind."

My heart was racing. I wanted to get away from them.

But before I could move, Howard said softly, so softly that I had to lean closer to hear him, "Ashlyn, you don't really want to abandon the club, do you?"

I was flooded with the overwhelming desire to please him and instinctively peered into his glowing eyes. His magic flowed through my veins as if by muscle memory, and I was filled with warmth and contentment. "No, of course not," I said. "I would never leave the club." My Celestial power tingled in my chest, but it was smothered by Howard's magic taking center stage.

"Very good." Howard nodded once and reached for my hand. "Come with me. I have much to show you."

I heard the heirs yelling my name in the distance, but I paid them no attention. Howard's hand was warm. It was the perfect fit because this was where I belonged. I was part of their club now. Lights flashed all around us, beautiful rainbow colors that filled me with the kind of joy I'd never experienced before. Energy pulsed through my body. I felt powerful, invincible, supreme.

Then Howard's hand was gone. Something strong and vice-like gripped my wrist, and I was wrenched away from the comforting cocoon of light and energy and pressed up against something solid. I felt the loss of Howard like a stab through my heart. Tears welled in my eyes, and I whispered, "No, come back."

"Ashlyn." The voice was familiar, but it wasn't Howard. My

brain was foggy, my fingers still seeking out the professor's. "Ashlyn, it's okay. You're safe now." A gentle finger raised my chin, and I found myself staring into green eyes with golden flecks.

I gasped. *Ethan Weiss?*

Author's Note

Dear Beloved Reader,

First of all, thank you. Whether you're a longtime reader or new to my work, the fact that you've picked up *Frenemies Like These* means the world to me. This book is deeply personal—it holds a piece of my heart and a lot of my journey as a writer.

I first finished this story in 2021, when I was just dipping my toes into the world of writing novels. It was my very first manuscript, and I was so proud of it—but also so scared. Like many first-time authors, I found myself filled with doubt. Was it good enough? Was *I* good enough? I told myself it wasn't ready, and honestly, neither was I.

Over the years, this story wouldn't let go of me. Ashlyn, Kris, Shane, and the rest of the heirs kept whispering in my ear, reminding me of their magic and their struggles. So, I rewrote it. Then I rewrote it again. Each time, I learned something new—not just about the craft of writing, but about myself. Finally, after three rewrites and three years, I feel like it's the story it was always meant to be. And now, I'm ready to share it with you.

Writing *Frenemies Like These* was an emotional and magical journey. It's a story about friendship, betrayal, and finding your strength in a world that sometimes feels overwhelming. But it's also a story about hope—and I hope that resonates with you.

I'd like to give a special thanks to Joyce Bloemker and PollyAné Nichols over at ProofsByPolly for the developmental edit and the motivational push to get this book published.

If you enjoyed the book, I'd be so grateful if you'd consider leaving a review. Reviews help other readers discover my work, but even more than that, they're a wonderful way to connect with you. Hearing your thoughts and knowing this story made an impact is the greatest gift.

If you'd like to stay in touch, please visit my website (LilySkyy.com) or find me on social media—I'm on Instagram, TikTok, and Twitter, and I'd love to hear from you! You can also join me in the Lily Skyy Readers' Group, where we talk about books, share sneak peeks of upcoming projects, and celebrate the magic of stories together. And if you sign up for my mailing list, you'll be the first to know about new releases, giveaways, and exclusive content.

This book has been a long time in the making, and sharing it with you feels like the closing of one chapter and the opening of another. Thank you for giving these characters a place in your heart and for walking alongside me on this journey. Your support means everything.

Also, although this book is just publishing, books 2 and 3 in the series have already been written. Expect them to be released soon.

With all my gratitude and love,
  Lily Skyy